She could ha...

She *could*. She w...
that Raphael did...
she had to do was look at him to understand
that.

He was all animal grace and golden good
looks.

Tall, gorgeous women were Raphael's type,
Kate thought, not someone who was five foot
four if she stood on her tiptoes, someone who
did not have a bad hair day now and again but
was having a bad hair *life*.

The problem was…his eyes.

Raphael had a way of looking at her when he
said things, a steady way, with that smoky
green gaze, while one corner of his mouth
crooked up in a secret smile. Like there was
something shared between them…

Dear Reader,

Welcome to the May selection of Silhouette Sensations!®

First up, Beverly Bird and Terese Ramin bring us two fabulous rugged, sexy cops with a wonderful sense of humour and warmth in *I'll Be Seeing You* and *A Certain Slant of Light*—both are well worth investigating!

We also have two challenging, very original and deeply emotional storylines from the talented hands of Marilyn Pappano (*Rogue's Reform*) and award-winning author Carla Cassidy (*In a Heartbeat*).

And in *Heart of Midnight* and *Her Secret Guardian*, Fiona Brand and Sally Tyler Hayes round off the month with their two seductive, dangerous secret soldiers—determined to protect one special woman from jeopardy!

Enjoy them all and do come back for the best in romantic suspense next month, when we'll be hearing from Marie Ferrarella, Maggie Shayne, Marilyn Pappano, Ruth Langan, Jill Shalvis, Pamela Dalton and Virginia Kantra.

Take care of yourselves

The Editors

I'll Be Seeing You

BEVERLY BIRD

SILHOUETTE
SENSATION.

*First published in Great Britain 2001
Silhouette Books, Eton House, 18-24 Paradise Road,
Richmond, Surrey TW9 1SR*

© Beverly Bird 2000

ISBN 0 373 27100 X

18-0501

*Printed and bound in Spain
by Litografia Rosés S.A., Barcelona*

BEVERLY BIRD

has lived in several places in the United States, but she is currently back where her roots began on an island in New Jersey. Her time is devoted to her family and her writing. She is the author of numerous romances, both contemporary and historical. Beverly loves to hear from readers. You can write to her at PO Box 350, Brigantine, NJ 08203, USA.

Chapter 1

Perfection had its own kind of rush, Kate Mulhern thought. It was a tingling flow of adrenaline that made her want to hold her breath in anticipation of the final result.

She stopped moving for a split second in the kitchen of one of Philadelphia's finer Society Hill brownstones and looked—just looked—at what she had created. The china she'd selected for Dinner For Two, her unique catering business, was a fragile ivory with gold trim. On each plate a filet nested among roasted scallions with a touch of potato thins to the side. Perfect.

Kate smiled and got back to business.

She'd left the couple she was catering for alone for eight minutes now. They had their wine to keep them company—an excellent South Australian '84 Pinot Noir—but the man was rapidly moving through that. It was time to get on with the meal's centerpiece. Kate left the plates on the kitchen's center island and turned away to retrieve the orange béarnaise and julienne rind that would top the steaks.

A crash splintered the kitchen's quiet.

She let out a yelp of surprise and whirled around, her hand pressed to her chest. What she saw was preposterous! "Hey!" she yelled. "Hey, you! No, wait, stop!"

And the dog did.

It *was* a dog! In the kitchen? Her client hadn't mentioned that he had one. But she'd left the back door open a crack while the broiler had done its business—it was August, and Kate considered it to be in poor taste to hike her client's air-conditioning up without asking. So she'd left the door slightly ajar to let in what scant breeze there was, and a dog—some scrappy little Chihuahua type thing—had come in instead.

Kate's skin pulled into gooseflesh. Not just any dog, she thought. *That* dog.

It looked back at her and wagged its tail. Kate let out a strangled sound. The dog dropped the filet that was clamped in its jaws to bark once, a cheery hello, then it snapped the meat up again and trotted out.

Twelve and a half minutes down the drain, she thought, her blood still jittering with astonishment. So there was no time to dwell on the dog or what it had done. She was prepared—of course, she was prepared for any contingency, even this, the outrageous. She had two more filets in the fridge. *There go my profits.* Reputation was everything. She could salvage this. *Twelve and a half minutes behind schedule.* She had to move, had to get two more steaks in the broiler wrapped with the bacon she'd take off before serving them.

Instead, she rubbed her eyes with the heels of her hands.

It had not been *that* dog, she decided, finally turning back to the broiler. The dog she was thinking of had disappeared into Manhattan four months ago after turning her old roommate's world upside down. What had Shawna named the mutt? *Belle.* Belle had blasted into Shawna's life for two short weeks, leaving love, murder and mayhem in her wake.

Kate cooked new steaks, watching the timer impatiently. She wondered if she should make an excuse for the delay or just proceed blithely and hope no one noticed. She slid the filets onto two new plates, abandoning the filet that the dog hadn't eaten. Then she took a deep breath. She felt perspiration slide between her shoulder blades and hoped it didn't show. She picked up both plates and stepped over the shattered china on the floor. She didn't even want to consider what that plate had cost her.

She pushed through the door into the dining room, a smile pasted on her face. The sight in front of her made her pulse give another hitch. The man, her customer, was laying facedown in his hearts-of-palm salad.

His date—a voluptuous blonde in shimmering silver— came through the opposite door at the same moment and started screaming.

"Wait a minute, just calm down," Kate murmured. She eased the plates onto the table. Maybe he had just passed out. *Please, don't let it have been the food.*

But it wasn't the food. Kate's biggest weakness was detective novels, and cop shows. It was the only vice she indulged in, but she did it with fervor. A thin ribbon of blood ran down the back of the man's neck. She knew what blood like that meant. It was a gunshot wound to the back of the man's head.

This job was turning into a nightmare!

Kate forced herself to touch the man's wrist, even though her fingers shook. His skin was warm and she felt hope shoot into her blood. Then everything inside her recoiled.

No pulse. Kate tried again, and her heartbeat took off. *No pulse!*

The blonde's cries changed to howls. Kate did the only

thing she could. She stepped around the dead man and slapped the woman hard.

When the blonde's wails had subsided to hiccups, Kate ran to find a telephone. She fumbled with the buttons twice before she managed to punch in 911. A voice answered immediately—cold, detached, almost mechanical. Kate cleared her throat.

"Uh, yes. Please send someone immediately. There's a dead man in my salad."

Lieutenant Detective Raphael Montiel preferred to think of adrenaline as something hot and sharp that hurt the underside of his skin. It was rarely a pleasant feeling.

It drove him hard as he shot his aging Explorer around the corner of Third into Willings Alley. His left shoulder rammed against the window when he jerked the SUV straight again. He didn't have to look for the address. He knew the brownstone without the police cruisers that hurled red and blue light up against the walls of brick that bracketed the alley. He'd had his eye on the home's owner for a while.

Phillip McGaffney was dead.

Raphael cursed roundly, most of his fury aimed at whoever had taken McGaffney out—not that the killer had done so in the first place, because that had been inevitable for months now—because the SOB hadn't waited three hours and forty-two more minutes to do it. Raphael's suspension from the force lifted at midnight. Now, twenty minutes after the 911 call had come in, his dashboard clock remained stubbornly stuck at eight thirty-eight.

He'd flatten the man who called him on it. McGaffney was his. Two warring factions of Philadelphia's powerful Irish underground had just begun sniffing around each other thirty days ago when Raphael had taken his suspension in the teeth. He'd spent the last month staving off boredom by continuing to track every move the family made. Lou O'Bannon, the mob's kingpin, had died ten days into Raphael's suspension—of cancer, a virtual anomaly in his world. It had been a slow, natural death that had given Phil McGaffney and Charlie Eagan plenty of time to begin recruiting their supporters. Both of them fully intended to take over O'Bannon's throne.

It had been only a matter of time before full-fledged war broke out between the groups. But Raphael hadn't expected it to start this way, with Eagan's boys shooting right for the other guys' top dog.

He drove the Explorer into half a space between two black-and-whites. The SUV braked to a hard stop, and Raphael was out before it had settled back on its shock absorbers. He jogged across the alley and up the steps to McGaffney's front door.

"Where's Plattsmier?" he demanded of the cop manning the entrance.

"Not here yet."

But his captain would probably be here soon, Raphael thought. "Who's in charge?"

The officer grinned. "Fox."

Some of the constriction eased across Raphael's chest. Having C. Fox Whittington catch this stiff was good. It was very good. Fox was his partner.

Raphael passed the cop and went inside. He began stalking the first floor of the brownstone looking for Fox. Then he stepped into the dining room and his jaw sagged.

It was a long, narrow room with a cherry-wood table in the center. Dark wainscoting traced around the ivory-papered walls. The chandelier in the center of the ceiling was heavy with too much bronze that robbed the sparkling white light of its innocence. There was a door to the kitchen on one side of the room, a door to a hallway on the other.

McGaffney was facedown at the head of the table.

The blood that seeped from the gunshot wound at the base of the man's skull was congealing now, going tacky and brown. It was nothing Raphael hadn't seen before. The scene on the floor, however, rocked him a little.

The woman at the bottom of the pile was leggy—very leggy, he thought, given that the metallic fabric of her dress was pushed up nearly to her backside. It was all Raphael could see of her because there was a brunette sitting on top of her, deposited right on the small of the other woman's back. Her knees were drawn up and her chin rested in her hand. Every once in a while, the leggy woman kicked, but the brunette wasn't budging.

Raphael had no idea if the brunette was leggy or not. She wore navy blue trousers and a starched white shirt. Raphael had spent his childhood in parochial schools. He hated starch, despised it on mere sight.

"What the hell?" Raphael muttered.

The brunette's head came up at the sound of his voice. He had never seen hair like hers in his life, Raphael thought. It was a million shades of onyx shimmering to deep copper in the chandelier's light. He thought maybe it was supposed to be tied back or something, but who could tell? It was wild, with corkscrews zinging everywhere.

She reached a hand up to smooth it as though reading his opinion of it in his eyes. "She's bigger than me," she muttered. "It was a fight."

Raphael cleared his throat. "Come again?"

"It was a fight to keep her away from the table. From him. To keep her from messing up your evidence. Aren't you a cop?"

"Yeah." He'd even be an employed cop in another three hours or so.

The woman gave a heartfelt sigh. "It's about time you got here. She's all yours." And with that statement, she stood. The woman beneath her let out a yowl that stirred the hairs at Raphael's nape. Then she rolled onto her back, sat up and sprang to her feet.

"Philip!" she cried.

Finally, too late, Raphael understood why the brunette had been sitting on top of her. This came to him in the split second before he recognized the other woman. He should have known her from her legs.

Allègra Denise.

She hurled herself in the general direction of McGaffney's corpse in that long, ankle-length dress that draped her like a second skin and caught the chandelier's light. Raphael stepped quickly to block her. She hit his chest like a battering ram, and she had arms and legs that were everywhere.

"Whoa," he murmured. "Let's ease up here."

"That's what I told her," said the brunette.

"Phillip!" the blonde wailed again.

Raphael took an elbow in his gut, and one knee came perilously close to his groin. He tucked one of Allegra's arms behind her. He used it to lever her into a dining room chair, then he leaned close enough to her ear to inhale the sweet, clinging scent of her perfume. "Quiet now, or I'll let the lady sit on you again," he whispered.

"Phillip," Allegra whimpered.

"Cut me a break. You had dinner with Bonnie Joe Donnelly last weekend. How attached to Phil could you have gotten in, what, six days?"

Allegra blinked up at him, her eyes swimming. "How do you know?"

"I know." Raphael straightened away from her and looked at the brunette again. "And who the hell are you?"

He watched everything about her draw up and in. She couldn't be more than five foot four, but for a second she reminded him of his second grade teacher—a behemoth, stern, unforgiving and wicked with a ruler. Then he blinked, and she was petite again.

A voice came from behind him. "She's the caterer. Allegra here was having an intimate dinner with our pal."

Raphael turned to find C. Fox Whittington grinning at him. He grinned back. They just barely restrained themselves from several hearty slaps on each other's backs.

"You ready to get to work?" Fox asked, laughing.

"Better check with Plattsmier on that one." But a smile kept twitching at one corner of Raphael's mouth.

"No need. I'm wearing a watch." Fox looked at it and gave a groan that almost vibrated with pleasure. "Three more hours with the rookie."

The brass hadn't broken up other partnerships to cover a one-month suspension. They'd brought up a Homicide wannabe to replace Raphael during his time-out without pay. Raphael knew all about it. He and Fox spoke every other night or so.

There was an odd sound from the brunette. They both glanced her way.

"What?" Raphael demanded. Starch, drawn-up shoulders and that sound she'd just made. Like a *tsk*. All of it was like sandpaper on his nerve endings. "What's the matter?"

"You're having a kaffeeklatsch," she murmured. "But a man's dead."

"We'll take care of him, ma'am," Fox said politely. He looked at Raphael, then he tilted his head in the direction of the brunette. "She was in the kitchen when it went down. Why don't you deal with her? Under the circumstances, I'd better handle the scene myself."

Raphael nodded. Anything he found in the house would be inadmissible in court. He wasn't back on the payroll yet.

"An excellent approach," said a baritone from the doorway.

Raphael felt something wither deep in his gut. It was Plattsmier. He turned slowly, edgily, to face his captain.

"I could order you off the scene," the man said.

Raphael gritted his teeth. "What would be the point?"

"I'd make the commissioner smile."

Raphael snarled. The sound was out before he could bite it back. Fox put a warning hand on his shoulder, but Plattsmier only nodded sadly.

"You still don't get it," his captain said.

"Sure I do. Thirty days." Raphael bit out the words. "A chunk of change. What's not to understand?"

"I supported you."

Raphael was too angry to answer.

"I may well have done what you did, Montiel, in my younger days," Plattsmier said. "However, I would not have done it in front of an Eyewitness News Action-Cam. That's why the commissioner was distressed with you." He paused, then his temper showed. "It's why I couldn't save you a suspension. Damn it, do you think I wanted you out? If I'd wanted you out, you'd still be out. Internal Affairs wanted to suspend you for three months. And I wouldn't have let Fox catch this case. Then you'd have no way in on it at all. As it is, you've just got to cool your heels for another few hours and you guys will be a team on it." He paused, and some of the anger went out of him. "Between the two of you, you're the best I've got in the area of organized crime. So let's let bygones be bygones and do our respective jobs here."

Raphael heard what Plattsmier didn't say. The case was going to blow wide open. The city of Philadelphia was on the verge of an ugly mob war. None of them doubted it.

Which made Plattsmier right. They had work to do.

"Take her for now, like Fox said." Plattsmier thrust a thumb at the brunette.

Raphael glanced her way, and damned if she didn't do it again, that deep indrawn breath, that squaring of her shoulders. "I have a name," she said stiffly.

Plattsmier wasn't impressed. He rarely was. "Good," he said. "Give it to him." He pointed at Raphael and left the room.

Raphael looked at Allegra. He wanted to talk to her. Allegra traveled in these circles. She'd probably know more about this murder than Charlie Eagan and his supporters had forgotten. And all of that information would be pertinent to the case.

Three more hours.

While he chilled, waiting for the clock to chime midnight, he'd have to see what he could do with this shoulder-squaring brunette with the wild hair. "Let's go into the kitchen," he suggested.

He went ahead of her. As Kate followed him, her chest began to hurt and it felt hard to get air. A man had just been killed! She'd held herself together, had called the cops, had kept that crazy blonde from ruining any evidence the authorities might need. She'd done everything right! And this cop, this Montiel, seemed to think it was all just some kind of reunion with his pal out there in the other room.

Kate's stomach felt sour. If she didn't keep her hands tightly fisted, she knew they would begin to shake again. She bit back a groan as she stepped around the broken china on the floor and sat on one of the stools next to the kitchen's center island. She was cold to the bone in spite of the heat. Maybe the dead guy's air-conditioning had finally kicked on.

To keep her teeth from snicking together, she asked, "What did you do?"

Montiel glanced at her, then he poked his nose into the baking sheet with the potato thins. To Kate's disbelief, he popped one into his mouth.

"Stop that!"

He looked at her again. "What, you're saving them for McGaffney?"

"No! No, of course not. It's just…"

He watched her levelly. Kate found she couldn't explain why she was so appalled.

It was his irreverence, she decided. He stood there, not so much tall—maybe five foot eleven—but with the kind of presence that seemed to bleed life from everything else in the room. He had dark blond hair, golden really, and it was unkempt and too long. She doubted if he had shaved since morning. The T-shirt he wore, a well-washed and faded blue, was untucked. He had bottle-green eyes, but as he waited for her to finish her perusal they went to the color of the sea on a cloudy day. They'd hold secrets, Kate realized.

Where had she gotten that from?

The answer was there beneath his infuriating indifference to what had just happened. It was at odds with it. Kate had never had a talent for nuances, except maybe in recipes. She had never been very good with people, or with reading them. Yet she felt a certain intensity beneath Montiel's who-gives-a-damn manner.

He'd come to investigate a murder and he was eating her potato thins. But his eyes were darkening and turbulent.

"What did you do?" she asked again, more softly.

"With what?" he countered, moving on to munch a scallion.

"What did you do to anger the commissioner so you can't work until midnight?"

"Doesn't matter. We're here to figure out anything you saw or heard tonight."

He was eyeing the one remaining filet now. "Miss dinner?" she asked.

That brought his gaze to her again sharply. "What?"

"If you're that hungry, I'll reheat it. There's nothing wrong with it. It's just…stale."

"Stale."

"Prepared, then permitted to return to room temperature."

Permitted? Who used words like permitted in casual conversation? The fact that she did irritated the hell out of him. Coupled with the fact that he was exiled with her in the kitchen, it made Raphael's voice rough and gravely. "I coldcocked Gregg Miller on Eyewitness News."

Kate felt something like shock move through her system, feather-light and cold. She'd almost forgotten her question. "That killer? The one…"

"The one," he agreed flatly. "Then I caught a thirty-day suspension from Internal Affairs for my trouble."

"Why? Why did you hit him?"

"What he did wasn't enough?"

As near as Kate could remember, Miller had killed four women, had held the entire city in the grip of terror for the better part of a month. She hadn't really followed the news broadcasts all that closely. Between her catering business and her second job cooking at a diner, between all the chores one had to do in order to keep on top of life, there'd been precious little time for her to peruse the media accounts of the murders. But she knew Miller had been preying on single women in their late twenties and early thirties.

Kate frowned. "You'd need more," she decided.

"Who are you, Freud?"

That snapped her spine straight again. "You'd see death

in your line of work nearly every day, I would imagine. But you don't run about—what did you call it?—cold-cocking suspects all the time. Or do you?''

''Tell you what, you're better with these crunchy things than you are with analysis.''

Her stomach rolled again at the bite in his tone. ''You don't like me.''

''Do you like me?''

''Not particularly.''

Well, she was honest, he thought. He almost grinned. But she'd done it again. Words like particularly didn't belong in general conversation. Then Raphael heard himself answer her and he felt a dull inner pang even as his words hit the room.

''We were bringing Miller out of the van,'' he said, ''for his arraignment. I'd taken him in the first place, so I wanted to be part of the detail. He knew all about me through his spree, during the whole investigation. He made it his business to know who was closing in on him. So he turned around just as he was being led through the courthouse doors. He looked at me, and he said—''

Miller had said what Raphael hadn't yet told anyone.

Raphael hadn't made excuses for his behavior that day. What he'd done, he'd done. And he'd taken the fall. He clamped his mouth shut.

This had all the melodrama of an excellent story, Kate thought. ''He said what?'' she breathed.

''Don't tell me,'' Montiel drawled. ''You're heavy into cop shows.''

Kate blinked. How had he guessed? She almost denied it, but what would be the point? ''Books, mostly. There's a certain element of escapism there.''

''Element? Damn it, can't you just talk?''

''I am talking!''

''No. You're giving a lesson in vocabulary!'' And he

didn't know why it bothered him so much. Maybe it was just his overall mood. But he doubted it.

"I was just asking a question." She sniffed.

Raphael found himself answering her—again. "He told me that Anna was the best of the lot. He told me how she screamed. Damn it, he picked her because she was associated with me!"

There was a stretch of silence in the kitchen, drawn out enough to thin the air. Kate's heart hurtled over a beat. "Anna Lombardo?" One of Miller's victims, she remembered. Maybe the last. And then Kate understood. She cleared her throat carefully. "You knew Anna."

"Yeah." He took a knife from a drawer and cut into the steak. "I knew Anna. We'd been seeing each other."

"You loved her." It was, she thought, a heartbreaking story.

But Montiel laughed in a raw sound before he chewed and swallowed. "Not yet."

"I don't understand."

"I'd only met her two weeks before she died." But maybe it could have been something, he thought. They'd never know. Miller had strangled her with piano wire.

"Montiel."

The voice came from the kitchen door. They both turned sharply, almost guiltily, as though they'd been caught in the act of something they shouldn't have been doing. It was that man, Kate realized. Plattsmier. And the other one, Fox. Both stepped into the kitchen. Kate watched the three of them confer near the doorway.

Something was happening.

There was a lot of gesturing. Then something changed in Montiel's expression. His jaw hardened. His eyes went thin, but just before they did, Kate saw them shine like glass.

He turned to her. "Clean up your stuff, Betty Crocker. You've got five minutes, then I'm taking you home."

Kate came off the stool. "I don't need a ride."

"Good. Because you're not getting one."

Her heart was hammering almost as hard as it had done when she'd found the body. The air in the kitchen felt suddenly humid and heavy, and it made it hard for her to breathe again. "Then I don't understand what you're implying."

"I'm *implying* that I'll follow you in my own vehicle."

"To where?"

"To your home. We just covered that."

"But it's not necessary."

"It is if I'm going with you. I'm not leaving my Explorer here. And it looks as though you've got yourself one damned overqualified baby-sitter."

With that, he threw the fork he had been holding into the sink. It bounced right out again with the force of his strength. Impossibly, it landed prongs-down in a single scallion.

Kate closed her eyes briefly. It was that kind of a night.

Chapter 2

Kate broke all her own rules. She chucked the shells from the oysters Rockefeller into her client's trash—he was hardly in a position to pass on word of her unprofessionalism. She dumped the rock salt back into its bag without checking off a use on her master list. She did a cursory cleanup and grabbed a wine bottle off the counter on her way out the back door. She paused in the alley and chugged from it.

Then she looked around quickly to make sure no one—heaven forbid, Montiel—had seen her. She was alone.

Everything went out of her. Kate leaned weakly against her panel van. *What had happened here tonight?* And why was it necessary for that cop to follow her home? Kate could not remember a plot she'd ever read that had involved the authorities baby-sitting a witness, unless that witness had turned State's evidence. But she didn't have any evidence to turn.

Suddenly, her heart nosedived into her stomach. Was

she actually a suspect? Did they think *she* had killed that man?

She needed a lawyer.

"Okay, Betty Crocker, lead the way."

Kate came away from the van quickly as Montiel left the kitchen door and came into the alley. She tucked the wine bottle behind her. "Do I need a lawyer?"

"What for?" He jiggled the handle of her panel van. "Unlock this thing."

"Absolutely not."

He turned back to her slowly. There was a streetlight on a nearby corner. It flung mild light into the alley, just enough that she could see something tic at his jaw.

"You don't want to push me right now."

Kate held her ground but her voice quavered a little. "I simply want a few explanations before I allow you in my vehicle—and besides, you said you had your own."

"I do. It's out on Willings. You're going to drive me around. And damn it, you're going to stop elocuting while you do it."

When she opened her mouth to protest, he came toward her and he did it fast. Kate gave an involuntary cry and took a step in retreat. She brought her hand up to ward him off.

Unfortunately, it was the one with the wine in it.

His gaze flashed to it. "Misdemeanor. Slap on the wrist if you have no priors."

"What?"

"For stealing the wine. Is that why you wanted a lawyer?"

"I brought the wine!"

"Did you charge McGaffney for it?"

"Of course!"

"Then you're a criminal if you leave here with it. Unless he gives his permission."

"He's dead!" Then she realized that he was deliberately provoking her into forgetting her question. "Why won't you just talk to me?"

"Because you do it funny."

"I do not!"

He turned his back to her. "Come on. Drive me around to Willings and give me some vague directions in case I lose you in traffic."

"Some cop," she muttered.

A stillness came over him. "Come again?" he said neutrally.

In for a penny, she thought. "Aren't you trained for this? For tailing people?"

"What I'm trained for," he said without looking at her, "what I've spent fourteen years working my way up in the ranks for, is a hell of a lot more than what I'm doing right now. I'm not happy about that. So if you're smart, you'll stop ticking me off."

Kate knew suddenly that that wouldn't happen if they stood out here for days. She rubbed him the wrong way, and that made her heart sink in a way that was all too familiar.

"I just want to understand," she said quietly.

He finally looked at her. "Do you know who that guy was? The dead one?"

"Of course. Phillip McGaffney."

"Not his name. *Who* he was."

"I—" She broke off, took a deep breath. "No."

"Second in line for the O'Bannon throne."

"O'Bannon?" She knew the name from somewhere, but couldn't place it.

"Some say third in line. There are probably a hundred or so gun-wielding idiots in this city who think that Charlie Eagan damn well ought to replace O'Bannon instead. Ten to one, those are the guys who killed McGaffney."

Kate finally understood what he was talking about, and it almost knocked her legs out from under her. "You're talking about, like…the mob?"

"I'm talking about like the mob."

Kate gave up the effort. She sank slowly to sit on the street. "I served dinner to a member of the mob?"

"Don't lose any sleep over it. They eat just like the rest of us."

"I served dinner to a member of the mob." She looked up at him. "The woman?"

"She's known in these circles, too."

"I tackled her."

Though Raphael had thought five minutes ago that he would never smile again, he felt a grin pull at his mouth. "Wish I could have seen that part."

"She was being stupid."

"Allegra is known for it."

"Allegra…" Kate whispered it, giving a name to the very strong, very tall woman who had been trying to fling herself all over Phillip McGaffney's body. "I don't feel very well," she murmured.

Raphael lost the urge to smile. "You're about to feel worse."

"Why?"

"The way the department has it figured—and I agree with them—is that something went way wrong here tonight."

"Then tell me."

"McGaffney is…was…flamboyant. It wasn't his style to entertain ladies at home, especially when they look like Allegra. If he was home, he was alone. Everybody knew that. So tonight was out of pattern."

She still didn't get it.

"His killer—or killers—didn't know you or Allegra were there." He fought the urge to ask what exactly she

had been doing there. He hadn't seen anything in that
house that would have required a caterer. But that would
come later, after midnight. "We can't keep a lid on both
of you being here. Not indefinitely. The press are vultures.
That's why I'm going to stick close to you for a while
until this either blows up or cools down."

He reached and gave her a hand up. Kate came to her
feet unsteadily. "They'll try to hurt me?"

"Honey, you're as good as dead unless someone is
around to stop it."

Kate looked at him sharply. When she did, something
happened to the streetlight in the distance. It blurred and
tilted.

Raphael's instinct to protect started in his toes. She
swayed, and he grabbed her shoulders. "Hey—"

"Don't touch me."

Raphael jerked his hands back. Anger drummed behind
his eyes, giving him a headache. "That should be no problem."

"I didn't…I mean…" Kate trailed off and closed her
eyes. Damn him. He had all the compassion, the sensitivity, of a rock. He'd laughed with that other cop in the
dining room with a dead man no more than two feet away.
She could talk until sunup, and he wouldn't understand
that she felt as though any kindness right now would shat-
ter her.

In all her twenty-eight years, she had never really known
fear. Now it made her palms sweat even as everything
rational inside her struggled with what he'd just said, picking for some way to convince herself it wasn't true. *You're
as good as dead.*

She couldn't believe any of this.

Kate stepped around him, holding herself together. "I'm
going home."

"And that might be where?"

Did she have a choice? She'd let him tag along, she decided, until she could figure this thing out. "South on Second. The corner of Bainbridge. I rent space in a garage on Bainbridge for the van. It's called Lucky's."

"Not tonight it's not."

Kate made a strangled sound.

She went around to the driver's side of the van. When she got behind the wheel he tapped on the passenger side window. Kate ground her teeth together. She shot the key into the ignition and let the big engine rumble. "See you on Willings," she muttered. Then she put the van in gear and rolled off, resisting the urge to look at him in the mirror.

Raphael jogged through the town house and out the front door onto Willings Alley. Until this night, until this very moment, he hadn't known there could be so many facets to his temper. He felt reasonably sure that in the last hour he'd experienced all of them. The little fool! She'd driven around to the main alley by herself like there was no possibility whatsoever that someone could have waited on the corner for her, to end it then and there.

His Explorer waited for him. Raphael jumped behind the wheel with a second to spare before her atrocity of a vehicle lumbered into the alley. She beeped at him and kept on driving. Raphael swore and made an illegal U-turn to follow her. She was the most irritating, stiff-spined, starched, *tsking,* hardheaded, cop-show-watching, nosy fool he'd met in his fourteen years on this job. And she'd *sat* on Allegra.

Raphael grabbed the radio handset from his dashboard. "Who's got Allegra?" he demanded when he got reception and was patched through to the watch commander.

"Vince Mandeleone," said a disembodied voice.

Mandeleone. Fox's rookie partner for the month. He wasn't a rookie to the department, but to the Robbery

Homicide Unit. "I'm back with Fox in two hours." Even Raphael thought he sounded like a jealous lover.

"Yeah, that's the word," came the voice soothingly.

"So how come they're not sending Mandeleone back down?"

"He did some good stuff this last month. They're keeping him up."

That was okay. Raphael didn't want to hurt the kid, he just wanted his own space back. But something stuck in his craw. "They're letting him question Allegra?"

"Hell, no. I thought you meant who was making sure she doesn't get whacked over this. Fox is going to spend some time with her first before Mandeleone takes her home and bunks on her sofa."

"That'll last one night."

The voice cackled. They all knew Allegra, by reputation if not by experience.

"Anyway, Fox said to tell you to keep your cell phone with you. He'll touch base as soon as he's finished with Allegra."

"Will do." Raphael signed off.

He was beginning to get a feel for things here. When Plattsmier had assigned him to the caterer, all he'd heard was his own blood rushing in his ears. But now he could see how things would play out.

In two hours, he and Fox were legit again. They would be running this investigation. Raphael was just going to have to do his part with the rigid little brunette in tow.

She was going to be his personal albatross for a while. There was no getting around that. The commissioner wasn't going to let bygones be bygones quite yet. But Plattsmier, damn him, had accommodated them all—Raphael and the commish and himself as well. The commissioner would get his extra ounce of Raphael's blood by saddling him with the witness. And Raphael was on the case so it had a prayer of getting solved.

The panel van tucked into the driveway of a garage just ahead of him. He stopped the Explorer in front of the entrance. A moment later, he saw her heading up the tunnel again, coming toward him on foot. Her head was down and too much of that crazy hair spilled forward to hide her features. Not bad features, he thought grudgingly, as he remembered them. Small, almost delicate. Then his eyes narrowed. For the first time he realized that she was towing a small red wagon behind her, and it was loaded.

Raphael drove a shoulder against the Explorer's door and flung it open. He left the SUV idling in the street and jogged around it to meet her.

Whatever he had been about to say died in his throat when she looked at him. Her eyes were huge and bleak. They were indigo, he realized, more blue than blank.

"I don't even know your name." She whispered it as though it were the saddest thing in the world.

"Montiel." His voice was hoarse. Probably, he thought, with the restraint it took not to try to comfort her again. *Don't touch me.* He never made the same mistake twice.

"No, I meant your first name."

"Oh. Raphael. Rafe'll be fine." Then it struck him. He hadn't questioned her yet—that was by design. Once he'd gotten the lay of the land from Plattsmier, he'd known he'd do better to wait until midnight. But he hadn't even asked her name. He opened his mouth, and she cut him off as though reading his mind.

"It's Kate. Kate Mulhern."

"Kate." It was pretty. It made him think of sunflowers and Kansas. Oh, hell, maybe she wasn't that bad.

She waited for him to offer to take the wagon from her. It was heavy and hard to pull. It would be an overture, she thought, an olive branch of sorts so maybe they could get through this night somewhat amicably until his superiors let him leave her alone again. But he only watched her.

Kate pulled her shoulders back. She moved around him, dragging the wagon.

"So how fast do you think you can run with that thing behind you, Kate Mulhern?" His voice took on an edge again.

"As fast as I have to. But it's got to come with me. I'm not leaving it in the van, no matter…no matter…" She trailed off without pausing in her march.

What had happened tonight, he finished for her. He couldn't for the life of him figure out if she was as cold as the moon in January—what kind of woman would have the presence of mind to sit on Allegra after finding a body in her salad?—or if, in fact, she was falling apart. He didn't have the chance to ask her. She whipped around the corner of the garage entrance with the wagon, out of sight.

Raphael had to run to catch her. She stopped in front of glass doors on the corner. Pale light spilled from a dim lobby. He looked at his Explorer.

"Don't move an inch until I come back."

He went to the SUV. He parked it illegally in the nearest space and stuck his PPD card on the dashboard. It would do for the rest of the night.

He grabbed his cell phone and a tape recorder from the glove box and went to where she stood. She yanked open one of the glass doors and pulled the wagon in after her. It started to swing shut again before Raphael followed her, and it almost took off his nose.

He had a spare moment to look around the lobby. There were a handful of hot spots—a lot of fake ferns in one corner that could conceal a man, and a reception desk that someone could easily hide behind. There was no doorman.

Kate was punching the elevator button. He caught up with her.

"What's through there?" He nodded at a nearby door.

"Stairs."

"What floor do you live on?"

"The third."

There were too many ways up, he thought. He didn't like it.

"The elevator stops running at midnight," she said, as though reading his mind.

"Sounds like a real witching hour."

She looked at him quickly, and he thought she might smile. Then the elevator opened, and she simply nodded and towed the wagon inside. Raphael stepped in after her.

The elevator spit them out on the third floor. She moved down a short corridor and thrust a key into the lock of a door.

The apartment was something of a hodgepodge, and it startled him. He'd expected something stark and agonizingly organized. Rigid, maybe stuffy. Instead, there was a lot of wood, none of it matching. An old sideboard sat against one wall—it had been pressed into service as an entertainment center—and an afghan that was the color of the sun was draped casually over the back of the sofa. The rear wall was all windows, open to the summer night. The sounds of the city were close—a horn blared briefly, tires rolled over asphalt, a dog barked somewhere. It felt like a home.

"You live alone?" he asked. "No kids, no husband?" Extra people, he thought, would complicate things.

"No, there's no one. My roommate moved out in April."

She pulled the wagon into a tiny kitchen sectioned off from the main room by a breakfast bar. When she looked at him again, her eyes seemed very dark, almost black. She'd left one light on in the living room, but all it did was throw shadows across her face.

"How long are you going to be here?" she asked.

She bit off the ends of her words as though she was in a hurry to get them over with, he thought. But her voice was low, vaguely throaty. Raphael shrugged as though it had touched his skin. "I don't know."

"You're sleeping on the sofa."

"I wouldn't have it any other way."

That stung, even knowing, as Kate did all too well, that she was not the kind of woman who stirred men to passion. "I meant," she said, "that this is a one-bedroom unit."

"And I meant that the sofa's just fine with me."

Her hands were shaking again. Kate looked at them, then she fisted them on the counter. "You're waiting to question me until after midnight, aren't you?"

"Yeah."

Kate looked at a mantel clock that sat on the sideboard turned entertainment center. Healthy green plants were piled on either side of it. She took a deep, fortifying breath. "Then I'd better put on some coffee."

Chapter 3

The coffee was good. It was rich and dark, the way he liked it. After an hour, Raphael agreed to another pot, as much to give her something to do as for the fact that he needed the caffeine.

He watched her unload the red wagon and put things away, then rearrange it all in the cupboards and drawers. When she was done, every spice bottle faced forward, its label visible. He felt his eyes bug a little as he observed the process, and something happened to his blood pressure. Then finally the clock on the window seat began to chime midnight.

Her shoulder blades shifted under that starched white cotton as though she was bracing herself. "Okay, let's get this over with. I'm tired."

He wouldn't argue with her on that one. Raphael leaned forward to take the tiny tape recorder from his jeans pocket and put it on the coffee table.

She cleared her throat carefully. "I'll ask you again. Am I a witness or a suspect?"

"You're a witness unless you say something that would indicate otherwise."

"What if I lawyer up?"

It happened again, yet another facet of temper. This one was a small man standing inside each of Raphael's temples, battering with tiny, hot fists. "Lawyer up," he repeated.

"Ask for a lawyer."

"I know what you meant." He clenched his jaw. "How about if you leave the cop jargon to me?"

"Fine." Kate dropped onto the sofa opposite the small love seat he'd chosen. She clasped her hands together and bracketed them with her knees. Her eyes widened as he went through the routine for the tape—his ID, who he was interviewing, the location and the time.

He thought, in spite of himself, that she really did have beautiful eyes. The slant of light from the fringed lamp made them look almost black again, and they shone.

"Okay. First question. What were you supposed to be catering tonight?"

Kate blinked at him and said nothing.

"Care to have me repeat the question?"

"Of course not. I heard you. You just never struck me as stupid."

Raphael turned the tape off with a deliberate snap. "Can we leave the personal opinions out of this?"

"I wasn't—"

"Just answer my questions!" He lowered his voice. "Like you would if you were in one of those books you said you liked. You know, the ones where they lawyer up."

"Then you might try questioning me like they would in those books. What do you think I was catering? It was food. You ate some of it."

More tiny fists, Raphael thought. Boom-boom-boom at

his temples. With a careful, precise motion, he turned the recorder on again. "There was no party in that house tonight. What did McGaffney need a caterer for?"

"Allegra, I would imagine. I didn't ask. It's none of my business, except in the respect that it affects what I serve and how I serve it."

Raphael pressed his thumbs against the little men inside his head. "Ms. Mulhern. I'll ask again. What were you catering?"

Kate flopped against the sofa cushions, looking at him disbelievingly. "Filets with orange béarnaise sauce for the entree. The appetizer was oysters Rockefeller, followed by a hearts-of-palm salad. Well, you saw what he did to that." Raphael reached for the tape again, and she hurried on. "We never got to dessert, but I had pears in a caramelized brandy sauce for that course. Is that what you wanted to know?"

"All this for two people?" Raphael clarified. Something in his jaw ticked again.

"That's what I do."

"You cater for two people."

"That's my niche. Otherwise, I'd be just like every other caterer in Philadelphia. I needed to do something different if I was going to stand out, make my mark." She shrugged. "I've gone for as many as dinner for six, but then it starts negating my purpose."

Raphael began to understand. "So you do take-out dinners."

Kate stiffened. "Of course not. Restaurants do takeout. But what do you get? Food in little cartons that someone has to reheat—"

"And then it's stale."

She nodded urgently as she would at a clever child. "That's it exactly. And someone has to be in the kitchen to do all that, to spoon it all out and put it on the table. But I cater.''

"You bring it over and spoon it out and put in on the table.''

He might have just suggested that she shot McGaffney herself. She pulled her spine straight again. Somewhere Raphael thought he heard fingernails scraping down a blackboard.

"I prepare on the premises,'' she said stiffly.

"You took all this food over there and cooked it for McGaffney, and served it.''

"Yes. I do all the elegance and service and variety of eating out, but in the privacy and comfort of one's own home.''

"So how much did this cost him?''

"Two hundred and eighty seven dollars. Plus tax.''

Raphael felt his brows climb his forehead. "McGaffney paid three hundred dollars to have dinner at home with Allegra Denise?''

"He did unless his check bounces. What's wrong?'' She didn't like his expression.

"Why?'' he said, almost to himself. "Why would he do that? Did he call you himself to set this up?''

"I don't remember. But I can tell you in a minute.''

She got up and disappeared down a short hallway. Raphael waited, wondering. Why hadn't McGaffney just taken Allegra out, especially for that kind of money? Obviously, he had wanted to be alone with her. But why?

Sex came readily to mind. But knowing Allegra, McGaffney would have gotten that regardless. So he must have had something important to discuss with her. Inside word on the Eagan clan?

Kate came back with a notebook. "He called me himself,'' she said, waving it at him.

Raphael nodded. "When?''

"Two days ago. On Wednesday at three forty-seven p.m."

"You wrote down the time?"

"Of course."

"Why?"

Why not? There was no specific reason for it, but it didn't hurt to do, and who knew when she might need the information, like now? She stared at him without answering.

Raphael looked at her a moment too long. She made a good witness, but her ingrained sense of perfection was irritating the hell out of him. "Did he say why he wanted to engage your services?"

She seemed to think about it fiercely. "No."

"Nothing," Raphael clarified.

"He just said he was having a lady over."

"Did he say where he had gotten word of your business?"

"No, but I had a great review in the newspaper in June. Ever since then, I've been doing four or five dinners a week. I've even had to cut back on my hours at the diner."

"You cook at a diner, too?"

She nodded.

"Why? If you're doing five of these dinners a week, you're knocking back maybe fifteen hundred dollars, right?"

"Wrong. That's before costs. And paying the help. And taxes."

"Who helped you tonight?"

"No one."

"Then what does your help do?"

Kate sat back and rubbed her forehead. "Four out of five clients call already knowing what they want. You know, they'll request lobster or...or just something specific. They call with these silly, preconceived notions of what a gourmet meal should be. If I have to cook to their prerequisites, I can't always orchestrate it so that I can do the whole thing myself. I can't be serving if I need to be in the kitchen doing something to whatever's simmering there. On those occasions, I pay a second pair of hands to serve.''

''How many employees do you have?''

''Two now. They're on call. If one can't do it, the other one generally can. Actually, I just hired Beth four days ago.''

Raphael's antennae twitched. That was convenient. It would bear some looking into. ''Beth who?''

''Beth Olivetti.''

''Who's your other employee?''

''Janaya Thomas. She's been with me for about two months now.''

''But no one was with you tonight?''

''No. I just told you that. McGaffney gave me carte blanche to prepare whatever I wanted so I could streamline the meal.''

''Okay. Let's move on to that. To what you did tonight.''

Kate nodded, sitting forward again. She didn't entirely understand all his questions, but she was beginning to enjoy this—in a matter of speaking. It was intriguing, she admitted, watching him work through what had happened. ''I didn't hear anything.''

His eyes narrowed. ''Let me ask the questions, okay?''

''But that was what you were going to ask next, right?''

It had been, but he'd be damned if he'd say so.

''Anyway, I didn't. I just took the steaks to the dining room and there he was. Splat in the salad.''

''No gunshot.''

''No.''

The killer had used a silencer then, Raphael thought.

But she'd been right there in the kitchen, through a solitary door. "What about a...like, pffting sound?"

She thought about it. "I didn't hear anything like that. But then, there was the matter of the dog." As soon as the words left her, Kate felt her face go scarlet.

Raphael sat forward, his eyes narrowing sharply. "What dog?"

Kate got to her feet unsteadily. She looked warily at the door, where the little beast had once slept religiously whenever Shawna had gone out. *Love, murder and mayhem.* Belle had trailed those things behind her like a banner. And she had also saved Shawna's life.

As she had saved Kate's tonight.

It had been Belle, Kate realized. Because if she had taken those steaks to the dining room—the first steaks, twelve and a half minutes earlier—she could very well have walked in on the killer. McGaffney's skin had still been warm when she'd felt for his pulse. He hadn't been dead long.

Her heart caught, and Kate hit her chest with her fist to start it again. "Uh, I had just finished the steaks," she explained. "The first steaks, that is. There was a crash. She...this dog...came in through the back door I'd left open. She got up on the center island somehow and stole a steak and knocked one of my plates over. I had to cook two new ones."

Raphael frowned. "A dog came in and stole a steak."

"Correct." She really bit that word off.

"Did McGaffney have a dog?"

"Not that he mentioned." She bit her lip. "I don't think it was his."

"So where did it come from?"

"I just told you that. The back door."

"Uninvited?"

"Well, I certainly didn't offer her a nine-dollar-a-pound tenderloin!"

"Maybe it smelled the food." Raphael frowned. There was more to this, he realized. Unless he badly missed his guess, something really bothered Kate Mulhern about this dog. "Go on."

Kate shrugged meticulously. "There's nothing left to say. The whole thing set me behind twelve and a half minutes."

"Knock it off," he growled, deciding to get a little rough with her.

Kate flinched a little. "Knock what off?"

"You're hiding something."

"I am not!"

"Honey, I've been asking questions like this for a lot of years and I know evasion when I see it." Her eyes wouldn't quite meet his, he thought. Then she surprised him.

"Okay!" she cried. "Okay. You want to know the truth? I know that dog."

It wasn't what he had been expecting. "So you're saying what—it followed you there or something?"

"Or something." Then she gave a giddy laugh that bordered on the hysterical. "Four months ago, my roommate was walking to work. Some homeless woman stopped her and gave her a dog. That dog. And while Shawna was trying to figure out what to do with it, she was mugged."

"Yeah?" Raphael frowned, wondering what this had to do with anything.

"And Gabriel Marsden rescued her."

"Gabriel Marsden, the writer? The ex-cop?"

"The one who was on the run from that crazed Broadway producer at the time. The producer who was trying to kill him."

Raphael was starting to get it. A little. He remembered

the story. It had captivated newsmongers for broadcasts on
end.

"Shawna ended hooking up with him and they spent the
better part of two weeks running for their lives." Kate took
a deep breath. "With the same dog I saw tonight."

Raphael felt dazed. This was turning into the oddest
witness interview he'd ever conducted. Why didn't that
surprise him?

"Shawna named her Belle. Belle saved their lives—a
couple of times, actually. And then she just disappeared
into Manhattan once Gabriel and Shawna had brought the
killer down."

More cop jargon, Raphael thought, wincing.

Kate didn't tell him that Shawna and Gabriel had become convinced that the Chihuahua was…well, some kind
of an angel. "Anyway," she finished quickly, getting back
to McGaffney, "when I went out there the first time, with
the appetizers, McGaffney and Allegra were just sitting
there talking. And when I took those plates back, I thought
they might be getting, well, tipsy."

"Tipsy," Raphael repeated. Another word he rarely
heard in normal conversation.

"They'd gone through one bottle of the wine already.
His glass was empty."

He didn't want to admit that her powers of observation
were extraordinary. But she must have picked up on something in his expression. Kate shrugged.

"It's my job. I keep trying to gauge how things are
going, you know, to pick up on any little telltale signs. I
still feel a little anxious about all this. Success isn't all that
comfortable to me yet." Then, for the first time since he
had met her, she smiled.

The reflex was crooked, a little self-deprecating. And it
changed her face. He realized for the first time that there
was usually something hard and determined about her jaw,

and that it was part of what had been irritating him from the moment he'd found her perched on Allegra's back. But when she smiled, everything changed. There was a dimple at the left corner of her mouth—just one, without a matching counterpart. She looked wistful and soft.

He cleared his throat. He didn't want her to have a dimple. And if she did, then he damned well didn't want to notice it. "What about the next time you went to the dining room?"

"That would have been to take them their salads. And another bottle of wine."

"And after that?"

"I went back to get their salad plates. She was gone that time."

"Gone where?"

"He said to 'the little girl's room.'" Her expression told what she thought of that particular euphemism. "I took her salad—he wanted to keep his. I went back to the kitchen to finish up with the steaks, and…". She trailed off.

The dog, Raphael remembered. Then when she'd finally gone back after that, McGaffney had been dead. "So he was killed between the time you went to pick up the salad plates and the time you took the entrees out."

Kate was subdued. "Yes."

"If we could nail down just how many minutes passed—"

"We can. I served the steaks medium to medium rare, at McGaffney's request. They were two inches thick. Twelve and a half minutes in the broiler for the first set, then the dog did her thing, and it took me twelve and a half minutes to do two more steaks."

"Twenty-five minutes." He didn't know whether to be irritated with her again or amazed.

"Actually, less than that. I do most courses ten minutes

apart. So I went to get the salad plates when the first steaks had been in the broiler for two and a half minutes.''

Raphael stared at her, figuring out the time of death. She'd called 911 at eight-eighteen. Therefore, McGaffney had still been alive, by her calculations, at approximately seven fifty-five. Give or take thirty seconds.

She was a very dangerous woman to have left alive.

"Other than that, I was in the kitchen the whole time," she said. "I try to remain as unobtrusive as possible. So all I can tell you for sure is that the killer didn't come in through the back door." She frowned. "Are we done?"

For the first time, Raphael saw violet smudges beneath her eyes. He was reasonably sure they hadn't been there half an hour ago. "We're done. For now."

"Good." She looked at the mantel clock as she got up and headed for the kitchen. "I have to get up in five hours."

He didn't like the sound of that. In fact, it sounded a lot like an alarm was going to go off somewhere in this apartment at roughly six o'clock in the morning. Raphael followed her with his eyes. "What for?"

"I work at the diner from seven to eleven. The breakfast rush."

"Not tomorrow, you don't."

He should have recognized the warning signs by now. The way her shoulder blades shifted. The way she turned to him and stared.

"I can't call in on a morning shift. They won't have time to get anyone to replace me."

Raphael came off the love seat. "What if you were sick?"

"I don't get sick."

"What, you're Superwoman?"

She sniffed again. "No. I'm just reliable."

"Well, get over it."

She took a step toward him. "I will not. I have a life!"

"Not for the foreseeable future, you don't."

"I work!"

"So do I." He was getting angry again. "You make fifteen hundred dollars a week! What the hell do you need a diner job for?"

"I don't make fifteen hundred a week! I told you, there are costs. I've got employees to pay!"

That still left her clearing probably eight or nine hundred a week. This was insane.

"And I've got an obligation," she added.

"You work a second job you don't need because of an obligation?"

"Yes. No. Well, not entirely."

She made that sound again. It wasn't a sniff, not exactly. It was more a sharp intake of breath.

"I work two jobs to save money for my restaurant." And it galled her to say so, to let him in on…well, her dream. But his expression turned thoughtful, and he surprised her.

"Honey, my guess is that you might be better off just doing what you're doing."

The thought had occurred to her, too, just recently, since business had picked up so radically. Dinner For Two had been intended as a means to an end. But then, she'd never really expected it to take off the way it had.

She wouldn't give him the satisfaction of agreeing with him.

Kate turned off the light in the kitchen, then went and sat on the sofa near the pile of blankets and pillows she'd put out for him earlier. He sat beside her. Not too close, she noticed with that achy stirring in the area of her chest again. Well, she was used to that.

She looked at him out of the corner of her eye in the thin darkness. His eyes made something curl in the pit of her stomach. He was gazing thoughtfully at nothing, seeming to see only his own thoughts. But they were good eyes, she thought grudgingly, even when they hardened, like now.

Kate pulled her gaze away. "Just tell the press I didn't see anything. Then it won't be necessary for you to watch over me. These…these mobsters will read about it in the paper, then you can go on your way and I'll go mine."

Raphael laughed. "Sure. That'll work."

She drew herself up indignantly. "I fail to see why not. It's the truth."

"You think these guys are of a mind to say, well, if the cops say it's so, then it must be so?"

Put that way, it sounded ridiculous. "I don't want you here! I don't want you underfoot. You're going to…to complicate everything!"

"That's me, honey, one big complication." Raphael got to his feet again, feeling absurdly burned, just as he'd begun to feel sorry for her again. "All right, let me tell you how this is going to be. In five hours, you're going to call the diner. You're going to tell them you're not going to be in for a while, days at least. Take an unplanned vacation."

Kate opened her mouth to argue, then she closed it again prudently.

"Then you're going to stay figuratively handcuffed to me while I work this case, while I figure this out. Because that's about the only way you're going to get your precious life back. At the moment, I'm the only prayer you've got."

It made her stomach roll over queasily. But Kate rallied. "Your job is to watch over me, correct? Isn't that what Mr. Plattsmier said? That means *you* follow *me.* So I suggest you get some sleep so you'll be on your toes in order to do that. I'm a busy woman."

Kate stood from the sofa and walked toward the hallway. She tried not to hurry, as if she wanted to escape his reaction. As she passed the sideboard and the little lamp, she reached and flicked it out, plunging him into darkness.

"Good night." Then she went to her bedroom and slammed the door shut behind her. Purely for the satisfaction of it, she threw the lock just as hard.

Chapter 4

The exclamation of Kate's bedroom door shot through Raphael's head like a bullet. His accommodations sent his mood spiraling downward even more.

He bunked down on the sofa to find that there was a popped spring in the middle of her center cushion. In the thin darkness, it took on the proportions of the tire of a truck. The darkness was incomplete because a yellow neon sign pulsed right outside her living room window and wouldn't let shadows gather. Raphael considered closing the blinds but the August breeze was like the breath of an aging dowager—warm, fitful and without substance. Scant as it was, if he blocked it, he would suffocate.

Kate Mulhern didn't seem to own an air conditioner. Or if she did, she was hogging it for herself in her ramparted bedroom.

Raphael rolled, putting his back to the window, and punched his fist into the pillow. Then his cell phone rang. He sat up, grabbed it from the coffee table and snarled into it.

"Are we having fun yet?" his partner asked.

"She's a lunatic!" Raphael considered adding a string of adjectives but his mind went blank. He felt that overwhelmed by his situation.

"And here I'd thought she'd be just your type," Fox drawled.

"Yeah? What type's that?"

"Breathing." It was a low blow. They both knew the reason behind Raphael's somewhat frenetic dating patterns this past month. "It wasn't your fault," Fox said a silent moment later.

Raphael's tone turned caustic. "You taunt a killer, you can't expect him to strike back, is that it?"

"You didn't taunt him. We were closing in on him. Damn it, Rafe, you're smarter than this. What are you going to do, spend the rest of your life never going out with a lady more than once because some scumbag might decide to make her pay for her association with you?"

That was pretty much exactly what he had decided. There was no doubt in Raphael's heart that Anna Lombardo's blood was on his hands. Gregg Miller had targeted her, had chosen her, had strangled that calm, cool light right out of her eyes because of him. To warn him off. But Raphael was damned tired of talking about Anna tonight.

"What did Allegra have to say?" he asked.

Fox sighed, but he changed the subject. "Not a word worth repeating. She saw nothing, heard nothing, smelled nothing. She says she was in the bathroom and when she came back, Phil was dead."

It was pretty much what Kate had said. Raphael got up from the sofa. His stomach was rumbling. He headed for her kitchen.

"How about why McGaffney opted to dine at home tonight?" he asked finally. "Did Allegra have any insight on that?"

"Sure," Fox said. "Something about her knickers."

"That's a crock."

"It is. He wanted to ply her for information about what Charlie Eagan's boys have been up to. We know that. But we'll never get her to say so."

Raphael flicked on the kitchen light. He opened Kate's refrigerator, then stared.

"You still there?" came Fox's voice.

"She's got her leftovers labeled."

He saw a plastic container that said Beef. Raphael grabbed it and pried the lid off. Red and rare. He found bread, then horseradish sauce in a small glass jar that said Horseradish Sauce. He made himself a sandwich. As an afterthought, he grabbed a carton of milk from the refrigerator, as well. He opened a cupboard door. Where the hell were her glasses? He found metal utensils that looked like they could have been used in the Inquisition, but nothing resembling an object that one might drink out of. Disgusted with Kate's orderliness, he swigged from the carton.

"Did Allegra mention a dog?" he asked, swallowing.

"A what?"

"A dog."

"No," Fox said slowly, "I can't say that she did. Why?"

"There was one there tonight. Seems it wandered in through the back door while the lady was cooking. It stole a steak off one of her plates and beat it."

"A dog," Fox repeated.

"Right."

"You're thinking that it was some kind of a setup to divert the caterer's attention?"

"Well, it's weird, what with the timing and all."

"We've come across some far-fetched things over the years, but I think that's reaching."

Fox was probably right. "Damn, this is good." Raphael swallowed another bite of the sandwich and marveled. Then his voice darkened. "Let's wrap this thing up, pal. I don't know how many days of Betty Crocker I can stand."

"I'll make the rounds of Eagan's men in the morning."

"I'll take McGaffney's boys and see what I can find out there."

"Not to bring up a sore subject, but what about the caterer?"

Raphael licked the last crumb of sandwich from his finger. "She's coming with me."

"Sounds like a plan."

"Damned right it is."

Suddenly, the last of the caffeine rush from her coffee left him and Raphael was bone-tired. "I'll check in with you at midday," he said and disconnected.

He hit the light switch in the kitchen and flopped down on the sofa again. He stuck the whisper-thin pillow beneath his backside to provide some minimal padding against the torture spring. He covered his eyes with his forearm to shut out the pulsing yellow light, then, instantly, he slept.

The next thing he heard was her screeching.

Kate had not ever known that a man could snore in such a fashion. Oh, she'd heard it spoken of, joked about. But the constant, deep sound that came from her living room all night was beyond the realm of her wildest imagination.

Sometime just before dawn she got up to stuff an extra blanket against the crack beneath her bedroom door to buffer the sound. It helped a little, but she was still agonizingly aware that he was out there. He was invading her life, her world, her plans. Pervading everything that was precious to her, making her stay home from work. Or at least he was trying to. It remained to be seen who would be the victor in *that* little battle.

"Damn you, Phillip McGaffney," she muttered just as the alarm went off.

Kate rolled over and slapped her palm down on top of it. Then she was instantly contrite. Phillip McGaffney was dead. What kind of problems did she have compared to that?

Then a particularly resonant rumbling came from under the blanket beneath her door. At least McGaffney had not been forced to spend the night with Raphael Montiel chainsawing away on his living room sofa, Kate thought sourly. It was just possible the man had gotten the better end of the deal.

At least Montiel had left her alone. He hadn't—

Hadn't what? A thin laugh escaped Kate's throat. He hadn't been suddenly overwhelmed with lust for the single woman just beyond the locked and blanket-bulkheaded door? Not likely, Kate thought. He'd spent most of their interview the night before watching her with those green eyes squinting ever so slightly. Like she was a bug or a microbe on a slide, something he couldn't quite identify. He had not once glanced at her with anything resembling a gleam in those eyes.

"It doesn't matter," she muttered, getting to her feet, swaying slightly from fatigue.

Kate knew her assets, and she also knew that a man like Montiel would never appreciate any of them. She'd tangled with his type before—a man with that same lazy, confident sense of power—and she had been left almost literally at the altar by him in favor of a flighty, vapid, though admittedly physically perfect exotic dancer. She swiped a hand over her head to smooth her wild curls. Then she went grimly to the closed bedroom door.

The problem was that she knew relatively little about men, she realized. She'd been engaged for those six short months and had come out of that experience even more perplexed by the species than she had been before. She did know, however, that men didn't have to be particularly swept away by attraction to…well, to…want it. And mornings—well, men often felt particularly amorous in the morning, and it was not so much desire that got them that way but testosterone.

Kate eased back from the bedroom door. Better to be safe than sorry, she decided.

She retreated to her closet, then she went to her dresser, gathering clothing. She was not going to bounce back and forth between the bedroom and the bath with a towel wrapped around her. It was best to set a precedent, she thought, right here, right now. Who knew how much longer this situation would be necessary?

After she showered and had gotten dressed she tiptoed into the living room, past the sofa, then she stopped and stared. He was laying on his back. His right arm was flung over his eyes.

He had taken his shirt off.

"Oh, my," Kate murmured. The arm heaved over his face was corded and looked strong. She hadn't realized last night just how…well, muscled he was.

He hadn't used the sheet she'd given him. He still had his jeans on, and she was very grateful for that. But the snap was open, and the dark golden hair on his chest tapered down, narrowing into a V until it disappeared beneath the denim. Kate took in a deep breath and ran a finger under her collar. She took a step backward from the sofa, then two. *Coffee.* She needed coffee. Now.

She squared her shoulders and turned for the kitchen. Then she stared at her counter, and a sound of pure distress caught in her throat.

There was a carton of milk sitting out. A whole half gallon. And it was the good stuff, too, not two percent, not skim, but the carton she used in recipes. Her gaze flew around the kitchen. She knew every move he had made by the time she breathed again.

There were rye crumbs on the counter. His cell phone sat beside them. She hurried around the breakfast bar and yanked open the refrigerator door. Within another thirty seconds, she knew that both her roast beef and the horse-radish sauce had been decimated.

That didn't particularly bother her. She cooked for others to enjoy, after all. But the waste infuriated her—a perfectly good half gallon of milk!

"What have you done?"

Her cry went through Raphael's unconscious like a jet breaking the sound barrier. It boomed his heart into sudden overdrive. He rolled and groped beneath the sofa for the gun he had tucked there after removing it from his waistband last night. When he landed on his feet, he was armed. "What?"

Astonishment—and maybe just a little fear—punched the air right out of Kate's chest. "Put that away!"

Raphael looked around. There was no one in the apartment but them. "What?" he asked again.

"That…that *weapon!*"

Raphael looked down at himself. Sleep tried to cling to his mind like a sticky spiderweb, making his thoughts track too slowly. "It's been called a lot of things but—"

"The gun! Are you crazy? What kind of person are you?"

Raphael finally came fully awake. "Me? What the hell did you scream for?"

"I want a new baby-sitter." She turned her back on him smartly—he doubted if a trained cadet could pivot quite that cleanly—and went to the kitchen. She grabbed the telephone on the wall.

"Your hair's sticking straight up from your head."

Kate gave a cry and dropped the phone. She plastered

both hands to her skull. Of course it was. She'd stuck her fingers into it in dismay when she'd seen the mess he'd made of her kitchen.

She smoothed her hair frantically, then was appalled to realize that she even cared what he thought. She dropped her hands.

One wild curl had escaped her effort, he realized. It made him itch to touch it, to see if it would wrap around his finger with a life of its own. He was losing his mind.

"I don't want you here," she said.

"Yeah. We've been all through that." He snapped his jeans and tucked the gun into them at his back.

Kate struggled for reason. "I understand that the authorities think I'm in danger, but I want them to send someone else to protect me. Clearly, this isn't going to work."

Something vaguely uncomfortable gripped Raphael's stomach. He told himself it was just the way she talked. It was really starting to get to him. Clearly... Then again, he'd rarely been vetoed by any woman, for any reason on any job.

"Why not?" he heard himself ask.

"You're...you're..." Kate crossed her arms over her chest and wished he would put a shirt on. "Chaos," she finished.

"*I'm* chaos? *You* screamed."

"You wasted a whole half gallon of milk while I slept! And you woke up and pointed a gun at me!"

"I thought you were in danger!"

"Why on earth would you think that?"

"Because you were caterwauling!"

This time he could almost predict what she would do before it happened. That sniff. The immediate hoisting of her shoulders. "I was not caterwauling."

"You sounded like a cat with its tail trapped in a door."

Color flooded her cheeks. Raphael watched the phenomenon.

Then, finally, for the first time, he noticed the way she was dressed. She wore khaki slacks, socks and neatly laced sneakers. This was topped by a white turtleneck, albeit a sleeveless one. Except for her arms, every inch of skin from her chin on down was covered, laced, pressed, creased. She looked as though she had been up for hours already.

Raphael glanced at his watch. It was only twenty after six.

He scrubbed his face with his hands. He needed a shower and a shave. Of course, he had nothing with him to shave with, and she definitely didn't seem the type to keep an extra razor on hand for unexpected male guests. Let her call Plattsmier, he thought. The department was full of by-the-book rookies who would put her milk carton away after they drank from it, and they'd both be a hell of a lot happier if one of them was assigned to her. But Raphael doubted if any of them had ticked off the commissioner just lately, or if they knew a blessed thing about Philadelphia's organized crime netherworld.

Nope, he thought, he was stuck with her.

"Call in to your diner," he said. "Tell them you won't be in. I'm going to take a shower."

"No."

He'd already turned away from her. Now he looked back. She was holding the milk carton in front of her in both hands, as though it were a smoking gun.

"We talked about this last night," she said, drawing herself up again. "I have responsibilities. I intend to meet them."

Raphael felt his blood pressure creeping upward again and it wasn't even yet six-thirty in the morning. Then he realized that there was always more than one way to skin a cat.

He thought of her labeled food containers. Of her scheduling diary with the times of calls noted down. "Yeah? Counting the one to your commonwealth?"

Kate frowned. "What are you talking about?"

"You're one of two prime witnesses in a murder investigation. Seems to me you have a certain responsibility to the good people of Pennsylvania, too." Unless he badly missed his guess, this was one woman who had never missed a chance to vote. Hell, she probably wrote her comments in the margins of the ballot.

"I fail to see—"

"You're bait."

"I'm *what?*"

"Bait. You're alive. You might have seen something. In all likelihood, someone is going to come after you in an effort to remedy that problem. When it happens, I'm going to nail his—"

"Spare me the profanity," she said quickly.

"Backside to the wall."

"I take it self-confidence is not a problem for you."

"No. Not when it comes to my work."

That quelled her. A new flatness had come to his tone. It was unapologetic and brooked no argument. Kate felt like she was somehow losing this discussion. "What does that have to do with the Commonwealth of Pennsylvania?"

"The long and short of it is that by cooperating with me, you'll be helping to take a criminal off the streets."

She cocked her brows. It irritated the hell out of him. But Raphael was winning here, and he knew it.

"Let me get this straight," she said. "A killer comes after me, and you're there beside me so you can nail his—"

"—backside."

"—to the wall."

"Right."

"And no other officer could do this quite so well."

"I'm not an *officer*. I'm a detective. Big difference."

"I beg your pardon."

Raphael smiled graciously. "Bottom line, honey, you're stuck with me if you want to see justice served."

Kate nodded thoughtfully.

She should have been fighting it a bit more, he thought. This victory was feeling a little too easy.

"Okay," she said finally. "Go take your shower. I'll make us some breakfast. Then I'll let you come to the diner with me so you can play watchdog."

"Damn it—"

"Stop swearing."

"Get used to it."

"I will not."

"You're not *getting* it here! I need to look for this guy! I can't do that from a diner!"

"You just said he was going to come to me."

"He will. He'll try. I want to nail him first! I can't do that if I'm baby-sitting you!"

"That's your job!"

"It's my *assignment*. I can do it my own damned way. And my way is to keep an eye on you while I try to unravel this mess."

"Not without my consent."

He was going to kill her, Raphael thought. End of problem.

He's going to kill me, Kate thought. She saw his hands clench at his sides, and he did have that gun tucked behind him somewhere. She took a judicious step backward until her spine came in contact with the refrigerator.

She did not want to die. She most definitely *did* want

someone good watching her back until this was over. But that only made it doubly important that they set some ground rules here.

"Look," they said simultaneously.

Kate waved a hand. "Go ahead. You first. You will anyway."

"We need a plan here," Raphael replied.

This time her brows positively arched. "A plan? *You* want to make a plan?"

"Right."

"Such as?"

"If I had one, we wouldn't need one."

"Unless, of course, it was diametrically opposed to my own." His eyes went to slits. Kate held a hand up, palm out. "Okay, okay. Go ahead. You were saying?"

"Call in to the diner for one morning until we can figure out how we're going to do this."

She hated, positively *hated* to admit it, but it made sense.

"They'll understand!" he argued at her silence. "A man dropped dead into your dinner plate last night!"

"Actually, it was a salad plate."

"What the hell difference does it make?" he shouted.

Kate flinched. "One morning?"

"And then we'll take it from there."

Kate knew, somehow, that it was the best she was going to get. Besides, she saw an advantage to letting him win this one. It was a matter of give and take, she reasoned. Dinner For Two had an engagement this evening. Talking him into letting her do both seemed like something of a long shot. She'd give in on the less important of the two issues. The dinner engagement was something they could get into later.

"Okay." She put the milk down and reached for the phone. But she didn't punch in the number right away.

She watched him turn away and head for the hall, still shirtless. She took in those broad, bare shoulders. They moved nicely with his stride, with that grace that was all male. She contemplated the movement of muscle beneath skin that looked like pale bronze. Kate put the phone down again quickly and rubbed her palms on her khakis to dry them.

He paused at the door to the hall. "You wouldn't want to have kept that milk anyway."

"Why not?" she asked, startled.

"Because I drank right out of the carton."

He heard her make that strangling sound again. Raphael went on toward the bathroom, imagining her expression, grinning to himself. Regardless of the fact that he didn't want the prize, winning felt damned good, he decided.

Chapter 5

Regardless of her many irritating traits, the woman could flat-out cook, Raphael realized half an hour later. He'd come back from his shower to find *huevos rancheros* waiting for him. He didn't know how she had managed to do it so quickly, then he thought of her labeled refrigerator containers. Under the circumstances, they didn't annoy him quite as much.

Raphael dug into breakfast. Spices rolled over his taste buds, caressing them like a lover. There was the bite of the chilies, perfect enough to make him want to groan with pleasure. He almost felt guilty for using, and probably ruining, the razor he'd found in her shower.

He pushed his plate away and wiped his mouth with his napkin. "Listen, about that shower I just took—" But he was interrupted by a knock at her door.

The sound galvanized Raphael. It wasn't a conscious decision to shove his stool back and have his gun in his hand, the safety off, before his next heartbeat. It was fourteen year's worth of ingrained reaction to trouble. It was the image of Anna Lombardo's crime scene photos that flashed across his mind's eye before he took his first step toward the door.

"What are you doing?" Kate cried, horrified.

"Go to the bedroom. Now."

"I will not!" It was the second time in as many hours that he'd pulled that gun out! At first she'd been merely astonished at his lightning reflexes. But now he was waving the weapon around again like he was some kind of Wild West vigilante, and her heart threatened to stop entirely.

When he turned to her, there was something dangerous about the way he moved. Each motion was contained, violence restrained—not at all like he'd been in Mr. McGaffney's kitchen last night.

"Go to the bedroom," he said again, every syllable a warning.

Panic seized Kate by the throat, but she held her ground. "I'll do no such thing."

Then, suddenly, she was *furious*. Kate marched up to him and stuck her face close to his. "Stop this! Stop it right now! You're running around here like Billy the Kid! It was a knock on the damned door, not a gunshot!"

"Did you just swear?"

Kate reared back. "What?"

"I could have sworn I just heard you swear."

"So what?"

"What was all that earlier about watching *my* language? What, underneath all that proper and practical surface you're really a wild woman? That could make these next few days a lot more interesting."

It happened instantly, a feeling Kate had never experienced before in her life. It was complex, tangled and frightening. Too many things happened to her simultaneously. Her breath shortened in the same moment something warm swept upward from the very core of her. She felt her skin burn, her heart pump, her adrenaline race.

Was he *flirting* with her?

Then he turned away. The moment was gone.

"If you won't leave the room," he said, "then at least stand over there behind the breakfast bar where you can duck if you have to."

Kate found herself moving obediently on legs that wobbled. Then she got a grip on herself. "Please. I have friends," she said weakly, turning back. "I've got associates. I have a job tonight. It could be a delivery. You can't answer the door with that...that thing, ready to shoot somebody."

He looked at her sharply. "What job tonight?"

Kate bit her tongue. It wasn't time for that particular battle.

"Hello?" came a female voice through the door. "Katie, are you in there?"

Relief flooded Kate. It was Shawna, her old roommate.

She swept past him, and Raphael put an arm out to stop her. She ducked under it neatly, or maybe he just hadn't acted quickly enough. He felt a little off balance.

He frowned after her as she rushed to the door. At the sound of the voice from outside, her features went soft with happiness. Her mouth seemed fuller when she smiled. That single dimple came back, winking at him. Raphael realized with a jolt that when she was relaxed, she wasn't just pretty. She was knee-buckling appealing. He noticed that her turtleneck clung to small but uplifted breasts and her braided belt nipped a waist that his hands could probably span. She'd done something to her hair while he was in the shower, taming it off her forehead with a headband. Near-black curls fell to her shoulders.

He stared at it, wondering if he might like it better wild.

Then she threw the door wide and his heart caromed into his throat. He'd been standing there like a fool, staring at her, feeling as though he was seeing her for the first time. He wasn't ready for whatever might happen in the instant the caller had access to her apartment. But it was only a woman.

With a dog.

Kate made one of her strangling sounds.

"Good morning," Shawna said brightly, stepping inside. "Look who I found barking downstairs in the lobby! Isn't this wild? Belle came home. She's back!" Then her gaze fell on Raphael, and her eyes widened. "Who are you?"

"Uh…Rafe Monteil. PPD."

The woman, a beauty with thick blond hair and warm brown eyes, shifted the dog to her left arm so she could hold her right hand out to him. "I'm Shawnalee Marsden." Raphael shook the woman's hand, careful not to get too close to the animal. It growled a little and showed its teeth.

"It's that dog," Kate said faintly.

"What dog?" Then Raphael understood. "The one from last night?"

Shawna looked at Kate. "You knew Belle was back and you didn't tell me?"

Kate didn't answer. She felt faint. *Belle?* Then Shawna thrust her face up close to hers.

"Do you have makeup on?" Shawna demanded.

"I—"

"You *do*. You never wear makeup to work."

Kate flicked a gaze at Raphael and considered dying on the spot. Whatever had possessed her to put on lipstick and blush while he was in the shower? She wasn't trying to *entice* him, though that was how Shawna made it sound.

But she wasn't without her share of vanity. She'd just wanted to be…presentable.

"I'm not going to work," Kate said finally, hoarsely. "A few things have come up."

Shawna sized up Raphael again and grinned. "Do tell."

Kate felt her face heat even more. "It's not what you think."

Raphael finally got his wits about him. "Your friend witnessed a murder last night. I'm with Robbery Homicide. I'm here on business, not pleasure."

Kate felt something wither inside her. Whatever notion she'd had that he'd been flirting with her a few moments ago scattered like autumn leaves on a cold wind.

Business.

"What are you doing here?" she asked Shawna a little too sharply.

"You haven't called me in six days so I thought I'd drop by. Good thing, too." Shawna held the dog out to her. "Here you go."

Kate backed up quickly. "I don't want her."

"Of course you do."

"No, I don't."

"She really doesn't," Raphael said quickly. He knew a moment of abject horror as he realized where this was headed. The last thing in the world he needed right now was the stubborn and confusing Kate Mulhern, an ongoing murder investigation and a dog.

For once, Kate seemed to be in agreement with him. "That dog came back from New York looking for *you*," she said to Shawna. Then she went into the kitchen and began loading the dishwasher. Plates cracked and pans clanged. "You lost her in New York in April. Four months ago. Obviously, it's taken her all summer to find her way back to the last place where she was regularly fed. This apartment, where you lived at the time."

Shawna frowned. "You're so practical."

"Animals do that all the time."

"Belle is *not* just an animal."

Kate considered the short time the dog had lived with them in April. *Love, murder and mayhem.* "Maybe not. Maybe she's the devil incarnate."

Shawna put her hands over the dog's ears too late. Belle curled her lip and snarled. "Now see what you've done? You've hurt her feelings."

Raphael watched Kate slam a plate into the bottom rack without answering.

"How did you know she was back?" Shawna looked at Raphael again. "Didn't you say she actually came home last night?"

"Not here," Raphael explained, his head spinning again. "She turned up at the house where Kate was working." Scratch the idea that it was a setup, he thought. This pup was some kind of bad penny with a penchant for turning up unexpectedly.

"You see?" Shawna cried to Kate. "Why would Belle look for *me* at one of *your* jobs?"

Kate opened her mouth and shut it again. An odd sensation filled her stomach. There remained the fact that Belle had probably saved her life last night. "I don't know."

"Come with me," Shawna said. "We need to talk."

Raphael watched the blonde head toward Kate's bedroom. Then something amazing happened. Kate followed without arguing. Apparently she had the capacity to follow orders *some* of the time.

"Don't you see what's happening here?" Shawna demanded when they were alone.

Kate pressed her fingers to her temples. "You're going to do it again. You're going to get all metaphysical on me. That dog is *not* an angel."

"Then explain why she came back. That cop said you saw a man killed last night."

"He's not just a cop. He's a detective. He gets a little testy when you don't iron out the difference." Kate sighed. "And I didn't see the guy get killed. He was already dead when I got to the dining room."

Kate filled her friend in on what was going on.

Shawna let out a shaky breath. "Wow. Raphael Montiel."

"Why are you saying his name like that?"

"Don't you get it? Gabriel—" Shawna spoke her husband's name musically, enunciating carefully "—and Raphael."

"Gabriel and Raphael," Kate repeated. "So?"

"Archangels." Shawna whispered it as though imparting the Holy Grail. Then she squeezed Belle happily, and the ugly little dog licked her cheek. "They're both named after archangels. You're a clever one, aren't you, little Belle? It's just like her to throw both of us at men named after archangels."

Kate felt panic wrap around her windpipe. "You're crazy. Nobody's throwing me at him. He's horrible. He's rude. He was going to shoot you when you knocked on the door. He left my milk out!"

"It's about time someone shook up your orderly life. You really need to flex more, Kate. You two are obviously meant for each other."

Kate choked. "He doesn't even like me! I could deck myself out like a cheap hooker and I wouldn't appeal to that man!"

"I should hope not," Shawna said, frowning. "That wouldn't say much for his taste."

Kate groaned inwardly. She did not want to have this discussion. It could only hurt. "I'm not beautiful."

"Glamorous. You're not *glamorous*," Shawna corrected

baldly. "You're certainly pretty in a wild, down-to-earth kind of way. Besides, you're just letting that fool Jeff get to you again."

Kate flushed. But if she was, who could blame her? "He dumped me and ran off with the cupcake who danced at his bachelor party!" It had hurt, oh, it had hurt! She could still barely tolerate hearing his name spoken aloud. "He said I was everything he ever wanted. He said I'd make a great wife and mother. I was so organized, so capable, so efficient! Then he tossed me over for someone with a belly-button ring and ruler-straight hair, someone who couldn't even spell her own name!"

Shawna stroked Belle's head thoughtfully. "Let me tell you what I know about men."

"You hardly dated before Gabriel came along," Kate scoffed, "what with law school and working to put yourself through it. This may not be your area of expertise."

"My point," Shawna continued, "is that men are like those Rorschach tests a shrink gives."

Kate frowned. "Men are like Rorschach tests?"

"Exactly. They're black-and-white blobs."

"Blobs."

"When you first look at them," Shawna explained, "you think they look exactly like a cow. But what you're really looking at is two minstrels holding hands. What you see isn't actually what you get."

"Your point?"

"Jeff acted like he wanted a quality woman. What he really wanted was belly-button rings."

Kate stiffened. "That became apparent."

"You don't know yet what Raphael wants."

Kate thought of his easy and familiar demeanor with Allegra Denise last night. She thought she had a pretty good idea. "You're giving me a headache."

"What I'm trying to say is that the only way you can

ever really know what a man is thinking is to goad him into acting on it.''

Kate stared at her. She felt momentarily overwhelmed again. Whatever Raphael actually thought of her didn't matter. Jeff Migliaccio and what he had done to her no longer mattered. The names of archangels didn't matter, because *she* certainly did not want *Raphael*. Shawna was missing the point. He might look good—okay, yes, delicious—but she couldn't think of one single thing she actually liked about him.

''Anyway, no matter what happens, you're going to need Belle.'' Once again, Shawna held the dog out to her.

Kate reached and pushed the dog back. Belle nipped neatly at her finger. ''Ow!''

The dog began squirming. She was small and wiry. She wriggled free of Shawna's arms, though Shawna didn't particularly try to hold her. She hit the floor with a mild thud and yipped once. Then she trotted over to Kate's bed and climbed the bedspread. She was too short to jump up on the mattress, so she took a mouthful of the spread and pulled it downward. Then, delicately, she ascended it. She went to the pillow and lay down, wagging her tail once when she saw them watching her.

It more or less defied gravity.

''I didn't just see that,'' Kate murmured.

''Sure you did. I'm telling you, Katie, this dog's not of this world. If someone is trying to kill you, then I would very much recommend that you let her stay here for a while. Not to mention what she could do for your love life.''

''I don't *want* a love life!'' Kate took a step toward the bed and reached for the dog. Belle's head shot up, and she showed small, sharp teeth.

''Keep me posted,'' Shawna said, turning for the door again.

"No, wait—"

But Shawna was gone.

Raphael got up from the sofa and turned the television off when the blonde came back. The woman stopped beside him and looked over her shoulder in the direction of the hallway. Raphael followed her gaze. So far, there was no sign of Kate.

There was no sign of the dog, either. That worried him.

"Take care of her," Shawna said in a conspiratorial tone. "She's the best friend I've ever had."

"Kate or the dog?"

Shawna gave a quick peal of laughter. "Both. But don't worry about Belle. She can take care of herself." She wiggled her fingers in farewell and sailed through the door.

Kate appeared in the hall a moment later.

"Where's that animal?" Raphael demanded.

"Asleep on my bed."

"Ah, no. Damn it, do you have any idea how this is going to complicate things?"

"So you go move her." Kate held up her finger.

Raphael saw what he thought might be teeth marks. "She bit you?"

"She has a way of not doing things she doesn't want to do. I remember that part very clearly. Actually, Shawna thinks she's…never mind." Kate sighed, then she went to the sideboard turned entertainment center. She pulled open a drawer and took out a black pouchlike purse—big, roomy and eminently practical. "Let's go."

Raphael narrowed his eyes. "I thought you called in to the diner."

"I did. But now we've got to go to a pet store and buy a crate. If you think I'm going to let that little tyrant have free run of my apartment while you're dragging me around playing Sherlock Holmes, think again."

It was already nine o'clock. He should have been on the

street an hour ago, Raphael thought, shaking down some of McGaffney's men. But it had taken him three hours to convince her to call in sick to the diner—and to acquire a dog.

Raphael stuck the tape recorder and his cell phone in his pockets. Then, with a last unbelieving glance toward the hall and the Chihuahua who lurked down there somewhere, he followed her.

"You know, they make dog pounds for just this sort of eventuality," Raphael said an hour later.

Kate glanced over at him as they left a pet store on the corner of South and Broad. A couple of cold fingers tickled the nape of her neck. "Not a good idea."

He hefted the box that held the crate to get a better grip on it. Effortlessly, she thought, though she knew it was heavy. She had tried to move it herself. At least, she thought, he was good for manual labor when he decided to be a gentleman. But she'd practically had to kick him in the shin to get him to give the concept a try.

He stepped from the curb to hail a cab. When one slowed down near him, Kate quickly waved it on. Raphael looked at her disbelievingly. "What did you just do?"

"We've got another stop to make. We can walk. It's not far."

"What's not far?"

"The Italian market."

"We're not going to the Italian market. We're taking this crate back to your apartment, then we're going to hit the streets."

Kate bit her lip. He wasn't going to like this. But hadn't she called in sick to the diner? "We have to go to the market. I need prosciutto."

"Prosciutto."

"For the pear cornets."

"What pear cornets?"

"Are you always this slow? I told you, I have a job tonight."

He let the box go. It hit the pavement with a thud, the metal clanging inside.

"Of course," she said quickly, "you can hit the streets while I go to the market."

Raphael took a very deep breath. He kept his hands judiciously clear of the gun still tucked at his back. Ah, the temptation. "You're my retribution, aren't you?" He looked at the sky as though searching the heavens. "That's it. You're like my penance for every wrong turn I've ever taken in my life."

Kate crossed her arms over her chest. "Well, I imagine there have been a few."

"What do you know?" he growled. "You think a transgression is leaving milk out on the counter!"

"Not when some slob drank directly from the carton."

"You don't have any glasses!"

"I have a whole cupboard of glasses!"

"Where? You just tell me where I was supposed to find them!"

"Over the oven."

"What, you *bake* with them?"

"The oven is right beside the sink. Ergo, when one wants a drink of water, they merely need to reach over their head and to their right."

"Ergo? *Ergo?*" Raphael threw up his hands. "Go ahead. Go to the market and get yourself killed. Damned if I'm going to knock myself out over this. And take that crate while you're at it. *You* carry it."

He left her and started up Broad Street. In the instant he turned away, Kate felt a hundred guns aimed right at her back. Which was ridiculous. But her skin itched at a point halfway between her shoulder blades anyway.

"Come back here!" she shouted. He kept walking. "I'm sorry!" She had no idea what she was apologizing for, but panic was trying to crawl up her limbs. She looked around helplessly. For what? A gunman? Or would someone rush at her wielding a knife?

She was letting him get to her, and that angered her as much as anything. But then he stopped and looked over his shoulder at her.

"What? What was that you just said?"

The words tried to jam in her throat. Kate pushed them out again. "I'm sorry."

He took in her stance. She stood with the crate at her feet, her hands planted on her hips. Her expression would have given an armed mercenary pause. "No, you're not."

"Let's just talk about this."

"You don't know how to talk."

"*Please.*"

And then, damn it, he thought he saw her chin tremble.

He'd become a cop for a very good reason. The world was full of women, kids, innocents who needed someone who cared enough to fight back on their behalf. And in that moment, she looked like one of them. Vulnerable. Scared. She looked left to right, those midnight curls swirling at her shoulders. Her arms came up to hug herself.

Raphael felt an almost painful rolling sensation in his chest, like his heart had suddenly taken it upon itself to change position. He walked to her.

"Okay," he muttered, "calm down."

"I'm calm." She took in a long sniff this time, one that probably cleared out her nasal passages. "It's just... I didn't *do* anything."

Raphael felt his temper spark again. "You've done plenty! It's ten-thirty! I should have interviewed five guys by now! I should have a clue who ordered that hit last night!"

"But I didn't do anything to Phillip McGaffney!"

Well, he thought, that was probably true. It wasn't her salad that had done him in.

"And I've got a job tonight. I gave you the diner. I called in sick. But I can't turn away business for Dinner For Two. I need that prosciutto, and none of this is my fault!"

"This is all about prosciutto?"

"It's about my *life!*"

"Which, I might point out, I'm trying to save."

"What's it worth if I lose everything?"

Raphael scowled. He wanted to comfort her somehow, but he remembered her reaction last night when he had done just that. Not to mention the fact that he didn't know who might be watching them at the moment—which killer, which scumbag, might glimpse a personal moment between them and decide to pluck her clean away whether she actually meant anything to him or not. "I might have had this guy by now if you hadn't eaten up the whole damned morning being obstinate," he complained instead. "You could have had your life back already."

"Oh, get real. You would *not* have had him."

Several small percussion instruments began sounding in his head. "What, you're casting aspersions on my professional capabilities now?"

"Aspersions? And you think I talk funny?"

Raphael scrubbed his hands over his face. Aspersions, indeed. She was rubbing off on him. "I'm not a dumb cop."

"Of course not. You're a *detective*. But even detectives need some forensic evidence to go on, don't they? And you don't have any yet."

"How the hell do you know?"

"Because you've been carting that phone around with you all morning but you haven't talked to anyone even once! Wouldn't someone have called you if they'd found something?''

He'd just lost another half hour arguing about this. And he didn't even know what they were arguing about. ''The killer was one of Charlie Eagan's goons,'' he said finally. ''There probably won't be much in the way of forensic evidence. These guys tend to be real careful about stuff like that. Which is why I need to shake a few trees here. And the sooner I do that, the sooner you're rid of me.''

There *was* that, Kate thought.

''I don't have time to go chasing down prosciutto.''

''One hour, then we'll be back at my apartment. You can make phone calls while I get things together for to-night.''

''I can't do what I need to do over the phone.''

''Why not?''

''Because if I use the phone, people who don't want to talk to me can hang up on me.''

''So if you do it in person, you can bang a few heads to force the issue?''

''Now you're catching on.''

He meant it. Kate was appalled. What had happened to life as she'd always known it, where people reasoned with each other and drank out of glasses?

''Don't do that,'' he warned.

''What?''

''That thing with your eyes.''

''I didn't do anything with my eyes.''

''Yeah. You did. You closed them for a second.''

''It's called blinking!''

''Not the way you do it.''

''How do I do it?'' She widened them deliberately.

''Like you're suffering.''

''Well, the PPD has saddled me with *you*.'' His eyes narrowed. ''Although I have no doubt you can keep me alive," she added quickly, just in case he decided to leave again.

"Then *let* me."

"After the prosciutto."

It wasn't really the prosciutto he had a problem with, Raphael thought. It was what it meant. "Where's this job tonight?"

"Literally? You mean the address? It's a high-rise on Park Avenue. Twelve twenty-two, I think."

"How many ground-level entrances?"

Kate stared at him, flabbergasted. "How the hell should I know?"

He grinned suddenly. "Oh, stop."

"What?"

"You're swearing again, and I told you how that turns me on."

He was impossible! And, Kate was reasonably sure by now, he was teasing her on purpose, to divert her. But it didn't matter. Something slow and hot curled up and rolled over in the pit of her stomach anyway.

She could handle the flirting. She *could*. She was practical enough to know that he didn't mean anything by it. All she had to do was look at him to understand that. He was all animal grace and golden good looks, just like Jeff had been. He was so…well, contentedly male, she thought, so complacent and confident with himself inside his own skin. How many times with Jeff had she marveled and rejoiced that a man like that should want her? Now she knew better. Allegra was Raphael's type, she thought again, not someone who was five foot four if she stood on her tiptoes, someone who did not have a bad hair day now and again, but was having a bad hair *life*.

The problem was…his eyes.

Raphael had a way of looking at her when he said things, a steady way with that smoky green gaze, while one corner of his mouth crooked up in a secret smile. Like there was something shared between them that no one else would understand. Like he meant every word he said, and she ought to know it. Jeff had never looked at her that way.

"All right," he said finally. "We'll do your dinner."

"We will?"

"But there are conditions."

"Such as?" Her heart kicked. Was he flirting with her again?

"You can't take any help. No employees. It's just you and me, honey."

Just you and me, Kate thought dazedly.

"I don't want any other bodies to watch out for."

"Oh." Kate straightened her spine abruptly as though a car had just whipped around the corner and thrown cold puddle water at them. *Business.* "Of course not."

"All right, then. Let's go get your prosciutto."

He picked up the crate box. Kate nodded cautiously and walked on without him, but she looked back once, warily, to make sure he followed.

He was out of his mind, Raphael thought. This was going to shoot the holy hell out of the rest of the day. He was going to have to background check these customers. He'd need to get officers to stand on all the downstairs entrances to the building. But maybe he could touch base with Fox and get him to move on to McGaffney's boys when he got through with the Eagan supporters, he thought. They weren't *both* hamstrung by this infuriating, stubborn brunette.

It was her eyes, Raphael thought. It was that bleak, I'm-losing-it-all-here way those midnight-indigo eyes could turn down at the corners. She was a victim. And he just had a soft spot for victims.

It had nothing to do with the tight little way her hips

moved as she strode up the sidewalk ahead of him. Not a thing to do with the way her breath had quickened again when he had joked about being turned on. Or with that guileless, bemused smile she'd gotten on her mouth, the one that made it seem fuller, softer.

Raphael dug his cell phone out of his pocket while he followed her, and called his partner.

"Yeah," he said shortly. "We've got a little change of plans here."

Chapter 6

She could have used an extra pair of hands for the Morley dinner, but Kate definitely wasn't going to argue the point. She called Beth Olivetti as soon as they got back to her apartment and told her she wouldn't be needing her after all.

The Morleys weren't easy clients under the best of circumstances, and she would need all her wits about her to pull this off by herself. Denny Morley had made his money in merchandising, and the couple had more of that than taste. They had somehow gotten it into their heads that shellfish was *de rigueur* for an elegant dinner, and they requested their menus accordingly. Kate would not be able to streamline the meal as she had with the McGaffney engagement.

Her seafood delivery arrived and she spent the afternoon cracking open lobster claws and peeling shrimp. Her hands were beginning to cramp when she glanced over the breakfast bar at Raphael. She did not want to squabble with him

Beverly Bird 79

again and give him an opportunity to change his mind about this job. But still...

"You're dripping." He'd brought a huge hoagie home from the Italian market and he was eating it over the wrappings he'd spread out on her coffee table.

He looked over his shoulder at her from his seat on the sofa. "What?"

"You're dripping," she repeated. "Oil. Maybe an onion or two. On my floor, I believe. Or maybe my sofa caught it."

He looked at the cushions. "There's a pity. You might have to break down and buy a new one."

She was startled enough to forget she was annoyed with him. "Why would I want to do that?"

"So strangers can sleep on it without discomfort?"

"Strangers don't sleep on it."

He cocked a brow at her.

"As a general rule. And it's perfectly serviceable otherwise. Why would I want to throw away a thousand dollars on a sofa? Do you know how far that money would go toward outfitting a restaurant kitchen?"

Raphael thought that if he gave her any provocation at all, she would gladly tell him.

He popped the last bite of hoagie in his mouth and wadded the wrappings up in a ball. Then, incredibly, he took aim at her trash can with it. She jumped into its path and caught it in midair, grimacing at the slick oily spots. Then she began washing her hands to get the onion aroma off them before it could taint everything else she touched.

Raphael sat back and put his feet on her coffee table. Her magazines slid to the side when his heel made contact with them. Kate reached for a knife and began chunking the lobster, imagining that it was his throat laid bare on the cutting board.

She listened to Raphael talk on his cell phone, then he

clicked a button with his thumb and disconnected. "This is going to cost the city a pretty piece of overtime."

Kate's hands paused over the lobster. "Why?"

"Two officers in the lobby and two each on every entrance, one inside and one out. That's a grand total of eight."

Kate chewed her lip. She really didn't like the idea of what she was doing to the city's poor, beleaguered budget. "Is all that necessary?"

"You want to take the chance that it's not?"

She got that cold feeling at the nape of her neck again.

His phone rang. He grabbed it and muttered into it a few times and began writing something down. This time, Kate moved around the breakfast bar to peer over his shoulder and see what it was. Then her eyes widened.

When he disconnected, she couldn't hold her tongue. "You investigated the Morleys? How could you do that?"

"Background check."

The kitchen towel began whipping in her hands as she dried them. "That's an invasion of their privacy! If they find out—"

"He's got forty-two thousand dollars in his checking account."

Her hands stopped cold. "He what?"

"It seems like a regular monthly deposit. Maybe his salary. I'll check into his company next."

Kate sat down hard on the love seat.

"Watch the eyes," he warned. "You're doing that thing with your eyes again."

This time she didn't give a damn. "Just destroy me!" Kate cried. "Just…just put an ad in the *Inquirer* announcing that I killed clients with salmonella. It will be quicker." She gulped breath. "You're going to ruin everything I've spent four months working toward!"

"Maybe, but I'm not going to let you go in there tonight

if there's any chance that these people are associated with O'Bannon, McGaffney or Eagan.''

"With mob bosses? The *Morleys?* Are you out of your mind?''

"Honey, you'd be surprised.''

Kate opened her mouth and shut it again. *Don't argue with him.* What if he should change his mind about tonight? "Is there any way the Morleys can find out we poked into their private business?''

"Not really.''

Kate breathed again.

"Unless that guy at the bank is a pal of theirs and he tells them. Come to think of it, I might have used your name.''

Kate blanched. He laughed.

She fisted the dish towel around her hand to keep from hitting him with it. She closed her eyes briefly, then she realized that he'd probably say she was suffering again. Kate forced herself to smile weakly. She'd smile if it killed her.

Someday this would all be over.

"This dinner was booked a week ago,'' she pointed out in her best reasonable tone, "before McGaffney was killed. I can't believe that it's a setup to draw me in and off me.''

Raphael cocked a brow, his smile fading. "*Off* you?''

Kate flushed. "You know what I mean.''

"Do you advertise?''

She scowled, trying to gauge his point before she answered.

"In magazines, newspapers, the Yellow Pages, that sort of thing, to draw in business.''

"Rarely. It's expensive.''

He would have bet on that answer. "You probably do a lot of business by word-of-mouth. Friends telling acquaintances, hey, you ought to try this new catering service."

Kate thought about it and nodded cautiously. "But there was also that newspaper review. That kick started things. That's how the Morleys first came to me."

"So who do you suppose told McGaffney about Dinner For Two?"

"I—" It *could* have been the Morleys, she realized. Or the Cornwalls or the Santangelos. She had amassed a list of wealthy regulars after that review. Anyone could have passed the word on. Any one of them could be peripherally associated with the man.

Kate shivered a little. It was all so complex, so tangled.

Raphael caught the reflex. Her eyes changed, too. He realized that they went black whenever she realized the magnitude of the truth of her situation. He stood from the sofa abruptly before she could do it to him again, before those eyes could make something soft and protective start moving around inside him, rolling his heart right upside down.

Then she sighed heavily. It was as bad as that blinking thing she did with her eyes.

"How long is it going to take you to get all your food ready and get out of here?" he asked shortly.

"At least another hour."

"You've got thirty minutes."

"*What?* I can't! They don't want dinner until seven! I can't invade their home three hours early! And I've still got to skewer the shrimp and make the mayonnaise!"

"You can always cancel. Which would actually be the best thing."

"No!"

"Then get that pretty little tail of yours in gear. I want to get everybody, including us, in place early so I'm sure we have the lay of the land."

Kate started to argue. Then she registered his words. *Pretty little tail?*

No, she thought, she was *definitely* not going to start considering again if he meant it or if things like that just rolled off his tongue as a matter of course. Then again, her tail wasn't all that bad. It was one of her better assets. Though Jeff had never specifically mentioned it—he'd been too busy eating her cooking—she thought that maybe in that one tiny area, she might have given Miss Belly-Button Ring a run for her money.

Raphael leaned toward her and snapped his fingers in front of her eyes. Kate jumped. ''What?''

''Did you hear me?''

''Thirty minutes,'' she repeated breathlessly.

He looked at his watch. ''Nope. Twenty-nine now.''

He waited for a retort and didn't get it. She shot to her feet and hurried to the kitchen. Which, he thought, was probably just as well.

He was starting to enjoy her reactions just a little too much.

Kate called ahead to warn Betty Morley that she would be arriving early. She told her that their dinner was very complex and would need some special time, and each word of the lie felt as unwieldy as pebbles on her tongue.

At a quarter to four, they wrestled Belle into the new crate. It took a concerted joint effort. Kate put the contraption in the bedroom and closed the door against the dog's aggrieved barking. Then she towed her wagon out the door.

Raphael went ahead of her up the hallway. He checked the elevator before she stepped into it and held her back from leaving it when the car stopped. Kate rolled her eyes behind his back.

''I saw that.''

Kate started. For the first time in all the years she had lived in the building, she realized that there was a mirror positioned at the top corner of the elevator. She looked into it and stuck out her tongue.

It flicked, fast and almost unnoticeable, but Raphael caught it. He felt a flash of something instantly alert under his skin, tightening his flesh. And that ticked him off.

The lobby was deserted. He moved quickly across it, letting her hurry to catch up. As she followed him through the doors onto the street, he stopped suddenly. "Watch out!"

Kate jumped out of her skin. She dropped the wagon handle, and it hit the sidewalk with a clatter. She nearly lost her balance jumping backward.

He turned to her and grinned. Her heart pressed up into her throat. "That was a hideous joke!"

"Got your attention, didn't it?"

She *was* scared. But admitting it—giving in to it—just seemed so…weak. And it was senseless. Fear was a waste of energy and emotion. She was determined that she was going to plow her way through this…this accidental mess with her life intact. She would keep sane, no matter how paranoid he tried to make her.

"They'll make it painless for you," Raphael said. "You haven't done anything to cross them. You're what they call an 'unfortunate.' Something that shouldn't have happened but you did, so now your existence has to be rectified."

He watched the color wash from her complexion. He went on anyway.

"You won't feel a thing. It will be a quick shot while I'm looking the other way, say, checking to see which prosciutto looks fattier. *Watching your tongue slide in and out of your soft, full mouth.* Raphael snapped his fingers. "Just like that, and you'll be gone."

"Stop it," she whispered.

He put a hand out to steady her. He thought of touching her shoulder, of kneading out some of the tension he'd deliberately put there to make his point. But they were on the street, where anyone could be watching. And he remembered what had happened the last time he'd done it. *Don't touch me,* she'd said.

For a minute, Kate thought he was going to reach for her again, the way he had last night. And this time, she realized, she really *needed* him to. Because no matter what else he was, no matter what he had done to her world, he had also coldcocked a serial killer a month ago. And knowing that made her feel...safer.

She was, after all, his job. She had a feeling he would go at it full throttle.

If he touched her, she thought, she'd feel all that in the contact. And for a moment, just a moment, she craved the reassurance. But then his hand went back to his side. She bent for the wagon handle.

Her eyes were ready for battle when she straightened. Raphael felt a swish of admiration for her.

"Just let me do my job," he said quietly.

"I am."

"No. You're distracting me."

"How am I distracting you? I've done everything you said!"

You're here.

Raphael almost said the thought aloud. The words crowded his throat, but he couldn't say them because he couldn't explain them. In the twenty some hours they'd been forced together, something had segued inside him. She'd stopped irritating him so much as she...provoked him.

She confused him.

He'd already spent more time with her in one day than

he'd spent with any woman since Anna Lombardo had gotten her throat sliced, he realized. Enough time that, under normal circumstances, any initial flare of attraction should have worn off. At the very least, it should have been easy for him to turn around and walk away, quickly and cleanly, before things got too involved or complex.

But she was having the reverse effect on him. Somehow, she was drawing him in. She was growing on him.

Raphael turned his back on her and started up Bainbridge. "Come on. Let's go. Keep up with me."

Kate didn't need to be told twice. She ran to catch up, but her legs felt unsteady.

She didn't know what had been going through his mind when his face had changed like that, and she told herself that she didn't want to know. But for a minute, he hadn't looked like her worst nightmare. For a minute, he hadn't looked like chaos and aggravation at all. For a moment, he'd looked…vulnerable. Almost human.

It had startled her, and it poked at something soft deep inside her. By the time they reached the garage and loaded her van, a gunman was the last thing on Kate's mind.

By six-thirty, Kate remembered the other thing she really disliked about serving the Morleys. Betty Morley had never learned the gracious art of sitting back and letting someone else serve her.

She hovered in the kitchen as Kate skewered the shrimp brochettes and slid them under the broiler. Kate had to move fast to keep everything on schedule. Without missing a beat, she spilled rock salt into the bottom of the cast-iron skillet in which the main course oysters would nestle through their stint in the oven.

"A frying pan?" Betty Morley asked, leaning over Kate's shoulder to inspect it.

"It can hold up to high temperatures and it's got a handle for easy retrieval."

"How clever!"

Kate nodded and scooted over to the oven. The brochettes were nearly ready. She glanced at the woman helplessly. She had never been one for subtle social arts, and she had to fish for an approach.

"Are you enjoying the wine?" she asked, trying to send her back to the parlor.

The woman only moved beside her again to peer into the broiler at the brochettes. "Your associate says it's very good. And Denny likes it."

Her *associate*?

For the first time in a hectic ten minutes, Kate glanced quickly around the spacious kitchen. Raphael had been doing cop things here, moving around in the background while Kate struggled to prepare the meal and serve it by herself. He'd closed the vertical blinds on the single window—she imagined the gesture was against a sniper on some rooftop who might choose to shoot at her. But after his earlier lecture, she didn't want to think too closely about that. So she'd closed his presence out of her mind instead.

Now he was missing.

"No," she murmured. "Oh, no. He wouldn't." But of course, he would.

Kate grabbed the brochettes from the broiler and put them on a serving platter along with the dip she'd prepared earlier. She herbed the oysters and popped them into the oven, setting the timer for six minutes. She grabbed the brochette platter and stalked out of the kitchen.

When she reached the door to the parlor, she felt as though a bullet *had* caught her. Raphael was sitting in a Queen Anne chair directly across from Denny Morley.

They each had a glass of wine, and they were talking like long-lost friends.

Kate hurried over with the brochettes and slid them neatly onto the table between them. Raphael had wanted the drapes drawn in here, too, so she'd suggested candlelight. But instead of the Morleys enjoying it and some intimate conversation, Raphael was talking to Denny Morley about *football*.

"I want a word with you," she whispered.

Raphael looked up at her and smiled. "Sure. In a minute."

Her teeth ground together so hard she felt pain in her fillings. *"Now."*

He reached for a brochette instead.

Her hand snaked out automatically to slap his away. She caught the reflex just in time and smiled weakly at Denny Morley. He was already cramming shrimp into his mouth.

"Try one, Rafe. Go ahead," Morley said around a chew. "Help yourself. They're delicious."

"Actually, I was thinking of doing just that."

"Actually," Kate hissed, "you weren't."

"Sure I was."

"No. You *weren't.*"

He picked one up anyway.

She didn't know she was going to do it. She had never done such a thing to anyone before in her life. But there was something red-hot behind her eyes now. It stained her vision and hurt her head. She stepped around the Queen Anne chair and wrapped her fingers around his ear, the one Denny Morley couldn't see, and twisted.

"Excuse me," she said sweetly to Morley. "I just need to talk to my…" She would choke on the word. "Associate. For a moment. In the kitchen, please."

"Hey, take your time," Morley said. "Where's Betty?"

She's got her nose in my oysters. "I'll send her right out."

"What the hell do you think you're doing?" Raphael grated when he had finally swallowed the shrimp and jalapeños. He held his head at an odd angle.

"Requesting your attention. Should I be more persistent?"

It was the kicker, he realized, the *coup de grâce* to the entire last twenty-four hours.

He reached up and caught her wrist, bending it back the other way. But she only tightened her fingers, pinching harder. He could hear her breath coming faster. Or maybe it was his own.

"You don't want to do this," he murmured.

"Oh, I do."

"No. You don't."

"Get out of the chair."

"This is probably not the best approach to convince me."

"I tried everything else."

Clang. They heard the noise at the same time. Not loud in and of itself, but it was followed by a second one, and then the hollow, metallic sound of cast iron rolling over tile.

Her oysters.

Kate let go of Raphael's ear and forgot propriety. She ran for the kitchen, feeling tears burn her eyes. What Raphael hadn't already ruined, Betty Morley just had. Unless Kate badly missed her guess, the woman had just dropped the skillet that was supposed to be in the oven.

She couldn't believe this.

Raphael was behind her, pushing a little against her back to get her to move faster. But Kate was at full speed as she hit the kitchen door with her palms outstretched. She took three steps into the room and stopped with a jerk. She

shot a hand out to catch the counter, but it did no good.
The room tilted anyway.

Betty Morley was dead.

"No, no, no!" Kate screamed. "Oh, God," she prayed,
"please, not again!"

"Shut up," Raphael snapped, stepping around her.

Kate put her other hand out to him to hang on as her
knees went weak. Her fingers found air.

He was already kneeling beside Betty Morley. The
woman was flat on her back on the kitchen tile. She was
wearing the oysters. The cast-iron skillet was on the floor
amid a spill of rock salt beside her outstretched, oven-
mitted hand.

A keening sound started in Kate's throat. In the next
second, another shot rang out.

Kate shrieked. She saw Raphael in a blur, coming to his
feet, his weapon drawn. She spun, looking the way he was
turning. There was a spasm of movement in the opposite
door, the one that led out to the hallway. Something in
black, she thought. Some*one* in black. But then the gunman was gone.

Kate screamed again. Denny Morley burst into the
kitchen behind her, bumping into her, sending her stum-
bling toward the prone woman. She pinwheeled her arms
for balance. Raphael caught her.

"What in blazes?" Morley bellowed. *"Betty!"*

"She's fine," Raphael said.

Kate was going flaccid in his arms. He felt everything
ease out of her muscles, felt her knees bending as she
began sinking. She was making a sound she probably
didn't know she was making—something broken, a
pitched whimpering, and it was repetitive.

"She's alive," he said, his voice hard, his mouth near
her ear. "Come on, honey, come on, don't wimp out on

me now.'' He thrust his gun in his belt, found his walkie-talkie beside it and got it in his hand.

No one had died. But somewhere in this building, a potential killer was fleeing.

He brought the walkie-talkie to his mouth as he tried to hold Kate up. ''All units, this is Command One. Shots fired. Suspect fleeing. He is in the building. I repeat, *suspect is in the building.*''

Kate mewled and wrenched away from him. She headed for Betty Morley. Raphael's free hand snaked out and caught hers at the last moment. Her indigo eyes flashed to his, too wide, too stricken, impossibly dark in her white face.

''Oh, hell,'' he muttered. He dropped his walkie-talkie on the kitchen counter.

''She's dead!''

''No.''

''Command One, where will you be following?'' the walkie-talkie squawked.

Center stairs, Raphael needed to say, so they didn't shoot at him unintentionally. But Kate was twisting her wrist in his hand, trying to get free.

''I killed her!'' she keened.

''Damn it, she's not dead!'' Raphael shouted.

''Come again, Command One?'' said the walkie-talkie.

Her eyes were starting to go unfocused. She was in shock.

Raphael grabbed the walkie-talkie and brought it to his mouth. ''All units, I'm not following. This is Command One. I'm staying on scene.'' He dropped the walkie-talkie with a clatter. It kept muttering and spitting at him. He ignored it. It was something he had never done before in his career.

He reeled Kate in by her wrist. She took two unsteady steps toward him.

"I did this," she whimpered.

"Sure, but you've had headaches on your conscience before. Four of mine, at least. Don't worry about it."

Kate stared at him. She felt horror punch the air from her lungs.

He had been like this when McGaffney had died, too. Joking with that other cop, the one named Fox. They'd been having a jolly conversation over the body. Then she had tolerated it. But this woman… Betty Morley was someone she *knew*.

Denny Morley was on his knees, leaning over his wife protectively. The walkie-talkie was sputtering and crackling on the counter. Kate took it all in as she tried to breathe, but her breath shook. "Get an ambulance," she pleaded.

"I'll call for one as soon as you calm down."

"I'm calm!"

Kate left him and lunged for the walkie-talkie. Maybe Betty Morley wasn't dead yet. Maybe she could save her. She got the walkie-talkie in her hands, but she couldn't make sense of its buttons. It kept talking to her, demanding the attention of Command One. She pushed and prodded. And achieved nothing. She threw it across the room and spun to Raphael.

He caught her neatly. "She's not dead," he said against her temple. "She's unconscious."

"How could you—"

"*Look* at her."

Kate couldn't. Not ever again.

"That's not a gunshot wound to her temple. It's a bruise."

Kate began trembling.

"I took her pulse. It's steady. There's a decent dent in the bottom of the frying pan. Looks like a thirty-eight, but I could be wrong."

He'd seen it all in the five seconds he'd spent with the woman, but the evidence wasn't all that hard to assess. The gunman had shot twice. The first shot—the one that had come while they had been in the parlor—had struck Betty Morley squarely in Kate's frying pan. And, to Raphael's best guess, the frying pan had then flown out of her hand and had clocked her right in the forehead. The second bullet had gone into the wall.

Kate's teeth were beginning to snick together. He wondered if she'd heard a single word he'd said. Probably not. Her skin had a waxy quality that he recognized. It was the second time in twenty-four hours that she'd seen someone shot. Raphael swore.

Denny Morley was calling 911. Raphael looked into Kate's face. Her tongue flicked out, swiping over dry lips. Her gaze danced to meet his, then was gone. A fist gripped his gut. It was cold, then it was hot.

He caught her chin in his hand, pulled her face around and didn't try to pretend what he wanted to do. Which only went to show that he was out of his mind.

His mouth covered hers, hard, brutal, fast. Kate reared back, shocked, breaking the contact. Then something about her eyes went opaque.

Well, he thought, at least she was coming back to herself.

He moved in on her one more time. To cement the reaction, he told himself. His hand had never left her chin, but now he gentled his hold. When he found her lips this time, her own were soft.

So—what the hell—he kept on with it. He touched his tongue to hers, a game, a tease. She tasted better than the wine he'd had before all hell had broken loose. And that was when everything started going wrong for him.

He'd only meant to break her loose from the shock that wouldn't let her hear him, with the one thing sure to gal-

vanize every starched, *tsking,* orderly thing about her.
Sure, her tongue flicking out again had given him the idea.
But he'd had purely altruistic motives.

The hell he had.

He hadn't figured, had never anticipated, that her tongue
would hesitate, then dare to draw his deeper, into something dark and warm and sweeter than he'd known for as
long as he'd breathed. Or that something that was maybe
a groan would come from her sensible throat and have his
hand tightening on her face again, the fingers of his other
hand curling into that crazy hair. The fist she hit against
his chest stalled and seemed to forget what it was doing
there. She curled her fingers into the front of his shirt instead and held on and kissed him back.

Kate felt instantaneous reaction race through her body.
It made everything inside her go weak and tighten at the
same time. This was outrageous. It made her heart thud
once, soundly, against her chest, but then her pulse seemed
to stop.

And she craved.

She craved with all of her, and it didn't matter that there
was a woman on the floor, or that her brokenhearted husband was kneeling beside her. It didn't matter that there
were sirens in the distance. It didn't matter that this man
had not a shred of human decency in his bones, or that
this whole dinner engagement was irretrievably ruined.
Something at the core of her raced hot and fervid to her
skin, burning it, and her blood picked up to pound in her
ears.

His mouth turned urgent against hers, more demanding.
And his hand never left her face, though his touch was as
soft as the kiss of an angel.

Then someone threw open the kitchen door. It cracked
against the wall, and Kate reeled back, breaking their kiss,

a trembling hand shooting to her mouth. Paramedics, she saw, but her eyes wouldn't quite focus.

He had *kissed* her! *Here? Now?*

Her gaze whipped to him. "You're a maniac! You're insane! You're...you're...you're..." She trailed off, beyond words.

Raphael grinned. Her color was back. In fact, her color was high. "Glad to be of service."

"You're...you're...you're..."

Raphael turned to the woman on the floor, still draped in oysters. He bent beside the paramedics. Not by a gesture, not by a word, did he show that he was reeling.

Chapter 7

A good dose of smelling salts brought Betty Morley around. Kate thought briefly of asking the paramedics for some of her own.

He had *kissed* her.

She would have to deal with it later, she thought shakily. She would decide what it meant and what she needed to do about it. Right now, there was too much going on.

The stretcher the paramedics had brought for Mrs. Morley wasn't needed, but they insisted that she visit the medical center for precautionary reasons. Kate watched her and Denny meld themselves to each other as he helped her out the door. She felt a funny twist at the pit of her stomach as she considered what it would be like to be cared for like that, to be able to lean like that on someone strong enough to hold her up, someone who wouldn't rethink her virtues and bail on her at the crucial eleventh hour.

Then Denny Morley glanced over his shoulder and glared at her on their way out. The look of betrayal made a cry escape Kate before she could swallow it.

"Easy," said Raphael from beside her.

"They'll never use Dinner For Two again."

Raphael waited for her to realize that that was the least of her problems.

He saw it happen. The transformation was like an avalanche suddenly spilling down a mountain. In one moment, her expression was determinedly calm. Her eyes were as still as a winter landscape after the storm had passed. Then she blinked. Her eyes filled and her mouth trembled. When she pressed her fingers to her lips, he saw them shake, too. The color he'd pulled into her face just a few minutes ago began to drain again.

"They...he...the killer...thought she was *me*." A tear spilled out. Kate scrubbed at it furiously. "If Betty wasn't such a...such a pain, sticking her nose in my recipes, if that bullet hadn't hit the skillet, she'd be *dead*."

"Or you would be." So many *ifs*, Raphael thought. If he hadn't found Denny Morley's company a pleasant diversion from Kate's controlled chaos in the kitchen, if Kate hadn't come after him to give him hell for it. If he hadn't determined that the parlor was the most likely place for anyone to breach the security of the apartment, with three times as many windows as any other room in the apartment. Change any one of those things, and Kate Mulhern might well be gone from this world.

His physical reaction to that was dangerous. The rolling sensation that she could kick into his chest seemingly at will was mild compared to the way his heart twisted itself into something like a fist now. But he couldn't regret not giving more weight to the fact that the door in the kitchen led directly to a more isolated section of outside hallway, because if he had to do it all over again, Raphael knew he would have done everything exactly the same. Because he had never anticipated that Charlie Eagan wanted Kate dead badly enough to send someone right inside after her to do it at close range.

"Come on," he decided. "We'll go to my place." The security at her apartment was more porous than that here in the Morley home.

Sensation started to come back to Kate's limbs slowly. She stared at him.

He couldn't be thinking what she *thought* he was thinking, she decided. A woman had almost just died in her place. She had at least half of the Irish mafia trying to gun her down. And he wanted to take her back to his place? What for?

Because he had just kissed her.

Kate focused on that hard and fast because it suddenly seemed like the least overwhelming thing of all that had happened in the last thirty minutes. She had been kissed before—not nearly so…completely, but it had happened. She had *never* been shot at before.

"I don't think so," she said stiffly. Raphael's brows lowered in that way he had, making his eyes so thin she couldn't see what was going on there.

"You don't think so," he repeated.

"I don't want to go to your home."

"Care to tell me why not?"

She sniffed. "This is hardly the time or the place for that discussion."

Raphael glanced around the kitchen as though expecting to find that they weren't alone anymore. "It looks pretty good to me."

"A woman was just shot at! I just can't deal with that…with the *other* right now."

"What other?"

"I need time to think about it!"

"About *what?*"

"About why you kissed me!"

For a minute, Raphael felt as though someone had cracked *him* upside the head with a frying pan. A laugh started in his throat. Then panic suddenly tried to climb into his chest from his gut, and it crowded out the reflex. She was taking him—and everything he did—entirely too seriously. He didn't mean anything by it. Not by any of it.

But the fact that she was still dwelling on it, that she was still *analyzing* it fifteen minutes later had a strange sensation of possessiveness wrapping around his heart, and he felt the damnedest urge to smile.

"Honey, you were going hysterical on me. I kissed you to snap you out of it," he said before the sensation could spread.

Kate stared at him expressionlessly for a moment. Then her face flamed with color. She brought her shoulders back so hard and fast he thought he could hear her bones crack. "I knew that."

Finally, he did laugh. Hoarsely. "Yeah. That's why you kissed me back."

"I didn't want to hurt your feelings." *She'd been willing to die for more of it.*

Her blood went ice cold. Oh, she was such a fool! What other reason could there have been? What had she been thinking? That he had suddenly been overwhelmed with passion in the middle of a crime scene?

Then again, a man with a little more sensitivity might not have pointed it out.

Raphael ducked when a salad tong came flying his way. It landed in the wagon. He caught the bag of rock salt that followed it. So, he thought, they were back to normal.

"Kiss my...my—" She broke off. No word that came to her was vile enough.

Raphael waited to see what she would say this time, how she would finish that little retort when it was inching

so close to dangerous ground. Then the door opened behind him and the crime scene techs spilled in along with
an officer and his partner.

"Well, this little problem is certainly heating up," Fox
drawled.

For a moment, Raphael didn't know which problem he
was talking about. *Kate,* he thought first. The frustrating,
fascinating, innocent and utterly practical Kate Mulhern,
who was turning a simple baby-sitting situation upside
down.

"So where is the scumbag?" Raphael demanded, dragging his mind back to business.

"Don't have him yet," Fox responded unperturbedly.

"What do you mean we don't *have* him?"

"We're still looking for him. It's a big building."

"He's still *here?*" Kate cried.

Raphael's partner turned to her. "It's all right, ma'am.
We've got half the department on the premises. Wherever
he's hiding, he'd be crazy to come out now."

It was true as far as it went, Raphael thought, but he
and Kate were still leaving. "Put that stuff down," he
snapped as Kate began to spoon food back into her containers. "We're going."

"As soon as I finish here."

"You are finished. The techs can pack up your stuff.
I'll have a uniform drop it all off at the RH Unit and we
can pick it up tomorrow."

"That's not possible. Some of it is perishable."

"There's a refrigerator there."

"It's all work product. It's my job. I have to pack it
up."

"Except you're leaving."

She would deal with where he was taking her after she
had her utensils and supplies stored neatly in the wagon
again, Kate decided. In twenty-four hours, she had already

learned to take one issue at a time with him. He was entirely too volatile otherwise.

He was going to be volatile anyway, she realized a moment later.

Raphael stalked over to one of the counters. He began grabbing things—*soiled* things—and dropping them into the wagon. "Honey, we're going to get this show on the road if I have to carry you out of here."

"You'll do no such thing!"

"Watch me."

Kate had started to grab a dirty spatula from his hand. She backed off quickly instead, putting more than an arm's reach between them. His eyes were hot. Just with temper, she told herself. She knew better than to think anything else at this point. But Kate licked her lips unconsciously.

Half an hour ago, Raphael had felt sure that he'd give anything for a glimpse of the unrelenting practicality that had been driving him to the edge for a solid twenty-four hours. Fragility didn't sit well with this woman, and watching it happen to her had wrenched something deep inside him. But now that she seemed to be back to her normal, annoying, *tsking,* stubborn self, he saw a great deal of merit in that previous stunned, shaky quiet.

He thought about choking her. Then she licked her lips, and he felt his blood pressure spike from an entirely different emotion. She had him completely off balance…again.

Kate scooted behind Fox. "He's a maniac," she told the other detective shakily.

"Nah, just a little unpredictable," Raphael's partner said. "He's right, though. The guy's still here somewhere. You really ought to go."

"But my *things!*"

"Looks to me like Rafe is taking care of that for you."

Raphael was. Kate gave a cry of alarm and hurried to

the counter. She began grabbing items, as well, though she kept a good distance between them.

"She's a nutcase," Raphael said to his partner.

"Nah, just a little set in her ways," Fox responded. "She's right, though. We've got enough on our hands here without having to worry about taking catering supplies back to headquarters. Look at that, between the two of you, you're done already."

Kate glanced around quickly. He was right. Everything was in the wagon. It was piled haphazardly, but it was there. Although, she thought, she should really wipe up before she left. She reached into the sink for a dishcloth.

"Don't even think about it," Raphael growled.

Kate jumped and pulled her hand back. She doubted very seriously if the Morleys were ever going to use her services again anyway. She bent for the handle of the wagon.

"I'm still not going to your house," she muttered, looking at him over her shoulder.

"Sure you are."

"I am *not*. I fail to see the necessity."

"That's what you said about needing a baby-sitter. Tell it to Betty Morley."

That quelled her. This time, when she reached the door, Kate waited and let Raphael go into the hallway first. She did not stick her tongue out at his back.

When the door shut again with a crack, Fox looked at the officer who had come in with him and gave a gusty, grinning sigh. "Love. Ain't it grand?"

They drove in silence with Raphael behind the wheel of her van. Then he turned west on Spring Garden Street, and Kate sat up straighter. "I live south of here."

"I know."

"You're not taking me home."

"I told you that."

"You can't just...just *hijack* me."

"It's called kidnapping. And yeah, I can. If you don't like it, call the cops."

Damn him! She hated letting him win, and knew he had her. "Just tell me why I can't go home."

"Because there are as many ways up to your apartment as there were into the Morleys' kitchen." He thought about it. "And because you're too cheap to buy a new sofa."

"I told you why I don't want a new sofa!"

"Yeah, well, I guess you never had to sleep on the one you've got."

Actually, she had, back when she and Shawna had still lived together. The apartment only had the single bedroom so they had taken turns with it, rotating months. In the interim, each of them had slept in the living room. Still, Kate had never thought the sofa was *that* bad.

"So now I get to sleep on *your* sofa," she muttered. "Is that the deal?"

He took his eyes off the street long enough to slant a glance at her. "I have a few manners."

Kate lifted her brows. "Sorry. I hadn't noticed."

He locked his jaw and looked ahead again. "You can sleep anywhere you damned well please. You can sleep in the shower for all I care. But you're going to do it at my address where I can secure every single way in or out. And you're going to stop picking at me about it."

"I don't pick."

"You pick."

"I do not."

"Honey, you're a world-class nitpicker. In twenty-four hours now, you haven't once let anything just *be*."

"Twenty-five."

His gaze rounded to her again. "What?" he asked disbelievingly.

"It's been twenty-five hours now. It's nine-thirty. You arrived at the scene last night at eight-thirty."

"There. *There.* You just did it. Twenty-four hours, twenty-five, what the hell difference does it make?"

"Well, they *have* been some of the longest hours of my life."

"You're damned lucky you've got any hours left."

That sobered her again instantly. Kate settled back against the seat, falling quiet for a while. "So where exactly do you live?" she asked eventually. "Where are we going?"

"North of the university." His tone was clipped. "Outside the worst of the city."

"Because?"

He looked at her again. Was she going to pick at this, too? Probably, he decided.

"Is there a specific reason why you live on the other side of the river?" she asked when he didn't answer. "I mean, I would think that with your job and all, you'd do better to live right in the thick of things. You must get called out a lot. Wouldn't it be better to just live close by?"

"I see enough of the thick of things during working hours."

"Ah."

"Ah, what?"

"Just ah. As in, I understand."

He took one hand off the wheel to scrub the back of his neck, wondering why he was going to explain. This, he thought, was definitely picking. "I need to draw a line between me and the job. Too many cops let the street bleed into their personal lives. And it destroys them—their marriages, their lives, whatever."

"You couldn't keep the line there with Anna Lombardo."

"I didn't try hard enough." Raphael felt his heart rate pick up in anger and with something like helplessness—a feeling he disliked a lot. Kate had been doing this to him since the first words he'd spoken with her, digging too deep. "Here we are," he said shortly.

Kate watched him, amazed at the changes of expression that danced over his face in the glancing headlights of the passing cars. It looked like a series of photographs clicking by, one right after the other, freeze-frames of too many emotions—pain, temper, maybe, she thought, even guilt. She realized she wanted to know more.

Kate began to ask another question, then she registered what he had just said. He was pulling into a driveway. She turned to look out the window, curious as to what she might find. Given the disaster of restraint that he was, she expected a place falling in on itself. But his home wasn't that at all.

It was a town house, one in the middle. Thin light from a street lamp spilled over it and its narrow lawn, just enough that she could make out a lot of dark brick and a brass sconce beside the door. The mailbox next to it had a brass clasp—their headlights caught it and made it wink. The sidewalk curved toward the drive rather than run ruler-straight to the street. Spiky green plants bordered it, and the lawn seemed healthy enough.

So, she thought, he respected *something*. "It's nice," she said, surprised.

Raphael turned off the ignition and her old van belched and rumbled for a moment before the engine finally quit. "Well, there goes the neighborhood."

Kate thought she could actually feel her veins tighten. "Do you have any idea how much a new vehicle costs?"

"No, but I'll bet you're just dying to tell me."

She didn't know, not precisely. "A lot."

"Might sweeten your image," he said. "A shiny new van, your name emblazoned on the side."

A whole fleet of vans wouldn't help her now, Kate thought.

The truth made a large, painful rock cram itself into her throat. Her mind had been nudging at it all night, like a tongue at a sore tooth. Now reality rolled through her blood like ice water.

Two dinners, she thought helplessly, and two disasters. *Death, gunmen, shooting.* The mob! It would make the papers. Her name would be in there. No one would call her. The word would spread. *Use that caterer, and you're as good as dead.*

She got out of the van quickly. Everything that had happened was too huge, too painful to contemplate just yet. So she hurried around to the back of the van instead, throwing open the doors, pulling the loaded wagon toward her.

She'd have to take the perishables inside and store them in his refrigerator. She was working the wagon out of the van, thinking that she didn't even have her toothbrush or anything to sleep in, when she heard the bark.

Like it had been doing all night, her mind danced from the truth. Raphael has a dog, she thought. But the distinctive sound of that yip—pitched, squeaky, maybe reproachful—pierced her denial like a needle through skin.

Kate dropped the wagon. It hit concrete with a metallic crash, and food containers rolled merrily down Raphael's driveway. *It wasn't possible.*

She turned quickly to Raphael. He was moving up the sidewalk, jiggling his keys in his hand, then he stopped, too, with a jerk. "What the hell?" she heard him mutter.

"Belle," Kate said. *Belle?* "You didn't lock the crate!"

"*You* locked the crate!"

"No, I did not! She bit me again when I tried. You locked it."

"Yeah? So how'd she get through two closed doors in that apartment, even if we left the crate open?"

"Two? What two?"

"The bedroom. The front door. And how did she know to come *here?*"

Kate swayed and put a hand to the side of the van for support. Belle was back. Apparently, Belle went wherever she chose to go.

Hysteria crowded into her throat. It came out as a thin sound. Raphael heard it and started to turn to her, but he was loathe to take his eyes off the dog.

The critter was on his porch. Sitting on his doormat. As his gaze lingered on the beast, she tipped her skinny muzzle up and barked again. Raphael felt something mildly spooked crawl over his skin, and it did it with small, cold feet.

"There's an explanation for this," he murmured.

"She's an angel," Kate croaked.

Raphael finally took his gaze from the dog to look at her sharply. "Knock it off."

"Shawna says she's an angel."

"Yeah. And I'm the King of Siam."

"Actually, I don't think Siam has a king." His eyes went wild. Kate backpedaled quickly. "Okay, okay. I'm picking again. So how did she get here? Just tell me that!"

"How should I know? You're the one with the practical answers all the time!"

Kate stared at the dog who couldn't possibly be there and felt the night closing in on her. Everything that had happened, ludicrous and terrible and beyond belief, flashed through her mind's eye.

Betty Morley on the floor, draped in oysters.

Denny Morley looking at her with such anger in his eyes.

Honey, I kissed you to snap you out of it. And like an idiot, she'd let the truth spear right through to her soul, the soul she'd poured into that kiss only minutes before. Even though she knew she wasn't the kind of woman who inspired passion. Because for a moment, while he had been kissing her, she'd let herself believe in magic.

Now, to top it all off, Belle had somehow found them when she was supposed to have been in a crate half a city away.

All of it crowded in on her, overwhelming her. The stars swirled. Kate looked at them helplessly and gave a puzzled cry, because she never fainted. Then, before Raphael's astounded eyes, she swooned dead away.

Belle woofed softly and waited for Raphael to carry Kate inside, then she darted quietly inside on his heels.

Chapter 8

Kate opened her eyes to find Raphael's gaze on her. His eyes were as dark as a stormy sea. There seemed to be no green to them at all.

He was close, too close. It made her pulse hammer erratically. She could feel the soft touch of his breath on her cheek. Something sighed deep inside her.

"I'm fine," she said automatically.

Raphael saw her pulse flutter at her throat just a moment before her eyes met his. It reacted on him like a fist he'd never seen coming. "Yeah, they'll put those words on your headstone." He straightened away from her.

Kate paled even more.

Damn it, he was no good at this sort of thing, Raphael thought. He didn't have the knack for comforting and coddling and care. He *fixed* things. He avenged wrongs and set them right again—he didn't sit around and console the victims.

He'd kissed her to snap her out of hysteria. Guilt nibbled

at his gut. *He'd wanted to taste her.* He pushed the truth of that away hard and fast.

Kate rose unsteadily from the sofa. "It's just that I never ate."

Raphael kept his expression neutral. "You spent the whole afternoon in the kitchen."

"That food was for the Morleys."

He wasn't sure if that meant it hadn't occurred to her to nibble, or that she hadn't done so because it somehow went against that starched grain of hers. He decided he didn't want to know. "Eat now. There's got to be plenty left over."

Kate shook her head fretfully. "No, that's all—"

"Stale."

"Not finished," she corrected.

She looked at him as though expecting him to argue with her. She did it with a slight tilt of her chin, but something in her eyes told him she didn't have enough fight left in her to meet the challenge. She was finally figuring out that her life was never going to be the same until this mob war was settled, Raphael realized. For someone who had not only had her ducks in a row but saluting her, it had to be overwhelming.

"I need to make something," she said. Then she headed for the kitchen.

Twenty minutes later, he began to understand what the cooking was about. He went as far as the kitchen doorway to watch her. Maybe she *was* honestly starving, but there was more to it than that. He wondered if she even realized it. Just like she had this afternoon, she worked with quick, precise, sure motions. He knew that it was therapeutic.

When he moved cautiously into the kitchen, her expression was softer, less stricken, no longer dazed. She was humming to herself.

The smells emanating from his oven and range top had

his stomach rumbling, and *he'd* had that hoagie this afternoon and a healthy portion of the Morleys' hors d'oeuvres. Kate had found his stash of T-bones in the freezer. She'd unearthed some potatoes. They'd seen better days, but somehow she resurrected them. Like a phoenix rising from ashes, they came out of his oven diced and sprinkled through with peppers and green onions. She made a trip to her van and eventually served up two plates full of steak, potatoes and a salad. Then she stood holding them, looking vacantly around his kitchen.

"You don't have a table."

He didn't. The breakfast area was barren. "I...uh, haven't lived here very long."

"How long?"

"Two months." Why did that sound interminable now?

"And you never bought a *table?*"

"I was going to get around to it." He'd been thinking about it, actually, because if things had gone anywhere with Anna, he might have wanted to invite her over for dinner or something. Then she'd been killed, and he'd determined that no one was going to be having dinner in his home any time soon.

It occurred to Raphael that he'd thought about Anna more in the last couple of days than he had in all the weeks since her death. That annoyed him. It also panicked him.

"I eat at the coffee table," he said shortly and took one of the plates from her.

Kate frowned. "That's barbaric."

"Then stand there and eat yours. I'm going to get comfortable."

A moment later, she followed him to the living room. Raphael dug in and refused to grin with the pleasure of it.

He looked at her out of the corner of his eye as he chewed. She was sitting cross-legged at the far end of the coffee table, keeping as much space between them as possible. She was scowling at her plate. Periodically, she nudged the food around with her fork. For someone who'd been so hungry, she wasn't doing much about it.

"Would you put some of that in your mouth? I'm not real wild on the idea of you fainting all over the place while I'm trying to sort this mess out."

Kate looked at him sharply. "I don't faint."

"You did one hell of an imitation."

She put her fingers to her temples as though to still a headache. "It's not something that's ever happened to me before."

"Well, keep starving yourself and maybe you can fix that. Even Wonder Woman needed fuel. And you're not Wonder Woman." Though she made a good show of it, he thought. And damned if he wouldn't like to see her in that sexy little suit.

"What?" she asked warily, noting the changes in his expression.

Raphael opened his mouth to repeat the thought. Then he shook his head. He was not going to joke with her anymore. He wasn't going to lean over her on any more sofas, and he wasn't going to kiss her again. He wasn't going to provoke her to find out what intriguing thing might pop out of her mouth next.

He wasn't going to get that close, because she was starting to get under his skin.

This job was going to be over soon. He'd wrap up Eagan's complicity, find a snitch somewhere in the ranks with a grudge against the big guy. Kate could go back to her orderly world. And he'd go back to Remmick's, the pub he favored over on Eighteenth Street. Remmick's offered up plenty of women who knew a joke when they heard one, who knew better than to get short of breath and look at him with wide, innocent eyes when he made one. When the women at Remmick's kissed back, they knew they were doing it. And they knew how to walk away when the kissing was over.

Which might be why he never wanted them to distraction, he realized suddenly.

"What did I see that night?" Kate cried suddenly, jolting Raphael from his thoughts.

He put his fork down, and the steak was good, too. "I don't know. You tell me."

Kate pushed her own plate away angrily. "There was nothing. But there had to have been *something*, or they wouldn't be doing this to me."

Maybe, Raphael thought, maybe not. Even the possibility would galvanize these people. "What about between the time you called 911 and when Fox got there? Anything unusual occur in that time span?"

Her eyes narrowed. She was thinking. Hard. And for some reason, that touched him more than anything she had said or done yet. He felt his heart crack a little at her courage. For that stubborn—and yes, strong—determination.

"Actually, a couple of officers got there before him," she said finally.

Officers, Fox—what did it matter? His temper kicked all over again.

Kate caught his expression. "I went back to the dining room after I called 911," she said quickly. "Then Allegra came back, too, and she made like she was going to lift McGaffney's head out of the salad."

Raphael frowned. "She came back? From where?"

Kate blinked. "From the kitchen. She followed me when I went to call 911."

If the killer hadn't gotten out of the house earlier, Raphael thought, then he certainly did it then. He picked up the thread of her story. "So then you sat on her."

Kate shook her head fretfully. "No, not right away. First

I grabbed her arm to stop her. But she kept trying to yank away from me. So I kind of knocked one of her feet out from under her. And she went down. *Then* I sat on her.''

Something clicked hard in Raphael's brain. It almost hurt. ''Which side of McGaffney were you two standing on?''

She looked at him, startled. ''What?''

''Were you on his right or his left when you knocked her down? Assuming a position behind him, facing the same direction. Were you looking at the hallway door, or at the kitchen door?'' There'd been two entrances to that dining room, he remembered. And they'd been on the kitchen side when he'd found her perched on Allegra's back.

Kate's eyes widened. ''I was facing the hall.''

''Was that door open?''

''It—yes,'' she realized. ''It was.'' Because Allegra had come in through that door right after Kate had found the dead man. She was pretty sure Allegra had never closed it again. Neither had she.

Someone had been out there. Someone, Raphael thought, had been in that hall. And at some point, Kate must have looked squarely in that direction.

So the guy thought she'd seen him. *Who?* Someone she might recognize in a mug shot, Raphael decided. Otherwise, it *still* wouldn't be enough to easily ID the scumbag—unless the scumbag knew that his mug shot was already on file.

''I saw him,'' Kate whispered, stricken. ''I must have seen him through that door. But I *didn't.* All my attention was on Allegra.'' Her eyes were getting wild again.

''Okay, calm down. It's okay.''

''It's *not* okay! Someone wants to kill me for it and I don't even know who was there!''

Raphael dropped a piece of steak at the dog, who was

circling under the coffee table. Belle darted forward and caught it in midair, whining for more. When he didn't offer any, she went in the other direction. A moment later, Raphael saw her needle nose come up over the edge of the coffee table, her nostrils quivering as she caught wind of Kate's untouched plate.

Kate swatted at her without looking at her. The dog's brows came together and she growled, snapping her teeth at air.

"No one's going to kill you," Raphael said. "They'd have to get past me to do it."

Kate snorted. "Oh, I forgot. Mr. I'm So Good At My Job."

Raphael's eyes narrowed. "I am."

"I don't think Betty Morley appreciates your skill."

"Damn it, letting you do that dinner went against every fiber of common sense I had!"

"Then why *did* you?"

His blood pressure skyrocketed in disbelief. "Because you *picked* at me!" Raphael held up a hand. He reined his temper in. Again. "We've got two avenues here. First, tomorrow I'm going to have you look at some mug shots."

"I keep telling you, I didn't see anyone out there."

"Not consciously. Maybe you saw something unconsciously."

"If I did it unconsciously, then how am I supposed to recognize this guy in a picture?"

"Maybe his face will tweak something in your mind. Will you stop arguing with me? I'm the cop here. I know how to go about these things."

She looked down her nose at him. "I thought you were a *detective*."

"I'm—" He snapped the sentence off. She was doing it to him again.

"What's the other avenue?" she asked.

"Maybe it would be worth it to have you hypnotized."

Her back snapped ramrod straight. Belle chose the moment to stand up, brace her front paws against the table and with her nose just barely angled over Kate's plate, she lifted her steak.

"I don't like the idea of someone taking over my mind," Kate said quickly.

"What you don't like is not being in control."

Kate drove both her hands into her dark curls. "What are you saying now? That I'm a control freak?"

"If the shoe fits."

"Well, the shoe does *not* fit."

"You've been pushing *me* around from the moment I met you. *I want prosciutto. I decided I'm going to keep the dog,*" he said in a falsetto. "Who, by the way, just made off with your dinner."

Kate looked at her plate sharply. Her steak was gone. She gave a cry of pure frustration, then she put her head down hard on her forearms on the table.

"You think about everything you do before you do it," Raphael said.

Except once, Kate thought, suddenly miserable. She hadn't considered anything at all when he had kissed her.

He watched pink steal up her neck. And he knew what she was thinking…because he was thinking the same thing. If she had kissed him back like that in sheer surprise, what would she do if she *really* got swept away? Instantly, Raphael felt things gather hard and hot in the center of him, things that should not have been awake at all.

He got to his feet fast, taking his plate. He saw her sit up out of the corner of his eye. He felt her gaze on his back as he went to the kitchen. He put his plate on the counter and returned to the living room.

He wasn't going to tease her, he reminded himself. He wasn't going to provoke her. That was real dangerous ground, getting more shaky with every moment they spent together. "In the meantime," he heard himself say, "we could practice. You know, so you could get the hang of it."

She cocked her head a little to the side and her eyes went thin. "Practice what?"

"I could hypnotize you. I'm trained."

"*You* are?"

"A while back, a good many major city police departments offered that kind of instruction to isolated personnel."

"And Philadelphia chose you?"

"Philadelphia chose the best." He felt compelled to get that in there again.

"I don't think so," Kate said quickly. "It's *my* mind. I don't want anyone else...you know, tinkering with it." She didn't want *him* getting inside there. In fact, the very idea appalled her. It would be like having him peer right into her heart. And if he did that, what would he see in there?

He would know that she'd liked kissing him a lot more than she detested him.

Raphael came back to the sofa. This time when he sat down, he did it inches from her. "It's not true, you know."

She reared back a little, looking at him. "What isn't?"

"That a hypnotist can make you do anything your conscious mind wouldn't accept when you're awake. So what won't your conscious mind accept, Kate Mulhern?"

Wanting you. It leaped into her mind and had her heart kicking.

She wanted to feel again the way she had when he'd kissed her, with every nerve ending alive, throbbing, sensitive. She wanted that feeling of being unable to breathe for the wonder of it. Because nobody had ever kissed her

like that before. No one had ever made her feel like that.
And she had liked it.

But she didn't *want* to like it. Because it had meant
nothing at all to him.

Raphael watched something come over her face. A
whimsical softening. A yearning. A wistfulness. She
hugged herself. And when Raphael's heart rolled over this
time, it took his breath away and it was painful.

He shot to his feet. ''I think dogs need to be walked or
something, don't they?''

''Dogs?''

''Like that one who just finished your steak.''

''We don't have a leash.'' Everything inside Kate settled
again. For a moment, it had gathered, lifting, her very
bones feeling weightless with the way he had looked at
her. But now he wanted to walk the dog.

She watched him pick Belle up in the palm of one hand.
Her short legs dangled and she looked indignant. Actually,
Kate thought, she looked horrified. Then Raphael was out
the front door, dog and all.

Kate got up shakily from the coffee table. She hunted
up the bone that was left from the steak Belle had stolen
and started dazedly for the kitchen. Her hands shook for a
moment, then they steadied. She shoveled in a few mouth-
fuls of cold potatoes as she stood at the counter, and they
hit the pit of her stomach like rocks.

She had to get a grip on herself. It was just…just his
way to swerve the conversation like that. He was smooth.
He was as mellow and warming as good, aged red wine.

Kate began washing up the dishes. Ten minutes later,
Raphael still hadn't returned, but she had herself together.
He had said that his behavior meant nothing. If she allowed
herself to believe that it did, even in a secret part of her
heart, it would end up hurting abominably. It would hurt
far more than just his backhanded explanation for that kiss.

She was smart. She was talented in certain areas. She was *not* a bombshell, not a sex kitten like Allegra... Jeff had made that plain, and she would do well to keep it in mind. She dried her hands on a kitchen towel and smoothed her hair.

When the kitchen shined and there was still no sign of Raphael, she went in search of his bedroom. After all, he'd said she could sleep wherever she wanted. And she felt just as inclined tonight as she had last night to do it behind a locked door.

His bedroom was on the second floor, a single room at the top of the stairs across from a small sitting area and a bathroom. Something about it made her shiver. It was so male, so him. It was mahogany and deep, dark blue. The bed was king-size. But then, she supposed he would be as irrepressible in sleep as he was awake.

The dresser was heavy, large, masculine. She crossed to it slowly, running an exploratory hand over the top of it. It was surprisingly neat. There was nothing personal on top of it. Given the general disarray of his habits, she'd expected pocket contents from the last six weeks.

What else didn't she know about him? She realized that she'd wanted some peek inside him.

Where was some glimpse of the things that mattered to him? Turning, she saw a basketball on the floor in one corner. Beside it were a pair of high-top sneakers with the socks still stuffed down inside them. She had a sudden image of him running, dribbling the ball, sweating, pushing himself against any defender. Angling up, muscles straining. Poised for the shot, all male grace, then the ball would leave his fingertips. Something invisible punched her in the area of her chest. Kate decided, shivering again, that Raphael would be very good at basketball.

"What are you doing?"

Kate gasped and spun for the door. "You said I could sleep anywhere I wanted."

His eyes were wary for a moment. "And this is it."

She nodded stiffly. "This is it."

He finally shrugged. "Sure."

"I don't have…anything."

"Anything," he repeated.

"To sleep in. To brush my teeth with."

"Consider that problem fixed."

He disappeared again and came back with a brand-new toothbrush still in its neat cardboard box. Kate didn't want to consider why he might have such a supply on hand, but women like Allegra came to mind again. Then he went to the bottom drawer of his dresser and pulled it open. He extracted a T-shirt. "Good enough?"

Kate took it. Then she stepped cautiously closer to him and peered into the drawer. "Could I have those, too?"

Raphael scowled. "What?"

"Those sweatpants."

"They won't fit you."

"I'm not going to be walking around in them."

Raphael shrugged and pulled out the sweatpants. "Anything else?"

"Socks."

"In August?"

"My feet get cold." They didn't, but she couldn't have explained the truth to him if her life had depended on it. She simply didn't want him to have any image of her in here that wasn't layered in clothing.

Her feelings *weren't* just like they had been last night, she realized. Last night she had been worried about him suddenly and for some obscure reason deciding to take a shine to her. Tonight, she was worried about herself. About things she suddenly wanted and couldn't have. About what she might do if presented with them for all the wrong reasons.

"Socks," Kate repeated in a croak.

Raphael closed the bottom drawer, pulled out the top one and handed her a pair. "Anything else?"

Kate thought fast. "A bathrobe."

He gaped at her, then he pulled his mouth shut again and frowned. "You've already taken a shower today."

"I'm not going to take another shower. I told you. I get cold in my sleep."

Raphael went across the hall to the bath and returned with a hunter green velour robe. It matched the color of his eyes, Kate realized distractedly, and rubbed her forehead. She couldn't think of one other piece of clothing she could add to the image.

"That's it?" he asked.

"That's it."

"I have a parka downstairs in the foyer closet."

Kate felt herself flushing. "No, this is fine."

Raphael threw one backward glance at her before he closed the bedroom door behind him. Kate sank down on the foot of the bed, clutching the clothing to her chest.

Finally, she breathed again. After a moment, she got up and peeked into the hall. Then she scooted into the bath and closed and locked that door. Shakily, she began to brush her teeth and change.

Raphael went downstairs to the living room and moved the coffee table. He yanked out the sofa bed harder than he had to and looked at the stairs one more time. She was the most nitpicking, irritating, *tsking,* organizing woman he'd ever had the misfortune to meet. Why did he care what she slept in?

What he should care about, he thought, was that tonight he was actually going to get a good night's sleep. Giving her the bedroom was no hardship. He often slept down here, with the television droning him into unconsciousness. He'd discovered early on in his career that images from his day could dog him all night. He'd learned a long time ago to fake himself out. He tricked sleep into figuring he didn't care one way or another if it found him.

He'd tried a TV in the bedroom. It hadn't worked. The minute he laid down in that bed, most nights, images from the day assaulted him.

There were already sheets on the mattress. He started to undress, thought better of it and moved toward the stairs again. He needed a pair of gym shorts, but they were all in his dresser. He took the stairs two at a time to his bedroom door and raised a hand to knock.

He considered how she would look when she opened it, in sweatpants six sizes too large for her, in that T-shirt that would come to her knees. In his wooliest socks and his bathrobe. Preposterously, something stirred inside him anyway. He thought of peeling away all those many layers to find her skin beneath. And to see if she'd give up control. *Real* dangerous ground.

Then he heard her crying.

Raphael's hand froze just before it hit the wood. Through it all, through finding a body in her salad and another woman getting conked in the head with a frying pan in her place, through a man shooting wildly before he dodged out the door and a dog arriving at his door that should not possibly have found them, through it all she had never really cried. But these sobs were deep, as though wrenched clear up from her chest by a violent hand.

He tried to open the door without knocking. It was locked solid. Raphael banged on it hard. Kate flung it open suddenly, as though waiting for him.

"Hey," he said quietly. "Easy does it."

"Go away." But she didn't make a move to close the

door. She brought up a fistful of his bathrobe and pressed it to her mouth.

His heart rolled over again. He looked past her shoulder. His sweatpants were thrown over the foot of the bed. He looked down. Her legs were bare.

Well, hell.

"I...I...can't take any more jobs," she choked.

Raphael doubted if anyone would be calling her catering service when this hit the papers anyway. "No."

"I tried so hard! I almost could have done it. Another year or two with the catering, and I would have had my restaurant."

"So now it will be another year or four."

"I c-c-can't put anybody else in jeopardy like I d-d-did tonight."

"Not for a while. But the quicker this is over, the sooner you can rebuild."

She didn't say anything else, but she gave a deep, shuddering, soggy cry.

Oh, double hell.

He thought she would probably push him away, but maybe she was too beaten with the truth now that it had finally hit her. For whatever reason, when he held his arms out to her, Kate flung herself at him and burrowed into his embrace. And she cried.

In that moment, Raphael could have killed the men who were doing this to her. He could save her life, but he couldn't save her business. So he stroked her hair and he ignored the roll of his heart—up, down, back and forth. And he knew that whatever precipice he had been standing on the edge of all day, he was in the process of going right over it.

Chapter 9

It was too easy, Kate thought. Too easy to hold on to his strength while everything else in her world fell apart, and too easy to breathe in the scent of him. And what exactly was it, anyway? Something subtly musky, she thought, like the hot August night air still clung to his skin from his walk. And when his hand smoothed her hair, it was far, far too easy to forget that the last time he had touched her, it had simply been to bring her back to herself.

This time, she knew, he did it out of pity. Kate pulled back from him when what she wanted desperately was to stay in his arms.

Raphael shoved his hands deep into his pockets. "You forgot your pants."

Kate looked down at herself quickly. She *hadn't* layered herself in all that clothing she'd taken from him. One minute she had been fine, and the next everything had piled in on her and she had fallen apart. But did he have to mention it?

She wiped her tears away with her finger, fast and furiously. When she looked again, Raphael was grabbing something from the dresser. Then he was just gone, leaving her feeling hollow. The dog stood on the threshold where Raphael had been a moment ago, looking aggrieved from her bathroom trip.

"I guess this means you're sleeping in here?"

The dog barked in response. It was uncanny. Kate scrubbed her hands over her arms against a chill and went to shut and lock the door again.

Kate generally got up before the sun did. She usually accomplished more before leaving for work than most people did in sixteen hours. But she no longer had work to worry about, and some part of her unconscious mind clearly registered that. When Kate awoke Sunday morning, it was to blinding, yellow-white sunlight streaming through Raphael's bedroom window. Her heart chugged in confusion until she remembered...everything. McGaffney's death. Betty Morley's close call. And the man who was systematically taking everything she thought she knew about herself and turning it upside down.

She was so hot in his bathrobe, she was sweating. Kate groaned and rolled over on her back. The velour twisted around her waist uncomfortably.

For a moment, she lay still and listened. There was no snoring this morning, just the distant drone of a one-way conversation. So he was already up and on the phone.

What was she going to do about him?

She was not going to let him get to her, Kate reminded herself. She got out of bed. All in all, it wasn't much of a plan. The problem was, she had never been one for passivity, Kate realized as she crept across the hall to the shower. Impasses annoyed the devil out of her. And waiting this out—just trying to survive Raphael and the trauma to her business until this was over—was definitely not her style.

She needed to *do* something. The answer came to her as she was dressing again in yesterday's clothes, and that alone had helpless discomfort plucking at her nerve endings. But when she went to find Raphael, she had a *real* plan.

He was on the sofa, his feet on the coffee table, the telephone to his ear. He wore gym shorts…and nothing else. Kate felt her heart kick, and the sound of her breathing changed. Which was ridiculous. She'd seen him without a shirt before—just twenty-four short hours ago, as a matter of fact. It made absolutely no sense for her reaction to be twice as potent now as it had been then.

Except, of course, now he had touched her.

For whatever misguided reasons, she'd felt that mouth on hers, she'd found a moment's peace in those arms. Kate fisted her hands at her sides against the thrumming of her blood. She made herself swallow. She was *not* going to think of any of that.

"Hey," he said, noticing her as he disconnected the phone.

"Um. Yes. Hey, yourself."

She focused on his feet. It seemed the safest thing to do. But then she thought of those sneakers on the floor of his bedroom and she had the most absurd flash—that basketball image again, his bronzed skin slick with perspiration, those muscles straining, and somehow, as she envisioned it, the gym shorts weren't there anymore at all.

Kate cried out and clapped a hand to her mouth.

"What?" Raphael came quickly to his feet, looking around the room. "What is it?"

"Nothing."

"You yelped like that over nothing?"

"I…uh, my nerves are a little…tight, I suppose. I'm going to make breakfast."

"Breakfast." Raphael kept looking around the room. "Now."

Kate gathered up all the determination she'd fostered in the shower as she began cooking. She was going to *do* something about all this, she reminded herself. She was going to help him put an end to this nightmare. She was going to actively participate in this investigation—as much as he'd let her—because the end result would mean getting him out of her life sooner rather than later. At which point, she reasoned, she would no longer suffer these sudden and inexplicable swerves of her mind—memories of his kiss, fantasies of him playing basketball *naked*.

Kate put her mind to what she was doing. Belle appeared and sat beside her right ankle, that skinny, rat-size tail beating a tempo against the floor as she looked up and licked her chops. "Finally woke up, did you?" Kate muttered.

"I could say the same about you."

She turned quickly at Raphael's voice. He'd gotten himself dressed. *Thank heaven, he'd gotten dressed.* He wore jeans again, and a white Polo shirt.

"I wanted to be at headquarters half an hour ago," he complained.

"What time is it?" Kate looked around the kitchen vacantly.

"Eight-thirty."

"It can't be. I never sleep that late."

Raphael pointed wordlessly to the clock on the stove. It was, to be precise eight thirty-eight.

Nothing about her was normal anymore, Kate thought helplessly. *Nothing.*

She held a finished plate out to him—steak and eggs,

all she could find in his kitchen. "I've decided I'm going to help you with your work."

Her announcement brought no response. Kate watched him warily as he took his plate and headed for the living room and the coffee table again. She followed him and took up her place at the far end.

"How?" Raphael asked finally, cutting into the steak.

"I...I don't know. I'll do whatever you let me do, I guess. Just...please, let's get this over with."

Raphael's heart rolled and he put his fork down without taking a bite. There was a thin thread of desperation in her voice that hadn't been there before. How much of it came from wanting her life restored and how much of it was a need to get him out of that life? He found that he didn't want to know. He didn't want to consider the faint lemony scent of her hair that he'd noticed last night when he'd held her in his arms. He didn't want to think again of what it had cost him—when it shouldn't have cost anything— to turn away and walk out of that bedroom, as though the way she'd suddenly jerked free from his embrace didn't mean anything to him at all.

The easiest way not to do any of that was to simply nod, so he tried it.

Kate sighed. "Good. That's good. So...who was that on the phone? What's going on?"

"That was Fox. The shooter got away last night. He said they never found the guy."

Kate dropped her fork suddenly and with a clatter. "He also said half the police department was in that building last night! How could this happen?"

Raphael felt a nerve tic at his jaw. "Hey, don't look at me. I wasn't the one peeking into stairwells, looking for the scumbag. *I* was cleaning up your pots and pans."

"Are you blaming this...this...atrocity on *me*?"

"Atrocity?"

"Yes! He was in the building! You let him get away!"
She shoved her plate away. "For that matter, how did he
get into the building in the first place? I thought you said
you had officers on all the entrances!"

"Sure did."

"Sure did? That's it? That's your explanation?"

"If you'd let me get my two cents in and stop throwing
words around like *atrocity*, I'd give you my explanation."

Kate noticed that his teeth were grinding his words flat
again. She folded her hands neatly and exaggeratedly on
the table in front of her. "I'm listening."

"My take on the whole thing is that the guy was already
in the building when we got there. Before the officers arrived, and before you and I did. He was hiding somewhere.
We had the building perfectly secured by four-thirty. No
one got in after that point."

Kate felt some of her air leave her. "You're saying he
went in *before* four-thirty?"

"It's the only explanation." Damn it, if her eyes started
going wild and helpless again, he'd kill her himself. "After
he hit a bull's-eye on the frying pan, I'd say he probably
went back to that same spot and laid low until after all our
men left the scene." It was all he'd intended to tell her.
But then she shuddered. "Fox says they checked every
empty unit in the high-rise, and all the common areas, as
well. They combed through the basement, the trash chutes,
the generator rooms, and got nothing. Fox is running down
the list of tenants and owners today. One of them is going
to have friends in low places."

"He—the…the shooter—knew a resident?"

"He had to have done his hiding and waiting in one of
the apartments. Fox says they knocked on all the doors but
they didn't force entry into any occupied ones."

Something horrific was beginning to dawn on her, something that started a shaking sensation deep in Kate's bones. "So he couldn't have followed us there."

Damn it, she was going to do it again. She was going to go all overwhelmed and helpless on him. He wasn't sure he could stand it. "No way that I can see."

"He knew my schedule, knew I'd be there? *How?*"

"Honey, these guys can find out anything they have a mind to."

Kate stood up quickly. He watched those shoulders go back again even as she wrapped her arms around her waist. Then she added something new to the repertoire. Those indigo eyes narrowed. Dangerously. She was getting mad, he realized, and his heart rolled over in his chest again.

"Can we do that, too?" she demanded.

"What?"

"Find out anything we have a mind to?"

"More or less. It just takes us a little longer because we're the good guys and we go through proper channels."

"We can't…cheat?"

His jaw dropped. "*You* want to cheat?"

"At this point, I think I'll do whatever it takes."

Raphael stood, as well, and fought the urge to hold his arms out to her again, to bolster her determination with his own. In that moment, he thought he'd do anything, as well, just to stop her from shaking. Because he was pretty sure that was what she was doing somewhere behind those arms that were wrapped so tightly around her waist.

He picked up both their plates instead. Sanity, he thought. He'd stay sane if it killed him. "I'll clean up," he said. "It's your turn to walk the dog."

Thirty minutes later, Kate figured out why he had been gone so long while he had been doing this particular chore last night. She and Belle made their way around the perimeter of Raphael's backyard at a crawl. Periodically, the dog would stop and inspect a lawn chair or a lush clump of weed. Then she would stare at Kate.

Kate waited. And waited. Then, disbelievingly, she caught on.

"This is ridiculous," she muttered, staring at the dog.

Belle showed her teeth.

"You're an *animal*."

Belle sighed and lay down.

"Oh, no," Kate said. "No, you don't. You're going to do this and we're going to get it over with if it kills me." Then she heard her own words, and a chill traced down her spine.

Kate looked quickly around the yard. It was like thousands of others across large cities throughout America. There was an apron of concrete that made for a tiny rear patio. Raphael had a barbecue grill there, but there wasn't room for much else. Just beyond the apron sat the lawn chair, and next to it was a resin table. There were two trash cans near the door, the lids on tightly. And encircling the little fifteen-by-twenty-five-foot space were young, spare shrubs.

There was no way to get into the yard except through the house. But that wouldn't stop someone from shooting right through the hedges.

"Oh, no," she whispered. "Oh, God."

Fear—this kind of fear—was totally new to her. It was stark and wild compared even to what she had felt yesterday, arguing with Raphael over the prosciutto on a city street. Kate's heart slammed. Panic took over.

She bent and grabbed Belle, planting the little dog on her feet again. Belle twisted around, aiming for her hand with flashing teeth, but Kate was quick. She let her go and turned her back on her. "Do it. *Now*."

She gave it a few seconds and glanced over her shoulder. Sure enough, Belle was finally taking care of business.

She'd been right. The dog had been waiting for some privacy. "I don't believe this."

Kate grabbed Belle in both hands and raced for the house. She met Raphael at the rear door and barreled into him. He caught her, and there was a yip from between them as the dog was pressed between their bodies. "Why did you send me out here?" she demanded.

"Because there's something weird about that animal. Is everything okay?"

"I could have been killed!"

And instantly, everything about him changed. His hands tightened on her shoulders, and the strength she felt there numbed her for a moment with both gratitude and a little alarm. She would not want him angry at her in quite that way. Then he set her aside, and he raced into the yard himself.

When he came back, she was still at the door, clutching the dog, but her heart was finally settling. In fact, she was mortified.

"There's no one out there," he said angrily.

"I never said there was." Kate sniffed.

"You never—" He broke off. "Then what the hell was that all about?"

"There *could* have been someone on the other side of those hedges."

"In the *Bakers'* back yard?"

Kate drew herself up to every inch she possessed. "That, I believe, is what I said about the Morleys before you pointed out the error of my ways."

"The error—" Raphael heard himself and realized he was stuck in repeat mode. "Bill Baker, my neighbor, is a municipal court judge."

"Oh, and of course, judges are *never* on the take."

She was right, and he hated it. "This isn't about Bill Baker."

"No, it's about why you just sent me to my death."

"You're alive. Until I choke you. You just scared the hell out of me."

"Me? Scared *you?* I was out there and all of a sudden I realized that one bullet—*one bullet*—could come tearing through those hedges at any moment and I'd be gone! That's what you wanted, right? For me to be scared? Well, you've got it. And presumably, you've got neighbors on both sides. What about the *other* side from the Bakers?" She shoved the dog at him without waiting for a response.

Raphael caught Belle out of instinct. It *had* been a stupid mistake. His only excuse was that he'd been off his stride all morning, so worried about what she was doing to him that he'd forgotten why she was with him in the first place. *It's your turn to walk the dog.* He'd flipped the words out without consideration. And she had a point. Bill Baker still didn't particularly concern him, but the town house on the other side was vacant. He'd been told that the people living there were retired and spent their summers at the Jersey shore.

Raphael made a growling sound deep in his throat and went to the living room. Kate was hunting around for her purse.

She realized that she didn't have it with her. She never took it on jobs. And, of course, she'd been on a job last night before she'd landed here in his home, in his bedroom, smack dab in the middle of his chaotic, kitchen-tableless life.

Another little cry of pure helplessness caught in her throat.

Raphael held the front door open for her with the hand that didn't hold the dog. One good day was all he needed to straighten this out, he told himself. And then she—and every crazy thing she had going on inside him—would be gone.

They went outside, then they both stopped cold on the sidewalk at the same time. They stared at her van. His SUV was still in her parking garage.

"Okay, here's how we're gong to do this." Raphael gave her the dog. "Your place will be our first stop. It's a little out of our way, but I'm not driving this thing all day."

Kate pushed Belle right back at him. "Okay. Just let me get my stuff first."

Raphael caught the mutt in one hand, nearly dropping her. Belle sounded a warning. "What stuff?"

"You know, my wagon and everything."

"You're going to go back inside and collect all that all over again? You put half of it in my refrigerator!"

"I want to take it home!"

"You're not *going* home! We're just going to your garage and changing vehicles." He shoved the dog at her. And Belle bit him, sinking her teeth into the soft pad of his palm, hanging on. "*Damn* it!" He shook her teeth off.

Raphael got behind the wheel of the van and started the engine. He'd left the keys in it last night, maybe subconsciously hoping that someone would steal the...the *atrocity*.

Kate hesitated until the van began rumbling backward down the driveway without her. She gave a yelp of disbelief and ran for the passenger door. Just as she grabbed it, Raphael hit the brakes.

"I hate you," she said tightly, throwing Belle into the seat then climbing up herself. She slammed the door shut, and the van began rolling again.

"Honey, the feeling borders on mutual more times than I can tell you."

Kate caught her breath. She made herself shrug. She was not going to let the comment sting. She hadn't really meant it.

But he did. The truth hit her like a sledgehammer. He was sort of...growing on her. Even during abominable behavior like this. And it hurt deeply, too deeply, that the transition wasn't mutual.

"I fail to see why we couldn't take just ten seconds for me to return my belongings to my own home," she said tightly.

"You don't know the meaning of ten seconds."

"If we finish this today, I'm just going to have to come back for all of it."

"Oh, man, and that'll knock your whole organized day out of whack, too." Raphael felt a small, sharp pain in the center of his chest that she was so anxious to put him behind her. She was going to *help* him with the investigation! Where the hell had that come from? Raphael turned the corner, heading toward the bridge. "If you'll be kind enough to just recognize someone from these mug shots, you might even get your *belongings* back by lunchtime. I'll have an officer deliver them all to your door personally."

Kate felt a burning sensation in the area of her heart. Well, that made it clear enough. He didn't even want her to come back here for her possessions. He couldn't wait to get rid of her. She bit her lip. Unconsciously, she smoothed a hand over her unruly curls. She hadn't put on makeup this morning. She didn't have any with her. Not that it would have made a difference anyway.

She nudged Belle over in the seat. "Isn't your headquarters on the way to my garage? Wouldn't it make more sense to just stop there on the way so I can look at these pictures? The quicker I get it over with, the sooner we'll know if we've got a lead or not."

Temper punched behind Raphael's eyes. Maybe it was at the way she used that cop jargon again. *We've got a lead.* Maybe it was because she didn't even want to detour a few blocks south before settling down to the business of getting him out of her way. Raphael jerked the big van around a corner.

"Is that a yes?" Kate asked cautiously.

He nosed the vehicle into a municipal parking lot without answering. He parked and watched her open her door and slide down off the seat before the engine had even quit sputtering. Then she set off across the street without him, her black curls bouncing, her hips moving in that tight little way that had entranced him from the start. Her spine was as straight and regal as any princess's.

It had happened, he realized. In spite of all his intentions, in spite of the many, many ways she managed to irritate him, somehow it had happened. She had him tied up in knots. She had turned him inside out. She had him furious and confused, and yeah, half of it hurt a little.

Damn it, he was crazy about her.

Chapter 10

Kate flipped each page of photographs over with exquisite care. She propped her chin on her hand. There was no stirring of her subconscious. There was…nothing.

Raphael stood on the other side of the table, watching her with an expression she couldn't quite read. It was strange and sort of bemused. She felt *him* clearly enough. His gaze was like a physical touch, brushing feather light over her skin. She finally let out a gusty breath of frustration.

"You're distracting me."

Raphael took a step back so that he was leaning against the wall next to his desk. "I haven't said a word."

He didn't have to. Paradoxically, she wanted desperately to feel a nudge of recognition from the photos for the same reason her mind kept straying from them. She had to get him out of her life by sundown. She didn't dare spend another night in his bed.

She'd weathered his comment about kissing her to snap

her out of hysteria. But then he had held her last night while she'd cried, and his comments in the van this morning had cut just a little more deeply than they should have. Who knew how badly his candid remarks would hurt if she was forced to spend yet *another* twenty-four hours with him? Only yesterday morning, he had infuriated her. That had segued into tolerance. And now she was fantasizing about him doing sports type things without his clothing on.

Kate grabbed the book in front of her and slapped it shut. She reached for the first one again. "One more time."

"What's the point?"

The point, she thought, was that she might see something in them this time if she could get him to leave the room. Instead, he planted his palms on the table and leaned toward her. Kate's pulse tap-danced as she caught that summery scent of him again.

"Kate, there's a time for determination and a time to just call it a day."

She started to argue, then she saw it in his eyes—green now, such a clear green. He had never really thought anything in these pictures would tweak something in her mind. At least, he had considered it a long shot. It was just a motion that needed to be gone through.

But for Kate, it was the only hope she had.

"I want to look again," she said obstinately. "If I don't come up with anything this time, then you can hypnotize me."

Raphael felt surprise jerk at his heart.

"Is there something to drink around here?" she asked. "Something that doesn't come from whatever place you've been feeding Belle from?" The dog was currently dozing near a paper plate in the corner. Raphael had emptied out a refrigerator somewhere in the building and had been using her for a disposal. In her sleep, Belle burped.

"Hot or cold?" Raphael asked.

"Huh?" Kate dragged her gaze off the preposterous excuse for a dog.

"Coffee or a soft drink?"

"Oh. A soft drink. No caffeine or calories, please."

"Then why don't you just use the water cooler in the hallway?"

Kate glared at him. He waved a hand and left.

Kate scrubbed her hands over her face and turned to the books again. When Raphael came back, she'd gone through the photographs one more time and there was still nothing. She was so distressed that she popped open the can of sugar-laden cola he'd brought her and drank it without noticing.

"Okay," she said grimly, looking at him. "Let's do the other, the hypnotism."

"Now?"

"Why not?"

He sat across the table from her and swigged from his own can. "Maybe tonight."

She didn't want there to *be* a tonight! "Please. Let's just try."

Raphael watched her. She pressed a hand to a pulse at her throat, then let it flutter back to rest on the table. He felt a stirring in his gut. What was that all about?

In all honesty, he considered her to be maybe the worst prospect for successful hypnosis he'd ever come across. Unless she gave up control, and he was no longer sure he wanted to be around to see that happen.

He leaned toward her. "Are you relaxed?"

Kate's hand went to her throat again. "Of course."

He reached out and trailed a finger along the line of her

jaw. And he watched that pulse begin beating madly. "How about now?"

Kate backed up, breaking the contact as the flow of her blood skipped at his touch. He didn't mean anything by it, she reminded herself. He was just making a point. "As much as can be expected while a crazed gunman believes I'm his worst nightmare."

"Not good enough."

"What do you want from me?" she cried.

Things he was damned if he was going to contemplate, Raphael thought. And he heard his own voice drop a notch regardless. "Tell me what it would take to relax you."

Too many things came to mind, Kate realized, and none of them had anything to do with hypnosis. Candlelight, she thought. A good Cabernet wine. A fireplace, its orange light dancing over that bronzed skin of his...

Kate put a hand to her mouth and coughed as her heart tried to squeeze into her throat. "I...uh, believe I get your point. This atmosphere isn't conducive to hypnosis."

What was she thinking, Raphael wondered, to make that blush creep up her neck? Then he decided that it was better that he didn't know. He felt his gut twist a little.

He'd like very much to get past that control of hers, to peel it away from her layer by gentle layer until her muscles were liquid and every move, every reaction she made came straight and raw from her soul. Wanting that, and acknowledging it to himself, was going to make the time until this job was over an exercise in determination and willpower. But he heard himself push her again anyway.

"You didn't answer my question."

A tub full of bubbles, Kate thought. *That* would melt all this coiling tension inside her. She mentally transferred the wine and the candlelight into a bathroom. And somewhere in her soul, deep in a place that dreamed, she could feel his body behind hers in the tub, her back resting against that strong, sculpted chest, his hard arms around her. *Why stop there?* She thought about his hands for a moment, sliding forward through hot, slick, foamy water and over her skin, her breasts, then her tummy, then...

"Kate?"

She cried out softly, pushed back from the table suddenly and came to her feet.

Raphael jolted. "Damn it, will you stop doing that?"

For a mortifying moment, she thought he'd read her mind. Then she realized that his right hand had moved to the gun at his back and his gaze had flown to the door.

"What the hell was that about this time?" he demanded.

"I...nothing. I'm sorry!"

After a long moment, his hand moved away from his gun. She could almost see the hard readiness for violence go out of his muscles. He seemed to take a deep breath. "Apologizing gets easier with practice, doesn't it?"

She *did* still hate that smug look he could get. "If not the hypnosis," she said stiffly, "then what's next?"

It took him a moment to answer. "We hit the streets. Fox says he's getting nowhere with McGaffney's guys. They won't talk to him, so it's my turn. You carry the dog."

Kate soon tired of carrying Belle. Though the little beast could hardly weigh more than four or five pounds, her arms ached from the relentless burden. Kate shifted her back and forth, from side to side, as she and Raphael made their way down Eighth Street on foot. When she'd pointed out that they had a vehicle at their disposal and that maybe all this walking was unnecessary, he'd only said something about the van being mistaken for a Trojan horse where they were going.

"And where exactly is that?" she asked.

"Bonnie Joe's."

"Is he a friend of yours?"

"He owns a restaurant on Filbert. I thought you were so big on cop dramas."

"And your point would be what?" His legs were long. Hers were short. She had to take twice as many strides to keep up, and he wasn't waiting for her.

He crossed Arch against traffic. "If you want to talk to a mob bigwig, you can generally find him where food is being served."

Kate was intrigued. "That's really true?"

"True enough. When we get there, you're going to stay at the door and shut up."

"Inside or outside the door?" She did *not* want to be cut out of this.

"Inside, where I can see you and shoot anybody who approaches you."

Kate stumbled. He finally glanced at her.

"Just kidding."

"Ha, ha." She began walking again. "Why am I carrying this dog?"

"Because it was your brainy idea to keep her."

"That is *not* true. She decided to stay." She tucked Belle under her left arm and pinned her there to give her forearm a break. The dog growled.

"Shut *up*," they said to her simultaneously.

Raphael turned onto Filbert and Kate hurried after him. Halfway down the block, they came to the restaurant. Several windows with old-fashioned panes fronted the street. There was thick darkness behind the glass. The place looked closed. Kate shifted Belle again to glance at her watch. It was only half past eleven.

"They're not open yet," she told him.

Raphael banged a fist against the heavy oak door anyway. He looked over his shoulder at her. "And how many years have you spent following the power shifts and movements of these—'' He jerked around to face front again as the door opened under a second assault from his fist. ''Hi, Joe.''

The man was not an inch taller than Kate was, but he was round. She stared at him, amazed. He had to weigh three hundred and fifty pounds. He had hair the color of ginger ale, and muddy brown eyes. His face was florid.

''Son of a—'' Joe began.

''Hey, watch your language. I've got a lady with me.'' And that quickly, that cleanly, Raphael had his gun in his hand.

Kate's heart pounded in shock. She hadn't seen him move. He didn't threaten with it, but merely made sure it was visible. What did he expect to happen here?

She did not want to be part of this. And she wouldn't have missed it for the world.

''Now what?'' she whispered, leaning close to Raphael's back.

''Now you shut up,'' he said in an undertone.

''Who's she?'' Joe asked, peering around him.

''My lady, the one I just mentioned.''

My lady? Something curled in Kate's stomach, something sweet and languorous.

''She's my job, pal. And I take my jobs seriously. So we need to talk.''

The air left Kate, and everything else inside seemed to sluice out of her with it. Of course, she was his job. He mentioned that often enough. How could she forget?

The fat man stepped back from the door. The gun must have persuaded him. Raphael strode inside. Kate stood immobile for a moment, then she scooted in after him.

''Stay here,'' Raphael said to her. He pointed at her feet. ''Not an inch farther.''

''But—'' She broke off at the look of warning on his face. She stayed put.

Raphael and the man named Joe went inside. She could just barely make out a bar behind a stand of ferns guarding the entry. She'd had a vision of hard, practiced killers sitting around a big table. Shoveling food in, drinking Chianti. Wrong mob, she thought giddily. Apparently, the Irish did things differently.

Kate craned her neck around the ferns. There was a row of seven men on the stools in front of a long panel of what appeared to be teak. They all wore suits. A few lean, hungry types hovered behind them, and they mostly wore jeans. They seemed younger.

Joe went behind the bar. Raphael followed right after him. Kate grinned. She liked his style.

They were talking too quietly for her to hear. Kate tucked Belle closer to her chest and crept forward. A growl rumbled in the dog's throat, and Kate closed her hand over her muzzle.

She watched Raphael put his palms on the bar. She thought his eyes had gone dark again, but in the dim light and with the distance between them, she couldn't be sure.

"Who put the word out on the McGaffney witnesses?" he asked.

Kate shivered. It was *just* like in the movies.

"You got the wrong restaurant," said one of the men at the bar. "Sounds to me like you need to be talking to Charlie."

Kate noticed that all the men who were standing had their hands at or near their waists, where Raphael always kept his gun. *They were armed.* The giddy feeling washed out of her. This was for real.

Raphael didn't look at the man who had spoken. "This is the way I see it. This current problem is between you guys and Charlie Eagan. It's your war, your business. I don't give a damn if you all shoot each other from here to Poughkeepsie. It's less I have to worry about on the streets. But now you're involving innocent people, and you know how testy I get about that. I'm not crying over Phil McGaffney. But that woman last night? *She* bothers me. And the one over there by the door? Gentlemen, you don't want to know.''

"Who's she to you?'' asked a man at the bar. Kate's breath gathered into a weightless sensation of expectancy. She cursed herself a thousand times for being a fool.

"Innocent,'' Raphael said calmly. "She was at the scene when Phil got hit, but she saw nothing.''

A lot of gazes came around to speculate over Kate. She took a judicious step backward toward the door again.

"She saw who nailed Phil, hey, let her tell us,'' one of the seated men said. "We'll take care of it. Otherwise, we can't help you.''

"So what's the word?'' Raphael said, swerving the subject, having made his point. "Who took out McGaffney?''

"Do we know?'' said the first man at the bar. "If we knew, there would have been more action by now instead of all the waiting.''

Kate listened and frowned. He was saying that if these men knew which of Eagan's men had killed Phil Mc-Gaffney, if they could pinpoint exactly who had ordered the hit, a mob war would have been in full force by now.

"Then thanks for your time,'' Raphael said. He stepped around the bar and came toward her. He took her elbow and steered Kate out the door.

She blinked in the sunlight as they stepped outside. "That's it?''

He looked at her, scowling. "What did you expect?''

"Answers.''

"From here? These guys have no idea which of Eagan's guys hit Phil.''

She couldn't help it. Kate dragged against his hold on her arm and stamped her foot. "Then why did we even bother? This was just…just wasting time!'' And the light was thinning, the day getting older. They were *never* going to get this figured out by nightfall!

"Let me get this straight. You thought some great nugget of wisdom was going to pop forth out of all that?"

Kate hesitated, then nodded.

"Someone died, Kate. And no matter what I said back there, McGaffney was a human being and that makes me mad. But these guys aren't going to tell me who killed him." He frowned and looked up the street, as though thinking ahead. "We're going to make another four or five stops this afternoon. And no one is going to tell us anything. But they're going to talk among each other. And someone way down on the totem pole, someone maybe a little disgruntled and a little ticked off at somebody else, he's going to get an earful of it. And one of *those* guys is going to come to me and tell me what he knows."

Kate was horrified. "That could take days!"

"Depends on how fast we talk to a whole lot of people. You should have thought of that before the prosciutto." He turned away from her. "We've got a lot of cages to rattle and a lot of trees to shake before that one guy gets my message, so let's go."

He started walking again. Kate followed him, a little woozy from the blast of reality.

"You did okay with that back there," he said finally.

He was a few steps ahead of her again. Kate didn't try to catch up this time. She hugged the dog a little tighter to herself and smiled.

By five o'clock, her arms ached abominably. By six, her feet were in agony. She was more than ten strides behind Raphael on Eleventh Street, and Kate no longer even cared about keeping up. As long as she could see him ahead of her, she wouldn't lose him.

He'd been absolutely right. No one had told them anything. Detective work was *nothing* like in the books that were her passion. They'd spent the entire afternoon talking to this person, that person, then another one—and they had learned nothing worth knowing.

Kate was tired. She was demoralized. But with each useless interview, Raphael seemed to become more dogged. She watched him gaining ground on her again. A man had died, a woman had nearly been killed, and he fully intended to stand for them, she realized. No matter what it took, no matter how many seemingly useless questions he had to ask, he would do it. He was not discouraged. He was doing what needed to be done.

Kate pressed her free hand to her heart. She was actually starting to *admire* him. Fantasies were one thing. A misguided kiss was more of the same. Not hating him anymore...well, she could accept that. But *respect?*

Kate stopped cold in the middle of the sidewalk. Raphael went on for several strides before he realized that she was no longer trailing behind him. He stopped and looked back.

"What are you doing?"

"My arms hurt," she shouted. "*You* take the dog."

But instead of coming toward her or answering, he looked at his watch. "Want to stop by your apartment and pick up some of your things while we're in the neighborhood?"

Kate looked around. She was so numb from fatigue that she hadn't even realized they were only a block or so from her apartment. The thought of clean clothes galvanized her. She started walking again.

The feeling dissipated as soon as they crossed her lobby. Sure, there were clean clothes up there. There were also the remnants of her life. She wasn't sure which she dreaded more—finding a lot of calls for Dinner For Two on her answering machine that she would have to turn down, or finding no calls at all.

"I want to stop and buy a newspaper after we leave here." She stabbed her finger on the elevator button. "I want to see what they have to say about all this."

"What's the point? You were there. You saw the whole thing go down firsthand."

Her temper kicked. "Maybe I want to see if they spelled my name right."

And he was just as determined that she would never know.

There'd been a paper behind the bar at Bonnie Joe's. He'd caught a glimpse of the front-page headline. The big banner was all for the rumbles of war amid the Philadelphia Irish underground. And beneath that, in just slightly smaller print, there had been a howl about the connection to Dinner For Two. It hadn't taken the press long to follow the trail of Kate's bread crumbs from Phil McGaffney to Betty Morley.

"You've got ten minutes," he said, to take her mind off it.

Kate swung around to face him as the elevator doors opened on her floor. "It's six-thirty at night!" she cried. "Even *you* have to give up at some point!"

He gave her a little nudge, sending her off the elevator. "We're done for the day."

"Then why are you timing me?"

"Because every minute we stay here is a minute someone can figure out you *are* here. If you were trying to find someone, where would be the first place you'd look?"

Kate ground her teeth together. She hated him being right all the time.

She hated being afraid more.

But she was. He had spooked her—again. She whipped through the apartment in record time, throwing clothes and toiletries into a small overnight case. She refused to drag her big suitcase out of the closet. For one thing, it was the one she'd come to Philadelphia with from the Midwest so many years ago—full of dreams that were dying now. And somehow, she thought, if she packed *that* many clothes, it would be like admitting she was going to be with Raphael for a while.

She saved the kitchen—and the telephone and answering machine there—for last.

Kate held her breath and looked at the little numeric display window. It showed a big, red zero. She couldn't help it. A small sound was wrenched from her chest.

"This will be the worst of it," Raphael said, watching her closely. "These first few days. But time will pass. And people will forget."

She looked at him, another thought suddenly coming to her, one that appalled her. "I never called into the diner this morning to tell them I wouldn't be in again!"

Raphael looked away from her, from the way her color drained. Then she grabbed the telephone. She tapped in two numbers, then her finger stalled. Slowly, making that sound again, she replaced the receiver.

"What good would it do?" she asked miserably. "If the diner hasn't already fired me, they'll just want to know when I *will* be back. And I can't tell them."

They'd know that already, Raphael thought, if they'd read the papers.

"It's all…gone. Dinner For Two. My job. My…my savings."

Raphael scowled. "What happened to your money?"

"I'm going to have to dip into it to survive! I have no income now!"

He hadn't meant to comfort her. He'd been carefully avoiding it all day. Now his hands went to her shoulders almost as though they had a will of their own. He thought about shaking her out of it. He only held her instead, his fingers kneading out some of the tension he found there. "Kate, this isn't a siege without end. Before the month's out, you'll have another job."

She made a strangled sound. "It's only August ninth!"

He ignored her nitpicking this time. "Dinner For Two will start getting calls again. You'll be notorious, and the bad guys will be behind bars."

She sniffed, not in that indignant way, but as though she was trying not to cry.

"I've got a little money put aside," he heard himself say. What the hell was he doing? Her net worth was probably three times what his was! She saved, he spent. That was what money was earned for, in his book. "I'll make you a loan to tide you over so you don't have to touch that restaurant money."

She stared at him, then, finally, her eyes started swimming. "That's…that's ridiculous."

He knew.

"I've *got* money. That's not the point."

"If it hurts you this much to use it, then I don't want you to do it."

Her stomach rolled. So did her heart. What was he saying?

That he cared. But she knew, somehow, that it said nothing particular about his feelings for her, except, perhaps, that he was starting to consider her a friend, or maybe he'd just always considered her a victim. And she knew that he would do the same thing for anyone in her situation, anyone who was scared and helpless against what was happening to them. Life's little trivial nuisances—like how much money *he* had in the bank—rolled right off his shoulders, unimportant.

It made a feeling swell inside Kate that was so treacherous, so dangerous, so far beyond tolerating him or liking him or even respecting him, she shook her head fast and hard and backed away. She couldn't let him see it in her eyes. She knew, in that instant, that she could fall in love with him.

"Let's go," she said, her voice still clogged. "It's giving me the creeps to be here."

He went to the door and held it for her, but he let her juggle her overnight case and the dog, making no move to take either of them from her. Kate opened her mouth with a caustic comment, then she laughed.

She felt the reflex climb all the way up her throat, and she let it out gladly because for a minute there, she'd purely been on the verge of losing her mind. *Loving him?* It was much, much better to enjoy the little grunt he made when she passed him and shoved the dog at his chest so hard that he had no choice but to catch her. It was infinitely better to hear him swear under his breath as he shut the door behind them.

This was safe ground.

Chapter 11

They picked up his Explorer from her garage, then Raphael followed Kate's big, lumbering van over the bridge toward his neighborhood. She'd refused to leave it in the municipal lot. So he kept close to her rear bumper, uncomfortable with the idea of her being in a separate vehicle.

Periodically it expelled bursts of noxious smoke from its tailpipe. Raphael closed his windows tightly and swore to himself. He decided that a tune-up probably wouldn't fix whatever ailed the van's exhaust system. It if were that simple, as meticulous as she was, Kate would have had it fixed by now.

He was coming to know her entirely too well, he thought.

On the seat beside him, Belle yapped once as though agreeing with his thoughts. He scowled at her, not sure how she'd come to be riding with him instead of in the van. "Why don't you run back to wherever it was you came from?"

The dog cocked her head and gave him…well, a pitying expression, he thought. Like she was saddened by the fact that he was stupid enough to believe it was even an option.

"I'm not buying it," Raphael muttered. "You're just a dog. Hell, you're not even a purebred. You're a mutt off the street."

She showed teeth. It was a little eerie, he thought.

"All you do is eat and sleep. Name one angelic thing you've done so far."

She yawned and closed her eyes. Dismissing him, Raphael thought, and the boring limits of his human mind. He was inclined to nudge her wiry little body off the seat onto the floor just for the hell of it, but she'd probably bite him again.

They reached his town house and Kate rolled her van into his driveway first. It was so big that when he tried to tuck the Explorer in behind her, about a foot of his vehicle protruded out onto the street. "Uh-uh," Raphael said, getting out. "This isn't going to work." He motioned back and forth between the two trucks.

Kate looked at them blankly. "You want to change them around?"

"Damned right I do."

"What for?"

"If anybody's tail is going to get smacked by a drunk driver, it's going to be yours."

"Does the judge typically drink and drive?"

"It doesn't have to be anyone who lives here. Traffic passes through." And it was the principal of the thing, he thought. It was *his* driveway.

He headed toward her, intent upon wrestling her keys away from her if she wouldn't cooperate. Then his cell phone rang.

Too much was going on right now to ignore it. His number was easily available and he'd talked to a lot of people today. It was possible that someone from within McGaffney's ranks had already turned. He paused to answer it, then he scowled. "It's for you."

Kate caught the cell phone as he passed it to her. "How could it be? No one knows I'm here."

Everyone knew, he thought. He had very little doubt that somewhere in that newspaper article, it had been mentioned that she was in protective custody. The rest was an easy leap.

She frowned as she followed him inside and spoke into the phone. "Hello?"

The bright, cheerful voice of Beth Olivetti answered her, the assistant she had hired before this nightmare had started. It seemed like a lifetime ago. "I called police headquarters and they said you were assigned to Raphael Montiel and gave me this number. How are you doing?"

Kate was mildly disquieted that the cops had volunteered such information so easily. Anyone could find her, she realized. Then again, Raphael had been giving the number out to people they'd talked to all day. He was always on the move and had to have a way for people to reach him.

She watched Raphael take the gun from his waistband and put it on the coffee table. His movements were all masculine grace, and there was a catlike awareness about him. She knew he was listening to every word. "As well as can be expected," she replied finally.

"Listen, I took the liberty of stopping by your apartment this morning. I figured that with all this going on Dinner For Two would be in a state of disaster."

Kate felt her heart squeeze. "I stopped there, as well, just a little while ago. No one's called us, Beth. Enjoy a little respite until this is sorted out. I won't be needing you."

"What do you mean no one's called us? There were

seventeen messages on your answering machine this morning.''

This time Kate's heart staggered. *Seventeen?* She knew immediately what had happened. Both Beth and Janaya had keys to her apartment because she ran the business out of there. Beth had cleared the messages off the machine before Kate had arrived.

She wanted to whoop with the relief of it. She wanted to cry. She couldn't take any of the jobs. ''Who were they from?'' she asked carefully.

Beth began reciting a list. Kate motioned frantically at Raphael for a pen and some paper. He brought her a crayon and a torn envelope from his electric bill. She looked at the crayon disbelievingly, then she set about using it.

Most of the clients had called more out of curiosity than anything else. But there were four dinner requests, as well. Kate almost sagged with relief. She couldn't take the work. She knew that. But she could return each call and salvage what business she could.

She disconnected and looked at the bright red crayon. ''You have a very weird life.''

Raphael headed for the kitchen. ''I dated someone last spring who had a kid. She brought him by sometimes when she couldn't find a baby-sitter. What's for dinner?''

Kate followed him, the crayon still in her hand. ''You date a lot.''

He glanced at her as he began opening cupboards. ''No, I don't.''

''Anna Lombardo, and now this crayon lady,'' she persisted. She had another thought. ''What about Allegra Denise?''

He stopped with a cupboard door in each hand and looked at her. ''Allegra?''

"You seemed so…familiar with her the other night. Have you dated her, too?"

Raphael gave a bark of laughter. "Not me. Not on a bet."

Kate felt an invisible hand around her stomach ease. She couldn't have said why she'd asked. Maybe it was an effort to figuratively smack herself upside the head. Kate had seen Anna Lombardo's photograph in the newspapers and had recognized her sort instantly. Like Allegra, Anna had been blond. She'd seemed sleek, polished, confident, with the kind of poise that seemed to bring men to their knees. Kate had guessed before she had read the article that the woman was some type of professional, and Anna had turned out to be a lawyer.

Kate wondered about the crayon lady, and knew without asking that she would have been blond, feminine, seductive, just the way Allegra was. Allegra knew her power over men and she knew how to wield it. Some instinctive guess told her that Anna had been the same way.

It was another very strong reminder to yank her head out of the clouds where Raphael was concerned, Kate thought. She wasn't even remotely his type—and he, at least, had made no bones about that from the start.

"What are you thinking?" Raphael asked curiously. A frown had gathered between her brows. For a moment, he thought, she looked absolutely bleak.

Kate tossed the crayon neatly so it landed on the kitchen counter. "I guess I'm crimping your style. Being here, I mean. I'm kind of…curtailing your social life."

It was an innocent enough comment. And memories of Anna rolled over him again like a series of snapshots being fanned out, one after another. He thought of the blood, of the pain and horror in her eyes when she had died, of the way she had looked when they had found her. "I've turned over a new leaf."

In spite of everything she'd just told herself, Kate's heart kicked. Maybe he had suddenly decided that he was going to go for practical brunettes. "What kind of leaf?"

He opened the refrigerator. "Are you going to cook tonight or not?"

"After you tell me about the leaf."

"I've discovered the glories of playing the field. With brief stops at each base."

Kate scowled. She was *definitely* not that kind of woman.

She watched him pry open the container that held the Morley's leftover lobster salad. "Don't eat that. It's two days old. It needs to be thrown out."

He popped a chunk into his mouth anyway, then he tossed one to the dog who was circling his feet, snapping her jaws like a miniature shark in a feeding frenzy. Belle caught the bite in midair, and they both stared at her.

"I left her in the truck." Raphael frowned. "Didn't I?"

Kate hesitated, then nodded. They'd been arguing about who was going to park where, she remembered. And then his cell phone had rung.

Kate glanced over her shoulder into the living room. The front door was slightly ajar. "There's our answer." She breathed again and went to close it. But she looked outside at the Explorer as she did. Both its doors were closed. She fought off a shiver and decided not to mention it.

When she returned to the kitchen, she took the lobster salad from Raphael's hands and began shoveling its contents down the garbage disposal. She had flour in the van, and enough staples to make a crust. She'd noticed a jar of mediocre spaghetti sauce in his cupboard. She had spices with her, as well, and could transform it into pizza sauce.

"What about you?" Raphael asked.

She glanced at him as she tapped a fingernail against an egg from his refrigerator, not entirely trusting its freshness.

He had his arms crossed lazily over his chest. One shoulder was tucked against the door jamb. He wore a slight five o'clock shadow that was more golden than dark. "What about me?" she asked carefully.

"There's no one serious. We know that. So do you date?"

Kate dropped the egg and swore. He cocked a brow at her as she grabbed a paper towel and bent to clean it up. "How do you know there's no one serious? You don't know me well enough to be sure." It bothered her considerably that he had guessed correctly.

"I know women."

She just bet he did. "Your point?"

"You haven't spent the last two days frantically calling some poor guy, assuring him that you're all right when he's actually enjoying the peace and quiet so he can see a ball game for once. You're not telling him that even if you *are* stuck in my home alone with me for the time being, nothing is going to happen because I'm ugly as sin."

Kate almost choked as she straightened. "Women do that?"

He had that half grin on his mouth again, the one that said he was enjoying himself. "Which? Call guys frantically, or lie?"

She couldn't help herself. Another peal of laughter rolled up her throat and escaped her. "You have an excellent opinion of yourself."

"And you're pretty clever at changing the subject."

"What was it again?" She found another egg and set about mixing dough in the bowl.

"Do you date? Or is that a waste of your precious, organized time?"

Kate's hands stalled before she made herself resume movement. It stung. She had known that the longer she stayed with him, the more his offhand remarks would hurt her. But she hadn't been ready for this one. "You don't know me," she said again, stiffly.

Raphael thought about it. He did, he thought, more and more with each passing minute. And right now, he was hitting pretty close to the mark. "There was someone," he realized. "Past tense."

Kate didn't answer.

"What happened?" He couldn't have said why he was so determined to know.

Kate was just as determined not to tell him.

"He moved your magazines? Left your milk out? Why'd you dump him?"

"He dumped me!"

Raphael was momentarily stunned into silence. "Why?" he asked finally.

Kate drove a fist hard into the pizza dough, punching it down. "I'm not Allegra."

He scowled. He didn't get it.

"He ran off with an Allegra."

"Then he was an idiot."

She had never meant to allow it, but her heart fluttered anyway.

"You didn't go after him?" Raphael asked.

She was appalled at the very idea. "No!"

Raphael nodded. "You wouldn't fight for anyone who didn't light a spark in you right from the start," he decided.

Kate's hands hesitated.

"If there was no—" he trailed off, hunting up the right words "—no passion or desperation, or the kind of need that makes you think you're going to die if you don't quench it—if there's nothing like that, it wouldn't be worth your bother."

She stared at him, feeling as naked as if he had suddenly peeled her clothing off, layer by layer. It was too true, but she had never understood the difference until *this* man had touched her. If left her feeling like crying.

"Glory be, Kate Mulhern," he said mildly, "underneath all that starch and practicality, you're really nothing but a romantic."

"There's nothing wrong with that," she said faintly. He made it sound like she was some sort of anomaly.

"No. It's just rare."

Finally, he understood the sense of panic that had been itching just under his skin all day. There remained the blatant fact that whether he intended to enjoy this woman or not, *she* had no such designs on him. She dressed like an Eskimo each night before going to bed, and she was certainly not feeling passion or desperation or need where he was concerned. She'd been trying to move mountains all day in an effort to be rid of him. No matter that she had kissed him back that one time. That had been purely surprise.

She wasn't going to come after him any more than she had battled the Allegra-type lady for her ex-boyfriend's heart.

That was good, he told himself. It was very, very good. Because crazy about her or not, that was where it had to begin and end.

Raphael's cell phone rang again, and he grabbed it from the counter and growled into it. A moment later, he passed it to her again. "Get your own number."

Kate cleaned her hands quickly and put the phone to her ear. "Hello?"

It was Beth again. "Did you call Faith Spellman back?"

For a moment, Kate's mind went blank. She watched Raphael stalk from the kitchen. What was wrong with him now? Something in her blood still hummed from the words he'd spoken. *Passion. Desperation. Need.* As the words had filled the air between them, everything inside her had heightened, sharpened, waiting. Then he had shut down again, leaving her feeling as though she was all dressed up for a party that had just been canceled.

"Uh, no," Kate answered Beth. "I'm making dinner. I'll do it later."

"Maybe you should take a minute and do it now. Faith called back a second time. She's crazy for you to do this cocktail party on Wednesday night."

"I can't do her party." Then Kate's mind jammed on something else. "How do you know she called back?"

"I'm at your apartment again."

"Why?"

Raphael came into the kitchen at the change in her tone.

"I left my purse here this morning," Beth said. "I came back for it and there was another message on the machine, even though you said there were none when you were here. So I took it."

"I'll call her now." She thanked Beth and disconnected. "This will just take a minute," she told Raphael. "I've got a job to turn down."

She said it with such grim practicality, it both irritated him and stabbed at something deep inside him. "What kind of job?"

"Beth said a cocktail party. I don't do parties anyway." She punched numbers in and connected with the Spellmans.

Raphael watched her face change as she talked. The grimness gave way to despair. But that went quickly to anger—the kind that boiled up whenever she realized the unfairness of what was happening to her life. He leaned over the counter toward her. "Call them back."

Kate slapped a hand over the phone. "Will you please refrain from interrupting me?"

"Call them back," he said again. "I want to talk to you for a minute."

"About what? Can't it wait until I explain to this woman that even if I had an up-and-running catering business right now, I still wouldn't serve hors d'oeuvres?"

"Why wouldn't you?"

"I just don't do that sort of thing."

"Not even under the circumstances? Not even to placate someone who might stick with you through all this? Honey, you've got to learn to bend."

Temper kicked in her. Hurt shimmied. She didn't know if she was angry with him for his unflattering estimation of her—again—or because he was right.

She was *not* so rigid that she couldn't adjust when the situation warranted it. "Um…could you hold on one moment, Mrs. Spellman?" Kate covered the phone with her hand. "Are you saying I can do this? You'll let me? It's safe?"

He wasn't sure, but he thought it was worth considering. "I'm saying I want to know what the job entails."

"Hors d'oeuvres."

"Nothing big? No…like, dinners?"

"It's a *cocktail* party."

"I know what a cocktail party is."

Of course, he did, Kate thought. Anna would have been familiar with the concept.

"For your own sweet sake, I'm trying to determine if these hors d'oeuvres might be something you can create in my kitchen and drop off there." Damn it, he was trying to help her. And every time he did, she found a way to make it drive his blood pressure up.

"I could do that." She sniffed. "Assuming I was your average caterer."

"Then *be* an average caterer! Make some of that precious money we were talking about today! Let this lady trumpet it all over town that Dinner For Two made a special exception for her!"

"Why are you shouting at me?"

"Because you are the most stubborn, argumenta-tive—" flushed, he thought, her skin was pink again "—rule-abiding, unflappable—" except her mouth was hanging open now, and what she really looked was inno-cent and shocked "—stuffy—"

"I am *not* stuffy! How dare you say that?"

"You sleep in sixteen layers of clothing!"

"I get hot in them, too! I lied!"

He stared at her a moment.

Then he kissed her again.

He hadn't known he was going to do it. But his temper yanked gleefully away from him, beyond his control, and suddenly her rejection of him seemed like the most im-portant thing in the world. It was stronger than his sense.

She'd react to him again. Damn it, she'd do it. Even if it was just born out of more surprise.

As kisses went, Kate thought as her mind spun away, it was awkward. He leaned over the kitchen counter and his hands found her hair, cupping either side of her head. Kate leaned into him, as well, instinctively, and the counter edged into her waist.

He chose the damnedest times and places, she thought. And then her mind wouldn't work anymore at all.

What she felt was…desperation. Heat rushed up in her, straight from her belly into her limbs, weakening them. The telephone clattered out of her grip, hitting the counter then bouncing off. She reached up and caught his wrists in both hands. Together they moved, a step, then another, blindly, until the counter was no longer between them, his mouth still on hers.

Then Kate did something she had never done before in her life. She gave herself utterly, hungrily and greedily, to sensation, without a moment's pause for deliberation or shock.

She had never really believed this might happen again.
Now that it had, she wouldn't waste a second of it. His
hands were still caught in her hair. He urged her head back.
She gave no resistance, couldn't. She didn't care that her
throat was laid bare to him, vulnerable. She craved his
mouth there, too. But when he moved his lips from hers
to skim his tongue along the line of her jaw, she cried
aloud and turned her face into his again.

She wanted that, yes, but she wanted to taste him again,
too, wanted so much more, wanted all he would give.

She swayed against him, and Raphael felt the surrender
in the way her bones melted. This, he thought, shaken, this
was what he had imagined—that control of hers peeling
back, and with a touch here or there, she would completely
unravel. He knew—extraordinarily, he thought—just
where to kiss her. He didn't need to learn her, to practice
to figure her out.

It would be here, he thought, that place at her throat
where her pulse fluttered at the oddest damned times. The
heat of his mouth touched her, and Kate went wild.

Now, she thought, here, this, right now. Her hands fell
from his wrists. She dug her fingers into his shirt front.
Wanting skin, wanting it next to hers, willing to tear
through fabric to have it. His mouth wasn't enough.
Though, yes, she thought, yes, it was glorious.

She dragged his mouth back to hers until their tongues
tangled again. She drove her hands into his hair and held
him there, demanding, the need inside her so raw and so
suddenly alive, she thought she would die if she didn't
quench it.

And then a voice squawked at them from the floor.

The telephone. Kate didn't recognize the sound at first.
But she was aware of the change it made in Raphael. His
hands caught her wrists and he held them tightly…and
then his mouth was gone from hers.

He put her away from him deliberately.

"I wasn't going to do that." His voice was roughened, hoarse.

Kate looked dazedly into his eyes and saw the lingering heat there. And something else. There was something dark and hard there...something angry.

What had she done? She had thrown herself at him. Mortification rose in her from her toes. Then reality sank in. "*You* kissed me! You did it first!"

"You were making me mad. I let it...provoke me." And even to Raphael, it sounded lame. "I'm sorry."

His words shattered her.

Kate closed her eyes, feeling the pain like the air she breathed. It filled her lungs then every fiber of her being. "Don't worry about it. The words get easier with practice."

"Wait. Damn it, I said that wrong." But she wasn't going to hear him, he realized. She was on her knees on the floor, grabbing for the phone. Then she twisted around and sank down to sit, her back against the kitchen counter as she cradled the phone in her lap for a second.

He'd hurt her.

Which was precisely why he'd had no business touching her, Raphael thought viciously. She wasn't the kind of woman who could take what she needed from him, then walk away. She wasn't like Anna, with that careful, charming wall always in place between them. She wasn't like the women he'd spent the last month with since Anna had died, women who had laughed unperturbedly when he'd waved goodbye.

She'd want—she'd take—all of him, and never be satisfied with anything less.

He *was* sorry he had kissed her again, abysmally sorry, because now he knew how she would lose control—suddenly, like an errant firecracker spinning out into the night, throwing off sparks and wonder. Now that he knew, it would haunt him every second of every minute they remained together until this was over.

Probably, he thought, it would haunt him long afterward, as well.

He was sorry because he had no business tasting her, no business making her spin out of control like that, when he had absolutely no intention of following through and risking what it might eventually cost her. *Blood. Death. Glazed shock in her unseeing eyes.* He was sorry because once would never be enough, not for either of them. And because for a moment—just a heartbeat—he was angry with Anna for dying and changing everything.

Raphael walked out of the kitchen. Then he paused because she was talking into the telephone again.

"I'll do it, Mrs. Spellman," she said breathlessly. "Of course, I'll do it. You've supported me since I started Dinner For Two." There was a pause. "Yes, of course, I'm fine. It was nothing."

Nothing. The word drove deep into his gut regardless of anything he'd just told himself.

"I can't stay and serve, but I'll drop everything off by seven o'clock and you can take it from there."

Raphael didn't look back, but he heard the slight thump of the phone hitting the kitchen floor again as she disconnected and put it down.

Her whole world was coming unglued, Kate thought. A drop-off job, of all things! Convenience food, a delivery!

And that was the least of it.

Misery remained a weight in her stomach. *He'd kissed her like it meant something.* But, of course, it hadn't. He hadn't wanted to do it. She'd driven him to it. Somehow, though she wasn't sure how.

She was going to have to stand up off this floor and

face him for another day or two anyway. Kate groaned aloud.

Say something, she thought frantically. Raphael was still standing in the door, his back to her, the muscles of his shoulders seeming hard, bunched, dangerous.

So Kate scraped up words to fill the quiet. Because sometimes, she thought, quiet could be the most painful thing of all.

''I hope Allegra's life is this much of a disaster.''

Chapter 12

I hope Allegra's life is this much of a disaster.

The words kept knocking around in Raphael's head, bothering him while Kate made pizza. The aroma began emanating from his kitchen fifteen minutes after he left it. He was blissfully amazed. He knew damned well that he didn't have the makings of pizza in his kitchen. Of course, she went to the van periodically, towing that little red wagon.

By her third trip, Raphael began to hate the thing no matter how good his kitchen smelled. It symbolized everything about her that kept him from enjoying the memory of that single, incredible, hot kiss. The wagon represented everything that made Kate who she was—a woman who wouldn't have any idea how to say goodbye when the fun and games were over, who would demand a whole lot more than he was willing to give ever again.

The truth of that kept him sitting in front of the television while she cooked, no matter how often he thought of wandering into the kitchen for a little conversation. He held the remote in his right hand, a can of beer in his left. He swallowed from the can as he clicked through the channels. And he thought, *I hope Allegra's life is this much of a disaster.*

The kicker was, he didn't think so.

On impulse, he grabbed the telephone—not the cell, because that was still in the kitchen and he wasn't going back *there* for love or money—and he called Fox.

"How are things in domestic heaven?" his partner asked.

"Just peachy." Raphael felt his teeth set hard against each other. He changed the subject fast. "Tell me something—how's Allegra doing?"

Fox chuckled. "More appropriately, one might ask how Vince Mandeleone is faring."

Raphael thought of the Homicide rookie who'd been assigned to baby-sit the other woman. "Heard from him lately?"

"Yeah. And he was gasping for breath."

"She'll kill him."

"Word has it, she's trying."

"But nothing's been attempted on her? There's been no trouble over there?"

"Not even an unexpected knock on her door."

Raphael had encountered *that* problem the very first morning with Kate. "So Allegra's world has been quiet as a tomb," he said.

"I was starting to wonder when you'd rouse from your libidinous bliss and question that."

"*Libidinous*?" Damn it, Raphael thought, if Fox were baby-sitting Kate, nobody would understand a word either of them said.

"It means—"

"I know what it means," he growled. "And there's nothing libidinous going on around here. Nothing."

"Actually, I was there last night. In the Morleys' kitchen."

Yeah, he'd kissed her then, too, Raphael thought. So, all in all, he'd managed about twenty-four hours without touching her. His mood darkened.

"The lady was…uh, tousled. I believe her color could best be described as the hue of a rose."

Raphael had been too busy dealing with his own reaction to notice hers. "Get a life and leave mine alone." He paused. "She was blushing?"

Fox hooted with laughter. Raphael waited grimly until the sound died down. Then he got back to business. "Eagan wants Kate. Not Allegra. Why?"

"Allegra's been passed from the arm of one of those guys to another for years now. Could be either Eagan or one of his goons has a soft spot for her still."

It was possible. "Or Kate was somehow more exposed to this particular goon than Allegra was." Which still gave them exactly nothing, Raphael thought. She hadn't recognized any mug shots, so whatever Eagan's guys thought she had seen…well, she hadn't.

The mouthwatering aroma of fresh, homemade pizza grew stronger, then it seemed to waft right under his nose. Raphael glanced over his shoulder. Kate was bringing their plates in from the kitchen. One thing about that practicality of hers, he thought. She didn't waste time holding a grudge, and he appreciated it.

His plate hit the coffee table hard and rocketed in a skid clear across it. Raphael reached out quickly and caught it just before it slid off the other side. "Uh, gotta go," he said into the phone.

"Take some more food for thought with you," Fox said. "How come McGaffney's boys aren't systematically re-

moving from this earth any possible hit man Eagan might
have used? It's been two days now since McGaffney was
hit.''

"They don't—'' Raphael began and broke off. He
frowned at his pizza. There went his appetite.

That was wrong, too, he realized. Philadelphia should
have been awash in a bloodbath by now. Fox was right,
but Raphael had been too preoccupied with his baby-sitting
duties to see it. He'd been too distracted by the lady who
was stonily avoiding eye contact with him as she sat at the
other end of the table and bit into her pizza.

He'd taken Bonnie Joe's explanation and he'd swallowed it neatly. *Stupid*. Joe's guys had said they didn't
know who'd done McGaffney. They'd implied that they
were waiting to find out. It was hogwash. Historically,
these guys had never needed to know for sure.

"Sit tight on your lady," Fox said, "because I've got
a feeling that sooner or later this is going to blow wide
open, and she's going to be right in the middle when it
happens."

Raphael watched Kate chew in precise, small bites. If
God truly had mercy, he thought, it would happen
sooner—before he got into more trouble here than he knew
how to get out of. He disconnected. He pulled his plate
close. Kate still said nothing.

He glanced at the television. "Football okay with you?"
Kate shrugged.

"Granted, it's just preseason. Doesn't count. I'll change
the channel. You can pick. Just…you know, no operas or
ballets or any of that stuff."

She wiped her fingers on her napkin and stood with her
empty plate. "Watch whatever you like. I'm finished."

Raphael closed his eyes briefly. When he opened them
again, she was gone. "You're not speaking to me, are
you?" he called after her.

He heard her plate hit the kitchen sink with a clatter. A moment later, when he heard her footsteps on the stairs, Raphael winced. *Come on, Bonnie Joe. Kill somebody already, will you?*

Kate knew she was being childish. A hundred times a day through the next three intolerable days, she told herself that. She was having a jilted-female hissy fit, pure and simple. It was beneath her.

And she liked it.

In fact, she was enjoying every minute of it. On Wednesday afternoon, as she finished the last of the Spellman appetizers, she realized that she was incredibly tired of always being strong and sensible. Damn it, she was also a woman who had been pushed away while in the throes of a resounding, passionate, desperate kiss. She was entitled to a little moodiness.

Under ideal conditions she would simply have shut Raphael out of her life after what he had done to her. Under normal circumstances, she wouldn't have taken his phone calls—presuming he even made them. If she'd seen him on the street, she would have turned around and walked the other way. She would have avoided him. But that was impossible when he was in her face virtually twenty-four hours a day, when his presence melted every nerve ending in her body hour after hour. He was so...*there*.

Since she couldn't avoid him, Kate ignored him. She was *not* going to embarrass herself again with moony, lascivious thoughts about his body or his eyes. She wouldn't consider the way he'd beaten the streets these last few days trying to avenge McGaffney and poor, concussed Betty Morley, never tiring.

"Here's how we're going to do this," he said, coming into the kitchen with a piece of paper. Kate looked at him quickly before remembering that she wasn't going to acknowledge him. She turned her attention to her onions.

"The Spellmans live in a row house on Twelfth," Raphael continued.

"I know. I've served them before."

"Yeah? So how many homes are there between the premises and each corner?"

She could figure it out if she had to, Kate told herself. But now she was too busy sliding canapés into the oven.

"Okay, I'll tell you," Raphael said when she didn't reply. "There are four to the north corner, two to the south."

Kate glanced at him. He wasn't going to take the hint and leave her alone. "And this means what?"

"It means we enter by the alley on the north side, facing south."

"Why?"

"A quicker getaway."

Kate threw her hands up, finally exasperated. "We're not robbing a bank here."

"After what happened at the Morleys, I want every last kink ironed out of this project. How long will the job take you?"

"How long will it take us to unload the van?" she countered.

"I'm asking you, damn it. And don't forget to add in time for small talk and polite exchanges of money."

Apparently, his mood wasn't any better than hers was, Kate realized. They grated on each other as a matter of course. They were total opposites. So why in the world had he ever kissed her in the first place? And why had it been so *good?*

"Twenty minutes." Kate snapped out the words. "Then we'll be gone and Faith can ruin my appetizers and I'll never even have to know about it."

"Okay. Then you've got twenty minutes to pull this off."

"What happens then? I turn into a pumpkin?"

"Then I pick you up, toss you over my shoulder and carry you out of there."

Kate started to argue and thought better of it. He'd do it. "Fine." Just please, please don't touch me again, she thought.

He raised a brow at her answer. The oven timer buzzed. Kate turned her back on him quickly and extracted the canapés.

Half an hour later, they were loading the van. It had long since lost its berth in Raphael's driveway. Now they had to detour around his Explorer, and privately, Kate did not consider that vehicle much more pristine than her own. She didn't know why he was so touchy about it being on the street.

They drove into the center of the city in silence. Belle was tucked on the passenger seat beside her. Once Raphael reached out and turned her radio from soft classical music to hard rock. Kate reached right out and snapped it back again.

They parked in the Spellmans' alley. Raphael went around to the rear doors and opened them. Kate left Belle with the seat to herself and hurried after him.

"No snitching," she warned. "Most of this stuff isn't finished yet anyway. Faith is going to have to heat it up the rest of the way."

"What are these?" he asked as she pulled out a tray and handed it to him.

"Crabbed-stuffed cherry tomatoes."

"They don't have to be cooked. Do they?"

"Don't even think about it."

He tried not to. But they looked good. He liked crab.

With his back to her, he slid one free from under its plastic wrap and popped it in his mouth.

Heaven.

He helped her carry everything into the home through the rear kitchen door. He noticed Kate's hitching sigh of relief when she saw that the Spellmans' housekeeper was still on duty for the party. Kate had already written down instructions for finishing off the hors d'oeuvres. Now the woman made notes of her own as Kate ran down the list.

In sixteen minutes, it was over.

"That's it?" Raphael asked.

"Just about." Kate's gaze skimmed the kitchen fretfully.

As if on cue, Faith Spellman sailed into the room. Sleek as a thoroughbred, she came toward Kate with her hands outstretched. Raphael almost laughed at Kate's wide-eyed, appalled expression when she realized that the woman was going to hug her. Then he had a treacherous thought. *She didn't do that when I held her.*

Kate extricated herself from the woman's embrace. She slid the check from her fingers. She looked at it, then her eyes popped all over again. "This is too much."

The woman waved a negligent hand. "It's a tip."

"You get tips, too?" Raphael interjected.

"No, I—" Kate looked at Faith Spellman. "I can't take this. I didn't do anything for it."

"How much is it?" Raphael took a step closer to look over her shoulder.

"It's an even extra hundred," said Faith.

Raphael raised a brow. Kate Mulhern was probably on the Fortune 500 list if this happened as a matter of course. "I should get half of that for talking you into this."

"You talked her into it?" Faith turned to him happily. "Everyone is just *dying* that Kate did this for me when her life is so obviously in danger."

Raphael gave Kate an I-told-you-so look. Then he glanced at his watch. "It's going to be in a lot more danger in about one and a half minutes."

"Stop it," Kate snarled in an undertone. She looked at Faith again. "Your housekeeper has everything in order. Everything should be fine. But about this tip—"

"She's very grateful." Raphael hooked a hand inside her elbow and began tugging her toward the back door.

She was going to kill him, Kate decided. "I have sixty seconds!"

She started to shake off his grip when they both heard it—a limp, bleating sound from the alley, followed by a more tenacious, strident wail. Raphael reacted without knowing—or caring—what the sound was. He let go of her and tore out the back door.

Kate knew. It was the van's horn. But it took her a moment to move. Alarm shot into her blood, then disbelief. She stood, dumbfounded, watching Raphael's back as he disappeared. "No, please," she whispered. "Not again."

Raphael reached in through the door and grabbed her hand. He hauled her unceremoniously after him.

Her momentum made Kate miss the bottom step outside. Raphael caught her without turning around, tucking her safely against his back. *No, no, I don't want to be close to him.* She didn't want to need the solid strength of him, not one more time, not *now*, not when she was over-whelmed again and terrified. But then the reality of the situation came crashing in on her, and she wrapped her arms around his waist hard.

Someone—something—was in her van.

The horn kept sounding, and the vehicle was rocking on its shock absorbers. Belle's barking came to them, sound-ing muffled and distant until the horn's resounding cry finally and abruptly ended. From inside the van there came a gunshot, then a horrible, bloodcurdling yelp.

"Belle!" Kate cried. Whatever was going on in there, she'd left the dog in the middle of it.

Raphael roared wordlessly as she jerked around him and ran. Kate was three steps from the rear of the van when something black emerged like a shot. She screamed and dodged. Metal clanged against metal as the doors hit the panels of the van.

A person, a man. Kate's mind wrapped around that and she absorbed the same black mask she'd seen on the gunman Saturday night. And Belle was still yelping in pain.

"Oh, no," Kate breathed, "please, God, no." *Please don't let me have killed an angel!* She scrambled into the van, going on her hands and knees to the front.

Raphael got off one shot as the gunman raced toward the south side—the short side—of the alley. And he missed. He was already turning to the van when his finger squeezed the trigger. That damned fool crazy woman who never listened to a word he said was *inside the van!* If anyone else was still in there, she was as good as dead.

He was going to lose her.

Raphael dove for the rear doors of the vehicle. He crab-walked to the front fast and found her there in the shadows, leaning against the back of the passenger seat. She was crying. And there was blood.

Words crammed in his throat and went unspoken. His knees felt weak. But there was no one else in the van.

"Easy, easy." He sat beside her.

"I k-k-killed her."

Kate turned a grief-stricken face to him. The tears she had shed the first night she had stayed with him had been gulping, wrenched from her as though she'd fought each and every sob hard. Now her cheeks were slick and wet and shiny. Tears rained from her eyes, unabashed. The sight tore at something inside him, then Raphael looked at the dog.

The dog. He'd forgotten about the damned dog. But she had given more thought for the beast than to herself.

He wanted to choke her. He wanted to crush her to him and hold her, needed to feel every pulse of her life. He found his voice again. "Let me see her."

Kate eased Belle from her arms into his. *So much blood.* But, Raphael saw instantly, it was all the dog's. It was on Kate's hands, her forearms, but nowhere else. It seeped steadily from the dog's tan and black nose.

Above that nose were two very baleful black eyes. This, Raphael thought, was one mighty angry Chihuahua.

"Okay," he said hoarsely. "Here. Take her back and just sit tight."

"Where are you going?"

"I'm going to drive. We need to find a vet." He climbed forward into the driver's seat. He turned the key in the ignition and stomped his foot an extra time on the gas pedal as Kate had warned him to do. The engine coughed to life and they rolled.

Raphael had no idea where to go. And that struck him as uproarious. Relief clogged his blood and made him feel nearly crazed with the need to laugh. Kate was alive. But the dog, that irascible little beast, had been shot in the nose, and somehow he had to find a veterinarian in the welter of Philadelphia's streets at eight o'clock at night.

He turned the van onto Callowhill for no particular reason, then he hit the brakes hard and stared.

"What?" Kate cried, her breath catching as she was thrown forward into the back of the passenger seat.

"It's a vet."

"That's what we're looking for!"

"Ain't it, though."

It was on the corner, its red neon sign hitching and straining to warm up and shine fully as though someone had just turned it on. It read 24-Hr Emergency Animal

Service. There was a parking space right in front of the place. In Philadelphia. On Callowhill. Off Twelfth.

Raphael dropped the van into the parking spot. There wasn't time to dwell on it. Kate was already scrambling out the rear doors, the dog cradled in her arms. She ran for the clinic.

Raphael followed her inside and looked around. The place was deserted. He looked at a clock on the wall behind the desk. It was 8:03.

The way he had it figured, an emergency veterinarian would do most of his business during hours when folks' regular veterinarians were closed. This place should have been rocking, but there wasn't another animal to be found. Raphael listened, but there weren't even any barks, snarls or meows coming from the door that led to the rear of the building.

A moment later, a woman wearing a crisp white lab coat came through the door. She was young and pretty and cheerful. "Hi. Have a problem?"

Kate thrust Belle at her. "She's been shot. In the nose."

The veterinarian took the dog quickly. She examined the wound, then she nodded. "Come on in the back. We can fix this."

Kate scurried after her. "Is she going to die?"

"Probably not, if you got her here in time. It looks like blood loss will be her biggest problem." She looked over at what stained Kate's arms and hands as though measuring. Kate looked at herself, as well, and gave another small cry.

Raphael finally began to follow them. He caught up with them in an examining room. The dog was laying flat on her side, but her gaze locked on Raphael when he entered, and those beady little eyes were still glaring. "Hey, beast, I got you here, didn't I?"

Belle's gaze seemed to tell him that *he* had done no

such thing. But there was not so much as a growl from her.

Kate gave a small, distressed sound. "She's got to be dying," she said again.

"No, no," the vet assured her. "The wound's superficial. We'll sedate her, then just clean it and stitch it up. The worst case scenario is that her muzzle might look a little...crooked now. She seems to have lost a small piece of it."

The dog moved her eyes to look at the woman with a pained expression.

"I don't know that she needs to be sedated," Raphael said. It was true. For the first time since he'd had the misfortune to cross the dog's path, Belle was completely, complacently quiet.

"But the antiseptic will cause a sting," the vet said.

Belle's ribs rose and fell in a hefty, long-suffering sigh.

The vet filled a needle and set about injecting it. Immediately, the dog came to life, twisting her head around, and growling. The woman jerked her hand back. "This is a problem. Normally, I would muzzle her so I could work on her without being bitten. But it's her muzzle that's the problem."

"If I were you," said Raphael, "I'd just do what needs to be done, and I'd do it in a hurry."

The dog lay quietly once the woman reluctantly put the needle down. The vet cleaned the wound. Once Belle's lip curled back, showing her teeth at the pain, but she didn't struggle or wriggle. Raphael watched, feeling another headache coming on. Then he stared. "Do that again."

"What?" the vet asked, startled.

"Not you. The dog. Do that again. Snarl."

Both the vet and Kate looked at him as though he had lost his mind. Raphael had. He knew that. But when the dog had pulled her lip back like that, he'd seen something in her incisors. He *thought* he had.

Belle growled again obligingly. And Raphael knew he was right.

"Don't lick," he said shortly. "Do you hear me, dog? Lick your chops and I'll kill you myself." He grabbed his cell phone from his pocket.

Kate's jaw was hanging open now. The vet was looking alarmed.

"There's skin in her teeth," Raphael explained. "Look for yourself."

Kate leaned closer. Belle kept her lip curled back nicely and held it there.

"This dog is amazing," the vet murmured.

"Yeah," Raphael muttered. "You ought to try taking her for a walk."

He raised a watch commander at headquarters. "I need a crime tech," he said, "as fast as you can get one to Twelfth and Callowhill." He looked at Belle's mouth again. The fairly good-size piece of flesh was still stuck there, between her teeth. "Good…uh, dog."

Her tail thumped once.

"I'm a cop," he said to the dazed veterinarian.

"A *detective*," Kate clarified with a bite to her tone, and he sent her a withering look.

"I'm bringing in someone to take that out of there and preserve it as well as possible," he explained.

Kate's eyes widened. She understood. It was just like in books, in movies. "DNA."

Raphael nodded and rubbed at the headache building behind his forehead. Damned if the dog wasn't going to nail this gunman almost singlehandedly. It was one for the books.

Not that he'd ever tell anyone about it.

Chapter 13

When they returned to Raphael's, Kate went straight to the shower. She stood under the steaming water and watched the blood sluice off her skin to spiral down the drain. She felt the heat melt her bones. Or maybe it was just exhaustion that had her legs feeling hollow.

She groaned as she turned her face into the spray and wondered how much more of this she was going to be able to stand. She'd long since moved past amazement and dismay over what had happened to her life. McGaffney had been killed. Betty Morley had been knocked unconscious. Belle had been shot. And someone wanted her dead. Kate could handle all that. But her bodyguard was a different issue entirely.

Somehow, she thought, in the middle of everything else, Raphael had changed all the things she'd taken for granted about herself. She'd survived Jeff Migliaccio—the hard way. She'd learned to be happy with what she was—efficient, talented, capable. Then Raphael had pushed her away in the middle of that kiss—*I wasn't going to do that,* he'd said—and the ache had come back, somehow even worse than before.

For the first time in her life, she wanted to be someone else. Not even Jeff had had that shattering effect on her.

But for the first time in her life, she cared more than sense that *this* man didn't want her.

Kate got out of the shower. She dried off wearily and snagged his bathrobe from the back of the door. There'd been no room in her overnight case for her own, not if she'd wanted to bring along a few days' worth of clothing. She shrugged into it and belted it, then she reached for the door handle to go downstairs and check on Belle.

The dog was on the sofa, ensconced upon a cushiony pile of pillows. An inch-long line of crisscrossed thread ran down the side of her snout. A bowl of food lay by her side—she hadn't even had to use her dissipated strength to stand and eat. Raphael had all but anointed her, he was so happy about getting that skin from her teeth.

"What are you doing?" he asked sharply.

Kate started a little at the tone of his voice. She looked at him quickly. He was standing at the living room window. He held a can of beer in his hand.

"Oh." She sighed. "I could use one of those."

"What?" His expression darkened even more.

"A beer. Is there another?"

"You want a *beer?*"

"What's wrong with you? You're talking in questions."

Kate went to the refrigerator to look for herself. She was pretty sure she had seen a few in there the last time she'd poked around. She collected one and returned to the living room. Then he startled her all over again.

"What are you up to?"

Kate paused with the can to her mouth. She cut her gaze to him out of the corner of her eye, then she drank. The beer was ice cold and mellow. Almost instantly, she could feel it loosen some of the knots inside her. She put it down carefully on the coffee table.

Something was bothering him. But she didn't have it in her right now to deal with it. "I'm going to bed," she decided.

"The hell you are. You're not going to sashay out of here without an explanation."

Sashay? "An explanation for *what?*" she asked incredulously.

He waved his hand in a wild gesture. "For *that!*"

Damn it, Raphael thought, he couldn't take any more. His nerves were already stretched out like rubber bands because of a convoluted case that he was damned if he could figure out because the chain of events was breaking all the tried-and-true rules he knew. And maybe because he wasn't paying as much attention to the details as he should have been. He'd been missing things from the start.

And that, of course, was all *her* fault.

She'd invaded his life, his home, filling it with the scent of pizza and whatever lemony stuff she used in her hair. *Woman* smells. A woman had a way of changing the very atmosphere when she moved in with all her woman stuff, he thought.

He could deal with that. He *had* been dealing with it. He'd been doing fine at ignoring it, that first kiss aside. And hell, that kiss had only happened because she'd been coming apart on him. He wouldn't think about the other embrace they'd shared.

Now, tonight, she'd gone and damned near gotten herself killed. And somehow, that changed everything.

"You could have gotten yourself killed!" Raphael shouted. "Of all the damned, stupid, idiotic, *female* things to do, that took the cake!"

Kate's mouth fell open.

"Jumping into the van like that! What the hell got into you? Did it even once occur to you in that—that *female* brain of yours that somebody else might have been inside that vehicle? Just because one goon jumped out, that didn't mean there wasn't another one still in there!" Air filled his muscles again just thinking about it. "And all because of a *dog!*"

For the first time in hours, Belle's head shot up and she growled.

"You're shouting," Kate said.

"I'm not shouting! I'm making a point!"

"You're shouting at me."

"Well, pardon me for assaulting your sweet little female ears."

Kate rubbed one of her earlobes. "You've also said *female* like it's some kind of affliction three times in the last two minutes."

"The hell I have."

"Yes, you have."

"Then go layer-up, for God's sake, and stop parading around like that!"

Kate went still. Something churned in the pit of her stomach. For a moment, she thought the single swallow of beer she'd had would come up.

She had never *paraded* in her life. And she was finished with "layering-up." What purpose did it serve, anyway? With that last kiss in his kitchen, Raphael had pretty much made it clear that there was nothing about her that could drive him past control.

She went to the table for her beer and drank again. Raphael watched her move. She did it with deliberate grace. Her motions were precise, but somehow fluid anyway. He knew she was angry. Spots of hectic color had bloomed on her cheeks. But would she let it rip? Of course not. She only got crazy over that damned dog.

He wondered if he was *trying* to make her angry, to push her to that uncontrolled edge again. Or maybe he was hoping that she would push right back until *he* found the edge. Either way, he knew he was crazy. But he remained furious with her anyway.

For the first time in all the days since she'd been here, she'd come bouncing out of his bathroom damned near naked. In his robe, and nothing else. It was the straw the camel just didn't need, Raphael decided. She'd treated her own life like it was about as valuable as fool's gold, then she left her underwear in his bathroom. Now she was swigging his beer like a sailor. What the hell was he supposed to do about *that*?

"Get dressed," he said, his voice dropping a decibel if only because it was strangled.

"No! I just told you. I'm going to bed."

He didn't want to know what she'd be wearing when she did, if she was planning on taking that robe off again to do it. "Nobody walked the dog." She'd have to put clothes on for that. "You should walk the dog."

"She did what she had to do in the vet's office."

He'd forgotten that.

"You're acting...bizarre," she said, frowning.

The words speared into his ears like driven nails. *He* was acting bizarre? He was fully dressed, and an occasional beer wasn't out of the question for him. He was the same man he always was, whereas *she* was behaving like someone he'd never met before in his life.

Raphael crossed the room without realizing he had done so. He stopped in front of her, close to her, standing over her...and she looked up, her mouth slightly parted in surprise.

It would have been so easy to sink into her all over again.

Four inches, he thought, and his mouth would have been

covering hers again. Now he knew how she tasted. Now he knew how quickly she could hurtle to that edge he wanted so desperately to drive her over. He heard her breath shorten. Her eyes widened.

Raphael swore.

He jerked away from her and went to the kitchen. His brain was pounding and his blood was too hot, rushing too fiercely. He grabbed another beer and pressed the can against his forehead.

Raphael stood very still in the kitchen and waited for the sound of her footsteps going up, then his bedroom door snicking shut behind her. It was a routine he was getting used to. Then there would come the metallic roll of the lock turning. But this time, there were the footsteps, then nothing else happened.

Thirty seconds passed, then a minute, finally two. Raphael left the kitchen and went cautiously to the stairs. He looked up. The door was open a crack. The bedroom was dark inside. What was *this* all about?

Maybe she was scared. Maybe she didn't want him to have to break through a door to get to her if anything else happened. It made sense. And instantaneously, with vicious force, everything inside him screwed tight all over again.

Oh, yeah, he thought, this was getting out of hand. Unfortunately, he had no idea what to do about it anymore.

Only two men within the PPD had known that Kate was going to take the Spellman job on Wednesday night, Raphael thought the next morning. He had known. And he had told Fox. He would have trusted Fox with his life—he had, in fact, on a few occasions. No leak had come from him. Therefore, Raphael decided, it had not come from the PPD. That meant that it had probably originated from someone in Kate's Dinner For Two network. It had been one of her clients or one of her employees.

It was time to start running down those lists.

He stood in the dining area of the kitchen where a table should have been and watched her over the rim of his coffee mug. She was relaxed this morning, he thought. She had left his bathrobe somewhere in his room, and he was thankful for small favors. Now she wore cutoff jeans and a white T-shirt as she made breakfast—omelettes, he thought, from the look of things.

He wasn't sure which was worse. The T-shirt was thin and he could make out the outlines of her bra beneath it. Therefore, she wore underwear today. That was good. The almost nonexistent proportion of those shorts was not.

He still wasn't sure what he was supposed to do about this…this *changing* she was doing all of a sudden.

"Kate?"

"Hmm?"

She was facing the stove and had her back to him. She looked over her shoulder when she spoke. Reams of dark curls shifted with the movement. She hadn't fought her hair down into manageability this morning, either. Why hadn't she?

"What?" she asked impatiently when he didn't answer.

"Uh, I'm going to need a complete list of everyone Dinner For Two has ever served. And, uh, that book, your phone log. You know, the one you showed me the first night where you write the time of the calls to the second." Somehow he knew she'd be able to lay her hands on all of it within three minutes of setting foot in her apartment. He waited for the swish of irritation that her fierce sense of organization always brought to him. This time it didn't materialize.

Kate cocked her head, frowning at him. "So you're saying the leak wasn't someone inside the PPD."

She was too quick. Raphael lied. "I don't know yet. I just want to turn over every stone. *Someone* knew you were planning to serve the Spellmans last night. My guess is that while we were in the kitchen the first time, he entered your van and just waited."

Kate cleared her throat carefully. "For me to go back there alone."

Raphael didn't answer. He didn't have to.

"He would have grabbed me then." Kate shuddered and hugged herself.

When she did, her curls shifted, catching the sunlight that poured through the window. He thought again of that open bedroom door last night. Was she *deliberately* throwing off come-hither signals? The thought hit him like a sledgehammer between the eyes just as he had taken a mouthful of coffee. Raphael choked. Kate looked alarmed.

"Are you all right?"

"I swallowed funny." No, he thought, she could have no way of knowing that he actually preferred her hair like that, all wild and untamed, hinting at that part of her that was buried deep, the part that had risen up with fierce abandon when he had touched her. She wasn't throwing off signals. It was just…indifference. They'd been thrust together for enough days now that she no longer cared if she had every hair in place.

"You're staring at me," Kate said. In fact, it disconcerted her enough that she almost burned the second omelette. She went back to it quickly and slid it onto a plate. Before she turned to him with it, she tucked an errant curl behind her ear.

And she wondered why she bothered. It didn't matter how good she looked—or how bad. She could have made breakfast stark naked, she thought, and it wouldn't have gotten a reaction out of him. No, that wasn't quite true, she thought, her heart squeezing suddenly and painfully.

He'd probably get angry with her, the way he had last night over the robe.

"Here," she said, shoving the plate at him.

Raphael moved quickly to catch it. He turned and went to the coffee table in the living room without another word.

Kate gnawed on her lip for a moment until the pain made her realize what she was doing. She looked at her plate. She was no longer hungry. She carried the plate into the living room and set it on the sofa beside Belle. The Chihuahua's nose twitched in sleep, then her head shot up. She eyed the omelette and dug in.

"What did you do that for?" Raphael demanded.

"I dropped it on the floor," she lied. She'd be damned if she'd let him know how much his indifference had started hurting—enough to rob her of desire for one of the things she loved most, her own cooking.

"Looks fine to me," Raphael muttered, scowling at the last of the omelette as Belle devoured it.

"I have my doubts about the cleanliness of your kitchen."

"*You've* been cleaning it."

That was true. Kate shrugged and dropped the discussion. She hurried upstairs without saying anything more. If they were going out, she'd have to do something about her hair.

When she came down a second time, Raphael breathed again. Her hair was captured by a headband. She'd changed the shorts for navy blue trousers, though now the T-shirt was tucked in and it seemed to cling to the swell of her breasts. He was going to have to live with it, Raphael realized. He was just not going to look.

They drove his Explorer to her apartment. He'd been right. She was in and out with the necessary records in three minutes flat. They took everything to headquarters and entered it into evidence. Then he divided her client list into thirds. He called Fox and Vince Mandeleone and gave them each a portion of it.

Raphael worked down his list while Kate prowled and paced, but she didn't say a word. He didn't know if that was good or bad. On one hand, it could mean that she was still so desperate for this to be over that she didn't want to make even a single sound and distract him from finding something. Then again, it could be some kind of woman thing, like playing hard to get and staying one step out of reach to drive a guy nuts.

God knew her silence was distracting enough in and of itself. And the way she *moved*. She made a few trips back and forth from the water cooler for Belle. He glanced up from a phone call once to absorb that quick, tight movement her hips made, the one that had kept him a little bit crazy from the start. Then she sat at Fox's desk and put her feet on it the way she had seen him do, leaning back in the chair with the dog on her lap. Belle laid her injured snout pathetically and comfortably between Kate's breasts, stretching that thin fabric even more tightly across them.

Raphael swallowed a groan.

He couldn't concentrate until he sent her out with an officer to get them some lunch. Then he worried that she wouldn't come back unharmed. The cop he'd sent was one of the best. Still…he wouldn't protect her the way Raphael would.

By the time they returned, *he* was pacing. He looked at her, then at the officer. "No trouble?"

"Not this time," Kate answered for the man, then promptly started feeding portions of her sandwich to the dog.

"You dropped that, too?"

Her hand hesitated as she began to tear off another piece. "I forgot to tell them to leave off the salami. I don't like salami."

"So take it off yourself. But don't feed a perfectly good hoagie to a dog."

Belle curled her lip at his suggestion. Kate sat down at Fox's desk again and sighed, putting the sandwich listlessly to her mouth. She bit off a small piece and chewed dutifully.

Something was definitely wrong with her, Raphael realized. He just couldn't put his finger on it.

He went back to the list. By half past four, he had touched base with both Fox and Mandeleone again. No one on either of their lists had any visible or even obscure connection with the Irish underground. Same with his own.

There was nothing. No link, no possibilities, no explanation for how a hit man could have been tipped off that Kate was going to be at the Spellmans' on Wednesday night. Which left one last, quelling avenue, Raphael thought. Faith Spellman or her husband had mentioned it to an absolute stranger. And if that turned out to be the case, they'd probably never find the link.

"Are you done?" Kate asked, watching his expression.

"Almost."

He opened the file she'd given him with her employees' information. He made another few phone calls, running the information through DMV and the PPD computer. Raphael found nothing new on Beth or Janaya, either. He sat back in his chair and rubbed his jaw.

"Who could it *be?*" Kate asked desperately.

He let his gaze move to her and wished he hadn't. Her eyes were almost the color of pitch now. He didn't know which was worse—having her look delectably appealing with that mussed hair that made it seem like she had just come undone in his arms, or this vulnerable, haunted expression that made him want to comfort her. It bothered him tremendously that *both* got to him. What the hell did that mean?

"Well," Kate demanded.

"Everybody's clean."

"This doesn't make sense!"

"Oh, the link is there. Somewhere. It's just hidden."

"So how do we find it?"

"We go over every name again and again until we see something."

"That could take forever."

We don't have forever.

Raphael knew that, too. Wholly apart from any desire either one of them might have had—might *still* have, he corrected himself—about getting this over with so they could go their separate ways, there was someone else involved who wanted to finish it even more quickly. Someone who had to be getting tired of holding his ground.

Two attempts had been made on Kate's life within four days. And she was still alive. Someone out there couldn't possibly like that.

Someone knew every move she made with Dinner For Two. But every client and employee came up clean.

Someone apparently didn't give a damn that Allegra Denise had been on the premises that night, too. Someone was focused entirely on Kate.

She knew something, Raphael thought again, or she'd seen something. But she had no clue what it was. It always came back to that.

Raphael got wearily to his feet. "Come on," he said quietly. "Let's go home."

Chapter 14

Kate sat in silence on the ride home, her thoughts in turmoil. Once Ráphael reached out to change the radio station from the one she'd set it on. She frowned at the gesture but made no move to flick it back, lost in her chaotic thoughts.

She had to do something about this.

It had been hounding her all day. Their situation had become intolerable. While he'd worked, she paced and fretted with it. While he'd made phone calls, she'd thought again and again of what Shawna had said to her on that morning Belle had turned up at her apartment.

Men are like those Rorschach tests a shrink gives. When you first look at them, you think they look exactly like a cow. But what you're really looking at is two minstrels holding hands. The only way you can ever really know what a man is thinking is to goad him into acting on it.

Kate's hands trembled a little. She fisted them in her lap. What was she thinking?

She was thinking about goading him. She couldn't go on like this, she realized. Not for one more minute of one more day. And Raphael had said just half an hour ago that they were no closer to knowing who had killed McGaffney today than they had been days ago.

There would be no quick escape from him. There was no end in sight to this investigation. And Kate knew, with a painful squeezing of her heart, that there was no way she was going to survive any more of the strange tension that had built up between them, any more of this heartache.

He'd kissed her…then he'd said that he'd done it to snap her out of her hysteria. He'd kissed her again—then he'd said he hadn't planned on it, that he'd only done it because she'd made him angry. Last night, she'd been sure he was going to kiss her a third time—but then he had stalked off to the kitchen, clearly upset.

He was, most definitely, a Rorschach test.

What to do? Kate knew—of course, she knew. Shawna had been right about everything else. She was probably right about this, too. Kate was going to have to goad him into action.

"Stop at a market," she said suddenly.

Raphael looked over at her. "Come again?"

"I feel like cooking. And there's nothing left at your house. I've used everything."

She had a point, Raphael thought. But he felt edgy and tense and didn't feel like a lot of unnecessary stops. He wanted a beer and the comfort of his own home.

Then again, his home hadn't been exactly comfortable since she had first set foot in it.

Besides, he remembered, cooking seemed to be therapeutic for her. And she'd been acting oddly all day—unnaturally quiet, jittery. If cooking would bring her back to herself, he'd do it. He paused at a red light.

"There's an excellent seafood place on Twenty-Third

just north of Arch.'' Kate thought aloud. Her mind was racing. ''And there's a market two blocks east of there. It's practically one-stop shopping. They'll even have wine.''

''A beer will do me.''

Kate set her jaw. ''We have to have wine.''

''What for?'' She was doing it again, he thought. She was acting strangely.

Because, Kate thought, beer wasn't right for the kind of mood she had in mind.

She would do what she did best, she decided. Well, she would *start* with cooking. She would make the mother of all meals—exquisite, romantic, everything he liked. *Then* she would edge into unchartered territory.

She would seduce him. And see…just see…what he would do when he was goaded.

By the time they'd gotten the seafood and had collected a cart full of fresh greens and wine at the market, Kate's insides had settled into a cold, hard block of determination. She could do this. She *would* do it.

She was terrified. And strangely elated, her nerves shimmering inside.

She was out of the Explorer before he'd even stopped it in his driveway. Raphael watched her march to the door like a petite, pretty soldier. Then again, no soldier he had ever seen had had hips that could move like that.

He felt strangely doomed, and couldn't understand it.

Raphael's dinner conversation eddied around Kate. She answered in monosyllables and didn't contribute much. She scarcely ate, though she'd outdone herself with oysters Rockefeller, Caesar salad and lamb kebabs with the little cherry tomatoes that he liked. He gobbled them up, but her stomach was in knots.

She couldn't do it. Kate knew precisely what would happen if she did. He'd push her away again, and she didn't know if she'd be able to stand it another time.

But she *had* to do it. Because if she didn't, sooner or later Raphael would find the hit man, and that would be that. This would be over. And she'd be left holding a whole lot of nothing.

She couldn't do it. She wasn't any good at all this sort of thing.

But if she could only find the courage, then she'd know where she stood with him once and for all. And no matter what happened, when this was over and he was gone, she would have the comfort of knowing that she had reached out and at least *tried* to grab something splendid for herself.

She couldn't do this. She had to do this. Because if she let someone so wonderful slip through her fingers like so much sand, without ever trying, she doubted if she would ever be able to look herself in the mirror again.

Kate heard her own thoughts ring in her head and felt like lightning had struck her. How had she gone from tolerating him to respecting him to liking him and now to...to needing him? No, not *need*, she thought quickly, sipping more wine, feeling the glow of it start to fill her. Need was such a strong word. *Want* was more apt. Yes, she wanted Raphael—she could admit that. But needing him was something else entirely. Need was terrifying. Need made it sound like she would never be whole again without him.

"Kate."

"What?" She jumped, snapping her gaze up from the deep burgundy wine she'd been staring into.

"I said, everything was great."

"I made coffee, dessert..." She trailed off. *I can't do this. I have to.* She was going to.

All she had to do was figure out what came next. Kate got to her feet. Suddenly, her skin felt on fire.

Raphael stood, as well, and picked up their plates from the table. She'd served lamb and oysters at a coffee table, Kate thought, and she hadn't even noticed the incongruity of it until this moment. And now *he* was cleaning up. They must be wearing off on each other. She laughed aloud, a little giddily.

"What's so funny?" he asked, looking up.

She swallowed, and her throat felt as dry as sand. "Uh, nothing. No, don't."

Raphael stopped in mid stride, a plate in each hand. "Don't what?"

"Just leave the...the...m-mess."

He looked at her oddly. "You want to leave dirty plates all over the living room?"

"I'll clean up l-later."

He frowned. "You're stuttering. Why are you stuttering?"

"I'm not stuttering."

"Yes, you are. You just said l-later."

"Don't make fun of me!" If he did, she thought she would die. That would be it. She'd never find the courage to go through with this. But he only shook his head, looking mystified.

"Okay," he said. "You're not stuttering."

"Yes. I mean, no. I'm fine."

He continued into the kitchen. A moment later, Kate heard the dishes clatter into the sink. Then he was back.

She had absolutely no idea what to do next, how to go about this.

Football, she thought, seizing on it. Of course, football. He liked football. If she could get him on the sofa, in front of the television, then turn the lights out, she could take a breath and figure out how to proceed. "Let's watch football," she blurted.

Raphael had just reached for the last of the bottle of wine on the coffee table. He went still in mid motion. Then he straightened again, empty-handed. "Kate. It's Thursday."

"I know that." She scowled.

"Football is on Sundays. Well, mostly Saturdays right now, because it's preseason."

No football? Damn, she thought. Double damn. "Oh."

He crossed his arms over his chest and narrowed his eyes on her. "Am I getting this right? You want to watch TV?"

Kate sighed in relief. She nodded emphatically.

"With dirty dishes all over the coffee table," he clarified.

She hadn't even thought of that, of how it would spoil the mood. Kate opened her mouth and closed it again, not sure how to answer.

"What's wrong with you tonight?" Raphael demanded.

What was wrong, she thought frantically, was what she knew—whether she was experienced at this or not—that sinking her hands into sudsy water and washing dishes and loading a dishwasher right now would be extremely counterproductive to what she had in mind. Kate finally made a decision. She picked up the wine bottle herself, her movements feeling jerky. "I don't want to waste this. Let's finish it."

"I'd been planning on it."

"You were? Good. That's good. That's great." She dropped down on the sofa, cradling it in her lap. "Where are our glasses?"

Raphael frowned, then he leaned down to the table and slid them toward her. In the next motion, he picked up more dishes. "Look, I mean, assuming this wouldn't really stress you out, I'm just going to move these. Because, you know, I kind of like to put my feet up on the table when I watch television.''

Kate's heart sprung like a rubber band being shot. Was he telling her no? Already? She hadn't even started yet! She was just laying the groundwork!

No, she thought wildly. He was just suddenly be-ing…neat. It was out of character, but there it was. Either way, she had no choice but to swim with it. Presumably, once he dumped the dishes, he would come back.

But what would she do if he *didn't*? No, no, she thought, he would. Where else would he go, and why? And any-way, the town house was only so big. She could find him again and start all over.

Raphael went to the kitchen. Then he stood near the sink with plates in each hand, and he stared at them. What in the hell was going on out there?

He half turned toward the living room, frowning. He almost went back to ask her. But that would be useless. A woman never coughed up her secrets until she was damned good and ready. Something was definitely on her mind, but he was just going to have to watch her for a clue as to what it was and tread carefully until he figured it out.

He deposited the dishes in the sink and went to the living room. Then he froze. She was drinking wine directly from the bottle.

Raphael forgot everything he had just decided in the kitchen and asked anyway. ''What's wrong with you to-night?''

Kate jerked the bottle away from her mouth quickly. ''You think something's wrong with me?''

Every male instinct in his body went on red alert. *Whoa. Dangerous ground. Really, really dangerous ground,* he thought. ''Did I say that? I didn't say that.''

"You said *exactly* that. You asked what was wrong with me."

He lost patience. "Because you're acting…different." Again. "It's not like I'm passing judgment on your entire character!"

Kate sat the wine bottle on the coffee table very carefully. "So is there? Anything wrong with me?"

There was absolutely no safe way to answer that, Raphael thought. He set his jaw stubbornly and remained silent.

"Please," she whispered. "I need to know."

Trapped. Okay, he could deal with this. "Nope. Not a thing that I can think of."

Kate licked her lips.

For a moment, Raphael stayed where he was, at the door to the kitchen. He watched her tongue flick in and out. There was an instant tightening inside him, a flare of heat through his blood. He studiously ignored both.

Then he found himself trying to remember again why he had to.

Because he wasn't ever going to get involved again, he remembered. Because of what had happened to Anna…a whole lifetime ago. Still, it was a viable reason. A *good* reason. And this woman, oh, yeah, this woman had involvement written all over her. He couldn't think about that quick flick of her tongue just now, couldn't dwell on teasing it with his own, because he couldn't do it. Sinking into that mouth of hers even one more time would be…involvement.

With her, with this woman, it would be everything. He'd known that for days now, since she'd unraveled in his arms in the kitchen.

Raphael crossed slowly to the sofa. He sat beside her, watching her out of the corner of his eye. His better judgment shouted in his head, pounding fists against the inside of his skull, telling him it wasn't a good idea to be here.

But where else was he supposed to go? He slept on the sofa. Figuratively speaking, this was his bedroom.

Then she reached over and switched the light off on the end table. And Raphael thought he understood what was going on.

The fire in his blood was instantly painful. His heartbeat was hard and hurting. *Think*, he ordered himself. He was jumping to conclusions. Had to be. She'd thrown off a whole lot of signals early on, telling him to keep his distance. What had she said that first night when he'd thought to steady her after McGaffney had died? He'd reached out to her, and she'd said, *Don't touch me*.

But now, lately, there'd been that bathrobe. And more than a couple of open bedroom doors.

"Kate…"

"We'll watch TV," she said quickly.

He reached cautiously for the television remote. He clicked a button with his thumb. Flickering colored lights filled the darkness of the room, shadowing her face, then throwing it into light again. He risked another glance at her. She was staring fixedly at the screen, then her eyes came around to his, and they were huge.

And in that moment, Raphael knew he was absolutely right about what was on her mind. He knew, because she looked terrified and unsure. And he was reasonably sure those words were not even in her vocabulary.

He had to get up off this sofa and walk out of the room. He wasn't right for her. He'd get her killed, sooner or later. And she wasn't the kind of woman who could walk away from this after it was over, not if they…if they did what he thought it was she was thinking they should do.

He watched her hand come up, moving as though in slow motion. She took the headband from her hair. Her curls cascaded free. She licked her lips. And then, God help him, she leaned toward him, her lips parted.

"Raphael, I don't know how to do this. I don't know how to have what I want right now. Please help me."

Her words drove to his soul. One minute he had air in his lungs, in the next there was none there at all.

The right answer was crucial. If he hurt this woman, he'd hate himself for a lifetime. She was honest, she was good. She was smart, she was spunky. She did not deserve to be hurt, and he would destroy anyone who dared to do it, including himself.

Raphael could not find his voice.

Kate waited a heartbeat, then two. She leaned closer, and she touched her mouth to his. "Okay?" she asked tentatively.

It was *not* okay. It was his undoing.

He remembered what he had said to her days before in the kitchen...before he had kissed her for a second time. She would have to feel something special to go after a man. *Desperation. Need.* He would have been able to withstand Anna's polished approach, he thought. He *had* laughed off Allegra's teasing advances on more than one occasion. But Kate's eyes were riveted on his, and her hand shook when she reached for him. *Because she wanted him.* He could withstand any clever female assault on his body. He had no defenses when Kate touched his heart.

She was strong. She was sensible. And she was coming apart...because of *him.* It was humbling. It was devastating.

Her mouth brushed his. She retreated, waited. He found his hand in those wild curls.

He heard her gasp—maybe in relief—and his fingers spasmed against her scalp. Then her mouth was sealed to his, hard and needy. And everything he thought he wanted for his life was gone. The lemon scent lifted from her hair and filled his head. There was the taste of the deep, red wine on her tongue. And he thought, from somewhere deep in her throat, he heard the purr of his name.

Please, please, don't stop this time. It was a prayer, a litany in Kate's head as she leaned into him, every muscle trembling, something hot pooling at the very center of her. If he stopped this time, she would die.

She would *want* to die. But he didn't stop. In a sudden, unexpected move, he dragged her closer, one hand at her waist, the other arm hooked behind her neck. Kate tumbled on top of him.

She wanted to ask again if it was okay. She was afraid to hear the answer. Then she felt it, knew without words, as his hardness pressed against her belly.

"Ah," she whispered, and almost wept with the joy of it. He wanted her. Her muscles went liquid with relief.

He felt her melting over him, as though whatever had driven her this far had suddenly abandoned her. Raphael knew it was his last chance to stop. He found his mouth sliding hungrily for her throat instead, for that pulse he had seen beat wildly at the hollow of it. This time he was going to feel it. He touched his tongue there, and it fluttered.

Excitement exploded in her. Kate dug her fingers into his shoulders. "Do that again."

His laugh was hoarse, raw. She was innocence. She was honesty. She wanted to be with him so much she was shaking.

He felt the change this time, felt the tympanic beat of her heart when his tongue slid over her skin again. He licked and soothed with a kiss and moved on. She cried out in protest, then whimpered when his mouth found the sensitive spot just beneath her ear. He had known it would be there. And that terrified him.

Not enough to stop him. Nothing could, not now. She moved over him a little more, shifting her weight, her legs straddling him. Raphael felt something threaten to explode at the core of him.

"You don't know what you're asking." It was the last protest he could make.

She leaned back from him. He watched her chin come up in the flickering glow of the television. "Oh, I do. Honestly."

And she'd take it all. Then she'd want more. And that, he realized, was exactly what he needed.

With an inarticulate growl, his mouth covered hers again. He didn't hold himself back. His tongue dove deep at the same moment his hand dragged her T-shirt free from her slacks. He felt her gasp shimmy through him against his mouth. Then he found skin, his palm sliding up over her ribs, and everything about her was small and delicate, and her skin was warm and flushed and heated. He closed his hand over her breast, over thin, gossamer fabric there, and she arched into his touch without pretense or guile.

There were fractured words and gasps. Kate heard them like echoes in her head, realized it was her own voice and marveled at that. She was coming undone.

"Please." She was begging, had never begged in her life and didn't care.

"Now." His voice was raw as he dragged the T-shirt over her head.

"Don't stop. Just…please, don't you dare stop this time, or I'll kill you."

He gave a laugh that turned into a groan. "I don't think anything could make me."

She'd unleashed something, Kate realized, and it gave her a thrill that was wild and exhilarating and wholly female…something she knew she would cherish all the rest of her life.

Somehow she found herself on her back. He was leaning over her, one of her wrists in each of his hands. He let

one go to tug her slacks down and off. Then one finger
hooked under her panties at her hip, his skin hot and rough
against hers. She thought her entire body throbbed. She
had never known that needing could be pain. She had
never known how it could tighten everything inside her,
every muscle, every nerve ending, coiling them smaller
and smaller into something that hurt. She watched, pro-
testing when he eased away from her, trying to pull him
back as he leaned away from her to pull at the fastening
of his jeans. She put her hand to his chest and felt his
heartbeat crash against her palm.

Then there was no more room for coherent thought. He
caught her hand away from his skin and dragged it to his
mouth. And even as he kissed her fingers, she felt him
plunge inside her with a suddenness that ripped another
cry from her throat.

He'd hurt her, he thought, dying a little inside, pulling
back. And then he felt her close over him, holding him,
and he saw her tremulous smile.

He drove into her again. And she welcomed him as
though she had been waiting for him all her life. Then she
came apart beneath him, wild and hungry, just the way he
had known she would.

Chapter 15

Kate breathed in deeply. That scent of something warm and summery filled her head. Not August after all, she thought dreamily, and not the night. It was him...purely, one-hundred-percent Raphael.

As it turned out, he had wanted her in a most emphatic way.

A smile curved her lips. She lay spent on her back, his weight heavy atop her. The arm she had wrapped around his neck a few moments ago was now more or less flung over his left shoulder. He hadn't moved, hadn't said anything, and she didn't want him to, not yet. She wanted to savor the moment.

She loved him.

The realization sent something hot and skittering into her blood. This kind of glow didn't come from just wanting him. It *was* a way of needing him. If he left her world, if he went away and she never saw him again, it would take her to her knees.

She finally heard the rumble of his voice, a vibration in his chest against her own. "You couldn't have just asked me?"

A gurgle of laughter broke in her throat. "What would you have done if I had?"

He would have stood half a chance, Raphael thought. As it was, he had gone down like a detonated building.

Something with claws seized hold of his nerve endings. *Panic.* It made him want to jump up, put some space between them. But the need not to hurt her was no less now than it had been when she had leaned into him with that plea in her eyes, her every muscle seeming to quiver.

"Exactly what I did, probably," he said finally.

Maybe it was the jagged edge to his tone. Kate watched him as he straightened to sit on the edge of the sofa, her gaze trying to cling to his. Something was wrong.

She sat up quickly, as well. She began reaching for her clothing.

"Kate, it's not—"

"It doesn't matter," she interrupted. *No, no,* something inside her screamed. *Just leave it alone! Don't say anything!* She found her panties and pulled them on without standing, finishing the motion with a little wriggle of her bottom.

Watching it, Raphael's mouth went dry as heat rose inside him all over again. "Yeah, it does." He realized that it mattered very, very much.

Kate shrugged as she yanked her top over her head. The movement was no less awkward than the other—*should* have been awkward, he thought—but the liquid heat inside him crested again.

"I asked for it," she said hoarsely. "You condescended. End of story." And it hurt so badly it stole her breath. *She would not cry.*

From out of nowhere, temper pounded him. "I did *not* condescend!"

Kate found her slacks and jumped up to drag them up her legs. "What would you call it?"

"I never stood a chance, damn it! You never gave me one!"

For an agonizing moment, she went still. Her gaze flew to him. She couldn't deal with this, not while he was still naked. The way he sat there was too intimate, too mouth-watering, more than she could bear while the conversation veered into something intolerable. "Get dressed," she croaked.

Raphael stood from the sofa, but he made no move for his jeans. Kate's tongue cleaved to the roof of her mouth.

"Don't change the subject," he growled. "We're going to finish this."

"We just did."

"That was only the start. That's the problem. You didn't let me explain."

"You're naked. Explain when you're not naked."

Raphael looked down at himself and swore. He finally grabbed his jeans from the floor. Then he glanced at her again. "You're a little late for that blush, honey."

"I'm not blushing." Kate put her palms to her cheeks. They were warm. But the heat was not from embarrassment.

How could she still want him after what he'd just said? But she knew, of course, she knew. She was helplessly, crazy in love with him. She *needed* him. He was the best person she had ever met—he had turned out to be true and strong, kind and selfless—and she needed him like the air she breathed. She would forgive him just about anything.

"I've got to go." She felt like an animal crawling off somewhere to lick her wounds. She wondered if they would be fatal. "Out," she continued mindlessly. "Anywhere. Away from here." Anywhere he wasn't.

She found her purse in the kitchen. She fell on it, digging for her keys. As soon as she got them, he snatched them out of her hand.

She'd never heard him coming up behind her. She looked at him wildly, and his expression had her heart pounding in an entirely different way from when he'd been standing there in the living room arguing with her in all his considerable glory.

"That van of yours is so big, you might as well paint a bull's-eye on the side of it," he snarled. "You're not leaving in it. In fact, you're not going anywhere without me."

"You have no right—"

"I have every right. I'm a police officer—"

"Detective—"

"—you're under my protection. That means you're stuck with me."

It was a handy excuse, he thought, but a lame one for what was really going on. He simply could not let her go.

A kind of desperation rose from the core of him. It had nothing to do with anyone wanting to kill her. It had even less to do with his job. All he knew for sure was that he couldn't let her walk out of here. Not like this, not now, not in anger. He couldn't let her walk away from whatever had just happened out there between them on the sofa, not until they figured out what to do about it.

More than sex. He knew it had been, and his mind reeled away from that truth even while his body gathered for more. He knew it even as he opened his mouth again to somehow deny it. It changed everything.

Kate made a move for the kitchen door. He reached out reflexively and caught her elbow. She whirled at him.

"Don't," she pleaded. "Don't make me do this."

He gave an ugly laugh. "But it's okay for you to make me."

Tears sprang to her eyes. "I didn't force you! I thought you'd push me away again!"

How could she believe that? *How?* "Honey, you've got everything upside down. Want to see how it feels? Okay, my turn." And with that he dragged her into his arms. What he couldn't say, he would show.

She needed to protest, Kate thought helplessly. There was the matter of her pride, if nothing else. And she knew, too, that if she made love with him one more time, she would be gone. She would never be whole again, never get back to herself when he was gone.

And oh, yes, she knew the truth now. Sooner or later, when this was over, he would go. She wasn't enough to hold him.

She had one last spiraling thought as his mouth crushed down on hers again. *Pandora's box.* Somehow, without even realizing it, she had opened it tonight. And now all kinds of hell were going to come flying out. But, she thought as his tongue sought hers, hadn't there been something left in the bottom when all the evil was gone? Something waiting, she thought.

She remembered what it was. *Hope.*

With a cry, she wrapped her arms around his neck. She felt his hands, deliciously rough, going for the snap of her slacks.

"You just had to get dressed again," he complained against her mouth. "Why do you always have to make things difficult?"

She gave an almost hysterical laugh and drove her fingers into his hair, holding him so he could not move his mouth from hers. She dared his tongue, feeling a little crazed. This was what he had done to her.

He finally dragged her slacks down her hips. Kate

stepped out of them even as she peeled away his. He tore her panties away with a snap of his strong fingers and started that trembling deep inside her again. Then she cried out as he lifted her and drove himself home.

He felt her whole body shudder, then melt over him, and he eased them both down to the floor. There was nothing sane in his head, no care for their comfort, or protection, or the ramifications of what they were doing, but his knees felt weak and he knew he would drop her.

What the hell was he doing? He was doing all he *could* do, he thought, all he was capable of—seeking the heat, the salvation, the sweetness that he'd tasted for the first time just a while ago. This time he could not tell either of them that she'd started it. This time he was claiming her for his own.

She moved under him, taking him in, deeper, harder, urging him on. Her fingers dug into his shoulders. Her teeth closed over a tender spot at his throat. His hand found her hair, pulling her head back, arching her throat. He started there and slicked his mouth downward to small, firm breasts that were so perfect. Her breath came in ragged bursts that matched his own.

He'd known she'd take and want more. And somehow, too, he'd known he would end up craving that.

She cried out, and he felt the tension inside her gathering and let himself go. They crashed over the edge together this time.

When she could breathe again, Kate spoke, and her voice trembled. "You couldn't have just left well enough alone?"

He couldn't have, Raphael thought three hours later. And he didn't see how anything was going to make him start now.

He'd gone over an edge. A steep, slick one. And he

knew, somehow, that there would be no scaling the wall again, no going back up to a place where life was easy.

Somehow, they'd made it upstairs to his bedroom. There'd be no closed doors tonight, either. He glanced at her as she finally slept, all that dark hair spilling crazily over his shoulder and the pillow. One of her legs was hooked over his. Raphael closed his eyes and fell after her into sleep.

He slept in his own bed. Without a television on. There were no street monsters chasing him down, just her warmth beside him.

His last thought was that he'd worry about how he was going to make this work in the morning.

Kate woke up because there was no snoring.

The low, rhythmic sound that had lulled her in sleep had evaporated and in its place was an incomplete quiet. She rolled onto her back, both arms outstretched. There were small twinges and pulls deep inside her that felt delicious and brought back memories of the long night behind them. The cool sheets touched her skin on both sides, and sunlight speared into her eyes when she opened them.

She was alone.

Kate sat up fast, brushing her hair out of her eyes. Raphael was gone. *Now what?* He'd spent the night with her, had stayed with her. That was good, she thought, and she had cherished it. She'd let herself believe for a while that everything would work out.

He'd wanted her. Not once, not twice, but so many times that she ached. And he'd stayed beside her. No matter what he had said last night, no matter what he had intimated, it was a place to build from, a place to start.

She had to believe that. *Hope.* The alternative was intolerable.

She heard him downstairs in the kitchen. In fact, she

heard a great deal when she listened. There was the clang of metal, then the sound of glass shattering. Kate winced and scrambled out of bed. She found his robe on the back of the bathroom door, pulled it on and hurried down the stairs as she belted it.

She stopped in the kitchen door and watched him sweeping up whatever it was he'd broken. "Why have you developed a neat gene all of a sudden?"

He looked at her. His grin made something coil inside her all over again. "I figure it's less time you'll spend doing it so it'll leave us clear for other things."

Her heart boomed once, hard, against her chest. Then it steadied. She'd been right when she'd woken. Something was wrong.

As she watched him, she couldn't put her finger on it. Outside of the cleaning up business, which was totally out of character, and that intimate grin that couldn't have happened yesterday before they'd shared everything they'd shared last night, he seemed pretty much his same old self. Kate moved into the kitchen cautiously and nudged him aside, taking the broom from his hand. "What broke?" she murmured, starting to sweep.

"A wineglass."

"Oh, good, not the coffee carafe."

"Nope. Feel free to make some."

Conversation was normal, too, she thought. So what was the undercurrent that bothered her?

She started the coffee and then poked into the refrigerator. There was very little there. They had really depleted his larder, and all they'd bought last night for dinner was gone. She turned away from the fridge to look at him again, and her heart stuttered.

He was leaning against the opposite counter with his arms crossed over his chest, watching her. And this time, she realized, his expression was just too…deliberately bland.

"What?" she asked cautiously.

"I've figured out how we're going to handle this."

Kate felt her heart slug her ribs again. "This? You mean…us?"

"We're both adults here," he said without answering.

"Seems like it."

"Intelligent."

She hugged herself. "I am. Most times, I'm willing to admit that you are, too." She turned away carefully to pour them coffee.

"I figure we can, uh, keep on with this, we can still enjoy ourselves here as long as it lasts, if we just stay…casual."

Something grabbed her heart and twisted it. "Explain casual."

"We both need to see other people."

She dropped the carafe. It shattered on the floor with a popping, explosive sound. Glass flew. Black liquid sprayed. Her eyes darted to his.

"I can't do…do *that*…what we did…with anybody else!"

He didn't want to feel it, that warm swell of his heart at hearing her say it. So he pushed on. "We have to, so nobody gets the wrong idea."

"Nobody *who*?" Her head was pounding. Her hands shook. Kate felt miserably naive. Inexperienced. Clumsy. She wasn't enough. He wanted…others. Just as Jeff had. *Two* men couldn't be wrong about her. She had her talents…and sex just wasn't one of them.

Every breath, every nerve ending inside her shattered like glass. She let out a strangled sound.

Damn it, Raphael thought, she was standing there staring at him as though he had just turned into a monster.

But it was the only way he could think of not to let her go. He couldn't let her go.

Kate dove for the dishcloth and bent to the floor, wiping furiously, not even mindful of cutting her bare feet.

"Wait." He raked a hand through his hair. "Maybe I didn't say that right."

"You said it fine. I'm not enough."

"No."

The vehemence in his tone froze her. Kate looked up. "Then *why?*"

"So nobody figures out that you matter. If I see other people, no one will ever know that you mean more than any of the others. It'll be like…you know, our secret."

She didn't understand. *You matter.* The echo of his last words rang in her head and tried to wrap around her heart. But if she did, then *why?*

"It's because of Anna." Another bad choice of words. He knew it the moment they left his mouth. Kate gave another small cry and shot to her feet.

The problem was, he was pressed for time. Each second that ticked off the clock somehow made matters worse. He had figured out how he could keep her in his life when he had woken before dawn and had finally had some quiet time to think about it. But he hadn't quite figured out just how to explain it to her. He'd gone into this part of it blind.

He grabbed pots and the broiler pan from the top of the stove, the remnants of their meal last night. He was buying time. Trying to find the words. He heaved everything into the sink.

"She died because of me," he heard himself say. "Because someone thought she mattered."

Kate went still. She was afraid to move. "You said that. Something like that." So very long ago, she thought, back

when she'd first met him. A lifetime ago. She hadn't understood then.

"Her killer chose her because of her association with
me. That's not going to happen again. It's damned well
not going to happen to *you.* That's why we're not going
to let anyone know we're...you're...I..." *Love you.* The
words poleaxed him. They jammed in his throat, and they
wouldn't come out.

"I'm what?" Kate whispered.

"Uh. Matter. You matter."

Matter? That word again. She was no longer sure if it
was good or bad. "Anna's killer is still behind bars. Isn't
he?"

"Yeah, yeah." Raphael started shoving everything from
the sink into the dishwasher. He turned the faucet on, and
water sprayed wildly every time it hit metal. "But there
are others. There are always others."

"You think some other bad guy is going to kill me
because I'm involved with you? That it's going to keep
happening again and again? That's crazy!"

"Once the first guy does it, it sets a precedent."

"There's been a study?" Kate asked incredulously.

"No. Not that I know of. But it follows." The sink was
empty. He turned the water off and began hunting up
something else he could whisk from the counter to clean.
"You know, it was all over the papers why Anna was
killed. The next really major slimeball I go after, well, he's
just going to remember what Miller did. And sure as hell,
he's going to grab whoever I'm seeing, whoever...
whoever *matters.* So humor me on this, damn it."

He finally turned to her. He wanted to beg her. It was
the only way he could see to continue this. And he had to
continue it. But when he looked at her, her eyes were wild.

"That's the biggest crock I ever heard!" She threw the
coffee-laden dishrag at him. It hit him squarely in the

chest, spraying thin brown-black over the front of his T-shirt. "Just tell me the truth!" she shouted. "Tell me. I'm flat-chested. I'm skinny. I'm short. I have weird hair! But damn you—*damn you!*—I know all that! So don't make up some stupid, convoluted excuse that makes it sound like you're so noble, like you're protecting me! At least give me the respect of honesty!"

He stared at her, dumbfounded. "I am being honest."

"It's all garbage!"

"You're not skinny and short. You're perfect."

The air went out of her painfully. Kate stared at him. He *meant* it. She saw it in his eyes. He meant it.

"I actually…like your hair." He turned back for the last piece of cookware on the counter, the baking sheet from last night's oysters. Now this, he thought, was awkward ground. He had never been any good at pretty words. But it seemed like there should be something else he could say.

"You like it," Kate repeated, swiping at it helplessly.

"Better without the headband." Somewhere, in some man's vocabulary, there was a way to say it. Raphael kept busy instead.

He found the bag she kept her rock salt in and started to pour it from the sheet. "I just don't want anyone to know that I do." He didn't want anyone to know what those wild curls did to him.

"Because if he's a slimeball, he'll kill me to hurt you?"

"Yeah." And it wouldn't just hurt, he realized. It would destroy him. He turned to tell her that, to *try* somehow to find the right words. And she was shaking her head hard.

"What now?"

"Just throw that out. The rock salt. I've used it a few times. It doesn't hold up for more than a few uses."

He was trying to bare his soul here, and she was talking

about the practicalities of *rock salt?* Raphael headed angrily for the trash can. Then he froze.

Midway between the counter and the can, sunlight speared in from the window at the rear of the room where a table should have been. It was the young brightness of the new day, sharp and clear and focused. It fell across the tray, and the rock salt dazzled.

It *really* dazzled.

"What the hell?" he murmured, staring at it.

"What's wrong?" Kate asked, moving beside him.

"What exactly is in this stuff?"

"I don't know." She frowned. "It's just some kind of mineral."

Raphael swore again and turned to the counter. He slid the tray onto it again as delicately as though it were made of the most fragile glass. He reached, his fingers closing over a large piece. "*This* is a chunk of rock salt?"

Kate stared at it, crowding behind him to look. And her eyes widened. "No," she whispered. "No, that's definitely not rock salt." Her gaze flew to his disbelievingly.

"Help me out here," he said hoarsely.

She knew what to do without being told. She nudged him aside from the counter. She knew rock salt. How many times had she used rock salt? Not enough, she thought wildly, to realize that what she had been cooking with this past week wasn't it.

She'd been cooking with…diamonds!

She gave a cry of pure amazement and began sifting through the tray. "Here." She gave him a gem, her fingers trembling so that she almost dropped it. Raphael caught it and put it in a bowl he snagged from the cupboard.

"Keep going," he said.

"I am, I am."

She pulled out seven, eight, fifteen, then twenty. Her pulse was pistoning. Every once in a while Kate made another small sound of shock. "How much?" she asked finally, still combing her fingers through the salt.

"Half a million so far. Easily."

She spun to him. "Dollars? *Half a million dollars' worth of diamonds?*"

Raphael nodded. He took her face in his hands. "Honey, it's not what you knew. It wasn't what you saw that night."

"It's been what I had."

He nodded. She'd been carting around a small fortune.

At their feet, Belle barked crazily, happily, and began cavorting in circles. Raphael shook his head and looked at the dog. "If you knew, why didn't you just say so?"

Chapter 16

Ten minutes later, Kate's hands still shook. *She'd spent a week baking diamonds.* No one had been trying to *kill* her, exactly. They'd just been trying to get the gems back.

What *had* been going on the night McGaffney had been killed? How had the diamonds gotten into her possession? Whatever had occurred, she thought, it had gone down virtually right under her nose.

Raphael had already been on the telephone when she'd retreated, dazed, to the bathroom, knowing that this development probably meant they would be going out somewhere soon. She showered and dried off frantically, afraid she would miss something. She was still zipping her slacks when she raced down the stairs. Raphael raised a brow at her, his gaze roving from her tummy to her eyes. He was still on the phone.

"I had the rock salt with me at McGaffney's!" Kate blurted. "That's where all this started."

He disconnected and looked at her as though she'd just told him that gravity existed.

"Then I took it home with me. Remember? I took it up to my apartment." He still showed no expression, but she desperately needed to work through this, to make sense of it. Kate drove her hands into her wet hair.

"We left it there on Saturday while we went to get the crate for Belle. Anyone could have grabbed it then and there! There was no need to shoot at anybody!" she cried, thinking of Betty Morley.

"They couldn't have known that the rock salt was in your apartment." Raphael finally spoke.

"They," Kate repeated unsteadily. "The mob?"

"Well, half of it, anyway. McGaffney's boys would be my guess."

She blinked, absorbing that. "Eagan didn't order the hit."

He couldn't have, Raphael thought. That was the missing piece to the puzzle—it was the point where he'd first started heading in the wrong direction. If Eagan had ordered that hit, then Eagan—or one or more of his goons—would be dead by now.

There'd been no further killing, Raphael finally realized, because McGaffney's guys had known exactly who had taken him out, and it had been one of their own. No retaliatory action had been needed. Now, in hindsight, it was the only thing that made sense.

As for Kate, her misfortune was that she had been standing between McGaffney's goons and her rock salt.

"They didn't know about that damned little red wagon you use to cart everything back and forth," he went on. "They probably thought you'd store all that stuff in your vehicle because you work out of a small apartment. Trust me, Kate, no one would ever anticipate that you're as orderly as you are."

Her eyes went to slits.

"My guess is that they *did* look in the van while it was

in your garage that day. But we didn't give them a lot of time to strike out in one place and launch a whole new search in another. We went back to your place so you could cook for the Morleys.''

''So why not send some gun-toting idiot *there?*''

''I was there,'' Raphael said simply. ''And I had a gun, too.''

''You were at the Morleys and you were armed! That didn't stop them!''

Raphael thought about it. By then, he realized, the gunman had to have known exactly where the rock salt was. He had to have known that Kate was cooking with it, and where. That would have minimized the risk, should have streamlined the retrieval effort.

And that meant he had been right all along. The leak had come from somewhere within Kate's Dinner For Two network.

''We took the van home—I mean, here.'' Kate caught herself, though oh, yes, his town house had started to feel like home. That realization almost shook her off her train of thought. ''We came back here after Betty Morley was shot at. Then I brought everything inside. Well, you did, after I fainted. Why didn't anyone just break in here to get it?''

''Same reasons,'' Raphael responded. No one had been stupid enough to take him on—armed—in his own home. No one had even particularly wanted to break and enter here. There wasn't a crime on the books that didn't jump several significant notches in severity when it was perpetrated upon a cop, and even the mob had a modicum of respect for that. Killing a cop would draw the death penalty, Raphael thought. Not necessarily so with your average caterer or her clients.

And there had been other ways. There'd been that inside contact they had within Kate's business.

Suddenly, Kate gasped.

"What?" he demanded harshly.

"I made herbed oysters for the Morleys!"

She was getting close to the crux of it, he thought.

"That was the skillet Betty was holding when she was shot at!"

Raphael nodded.

"It went flying! There was rock salt—*diamonds*—all over that kitchen!"

And whoever had cleaned up the floor later had probably thrown it all out, Raphael thought. The techies had no doubt ignored it in the interest of finding the bullets and fingerprinting the known areas where the gunman had moved. That part of the cache was irretrievably gone. But there had been plenty left, which spoke to how much there had been in the first place. Kate had used only a small portion of rock salt for that recipe—he knew, because he had been angrily swiping things off the counter himself to get her out of there. Most of the rock salt had been sitting in its bag on the counter—and Betty Morley had been standing right between the bag and the gunman.

She'd had to be removed. But it hadn't happened neatly or well, and then all hell had broken loose and the gunman had fled empty-handed.

Unless Raphael badly missed his guess, oysters would have enjoyed a sudden surge in popularity in the days to come. And Kate would have come under more and more pressure to take this special job or that one. *Who had been the McGaffney confidante?* Thinking about it, Raphael's blood hurt as it moved through his veins, like it had filled with chunks of ice.

"What are you doing?" Kate asked.

"Making one more phone call before we go downtown." She hadn't put it all together yet, but it wouldn't take her long, he realized. He wanted the last of the answers before it happened. And he wanted to be able to give her his full attention when the truth dawned. Because she'd blame herself, he knew.

Someone had known that Kate was doing the Morley dinner and the Spellman appetizers. And only two other people *could* have known about both jobs—her employees. It was time to start checking the DNA of everybody who had been in the house that night—and everybody who *should* have been there, had Kate not decided that she didn't need any help.

He raised Vince Mandeleone on the man's cell phone. "Where's the lady?" he asked, then he nodded at the answer. "Okay, while she's sudsing up and soaping down, I need you to take a little detour through her bedroom. I want a strand of her hair." It was the fastest, easiest thing to test, he thought. "If she has a hairbrush in there, great. If not, try her pillow. Then call Fox. He'll pick it up from you and get it to the lab in a hurry."

He disconnected. He looked at Kate and decided to make the call to bring in her employees in private, after they got to headquarters.

"What was that all about?" she asked.

"Process of elimination. The better half of police work. You've figured that out by now." Raphael found his keys, bounced them on his palm once, then headed for the door before she could think too much about his explanation. "Come on, let's roll."

"Right. Roll." Kate went to the kitchen, grabbed her purse and ran after him. Only once she was in the passenger seat beside him did she think to ask the obvious. "Where are the diamonds?"

His teeth flashed in a hard grin as he rolled the Explorer out of the driveway. "In my pocket. I've already put the word out on the street while you were getting dressed. You no longer have them. I do."

* * *

The normally quiet Robbery Homicide Unit was crowded with chaotic activity when they arrived. Kate took it all in, then she unobtrusively stepped back to press her spine against the wall. She watched the frenetic scene from the edges. And everything she saw made her stomach knot more.

It was over.

Something like despair rose in her throat, but she got a grip on herself. There was still time. All they knew for sure right now was *why* an armed man had been popping up at her job sites. It remained to be seen who that man was. Or why diamonds had been dropped in her rock salt in the first place. Still, as she watched Raphael, she knew he would have those answers by nightfall.

How had she ever thought he was indifferent? How had she ever believed that first night that he didn't care about the man lying facedown in her salad? The energy in him now was volatile. It etched his frown deeper. It made something in his eyes seem sharper, lit inside by a green fire. He moved around his desk restlessly, stretching the phone cord as far as it would go to grab something out of the fax. Occasionally, he would look up, cup the phone against his neck and give an order to someone in a voice that was notched just a little lower and more dangerous than she had ever heard it. He had something to sink his teeth into now, for the first time since this had started.

''There's a waiting room down the hall.''

Kate looked to her right. It was Raphael's partner, Fox. Unlike Raphael, he was calm, leaning one shoulder lazily against the wall. She wondered if he ever got perturbed about anything.

Kate gave her head a little shake. ''I want to watch.''

''There won't be much to see until all the DNA comes back.''

Something nipped at the pit of Kate's stomach with Fox's words. The DNA, she thought. There was something about that she needed to think through, something that bothered her. But Fox was waiting for a response. "How long will that take?" she asked.

"The way we're doing it? Maybe another four hours." At her frown, he shrugged. "We just want enough of a match right now for a warrant. There are a lot of different levels of DNA testing. DQ-Alpha just matches twenty-four points, and our police lab can do that. It'll give us a suspect. Later, we'll send the specimens out to one of those highfalutin brain factories where they'll do the more complex tests for trial evidence."

"Ah," she said, barely understanding because her gaze was drawn to Raphael again. Then she looked at Fox sharply. "*Four* hours?" Her legs were already achy from standing against the wall for so long.

"Close to that."

Kate sighed and let her gaze linger on Raphael one more moment. "I'll wait in the lounge then."

Fox nodded. "You'll be more comfortable there."

He watched her go a little speculatively. Then he observed his partner's gaze follow her out. For a long moment, Raphael seemed to forget who he was talking to and why. There was naked emotion in the other man's eyes. Fox grinned.

Oh, how the stubborn did fall. The dude's crazed dating days were over.

Kate dozed in a cracked plastic chair in the waiting room. When she woke, her spine felt as though someone had rammed a bent steel rod inside it.

How could she have possibly slept? she wondered groggily. Her only explanation was that she'd been awake through so much of last night.

Last night.

Her heart skittered away from the memory. It should have been something she cherished forever, she thought, sitting up and burying her face in her hands. It should have been precious, exquisite, always and forever shining in the corners of her mind. How many times in a woman's life was she loved like that? Raphael had known just where to touch her. And how. She replayed it in her mind, shivering a little. It had been as though they'd shared lifetimes together instead of a week. And even now, she could still feel the warmth of his skin against her palms.

Then he had tarnished everything with that crazy talk this morning.

Kate let out a low moan without realizing it. She looked at her watch. She was startled to see that nearly four hours had passed. She'd slept more soundly than she'd realized.

She got up and went in search of coffee. She knew from her visits here where it was. She found the little lunchroom tacked at the back of the floor. Then she glanced at the compact refrigerator and winced. It reminded her of Belle. In all the rush of this morning, they'd left the dog at home.

Not home, she corrected herself. She'd slipped with that same phrase this morning before they'd come here, and she'd just barely caught herself then from the blind and painful mistake of her tongue. It was Raphael's home, not her own. She would be going back to her apartment any time now.

Over. Something hurt inside her in a cold way, deep inside her bones. What had happened to her, that she didn't even want to go to her own apartment? Everything had happened, she thought, and everything could be summed up in one word: *Raphael.*

Kate found change in her purse and shoved it into the coffee machine. The liquid that came out was pale and tepid. She tossed it back in one long swallow anyway, grimacing.

Over. At least, Kate thought, she'd found the courage last night to instigate what had happened between them. She had those memories…and too many conflicting ones from this morning to contemplate now.

Kate crumpled the empty cup in her hand. There'd be time to sort through that and make sense of it later, she decided. For now, if Raphael didn't already know who the gunman was, he would as soon as the DNA results came in. Which should be any minute—

Kate's thoughts broke off.

She threw the paper coffee cup at the trash can suddenly and ran from the room. She raced up the hallway to the homicide unit. The DNA! Raphael had only asked for one hair, to her knowledge.

She found Raphael, Fox and another man hunched over Raphael's desk, studying something. She jerked to a stop just before she reached it.

"It was Allegra. You think it was Allegra. The only DNA you have to compare her hair to is what you took out of Belle's teeth."

Fox and the other man stepped back. Raphael's gaze found her. Something in her heart cracked at how tired he looked. He got to his feet. He caught her arms in his hands, his thumbs making gentle circles on her skin. Soothing her. Thinking of her first. Heat bubbled up inside to gather like pulse points beneath her skin where he touched her.

"No," he said finally. "I asked for three specimens. We just got the results back. One of them is a dead-on match to what we took out of Belle's teeth."

"Three?" Her mind swam around that, unable to make sense of it.

Raphael turned her around, nudging her a little until she was seated in his chair. He sat on the corner of his desk and scrubbed his hands over his face. "Kate, I need you to think about this. Were you ever, at any point, planning to make oysters for the Spellmans that night?"

Her gaze fastened on him. "Of course, I was. Rockefeller is one of Faith's favorites. But I changed my mind at the last minute. I couldn't be there to finish things off myself, and it's a reasonably delicate recipe to do right, so—" She broke off, and her eyes widened as she understood what he was implying.

As if on cue, more people entered the room. A dark-haired detective had an agitated Allegra Denise by one arm. Two other officers accompanied Beth Olivetti and Janaya Thomas, her employees. Kate sprang to her feet. She rushed at them. And in that instant one of them recoiled from her approach, and she knew.

Janaya had been with her from the inception of Dinner For Two. But she had hired Beth only four days before McGaffney had been killed. *When had this nightmare actually started?*

She spun to Raphael disbelievingly. And what she saw in his eyes nearly chopped her off at the knees. "You've known this all along."

He shook his head. He looked too haggard to argue about it, but something in his eyes sharpened and heated anyway. "No. Only since we found the diamonds this morning, and even then it was just an educated guess. It stood to reason that someone was tipping McGaffney's guys off to your Dinner For Two moves, suggesting the ones where you'd take the rock salt with you."

"Why didn't you *tell* me?"

"I wanted to be sure first."

"You were protecting me."

He raised one shoulder in a shrug, but there was nothing of Fox's laziness in the gesture. The movement seemed somehow dangerous. "And if I was?"

"It's my business! They're my people. It was my *mistake!*"

"No."

"I hired her in the first place!" She spun to Beth. "What were you going to do? Feed me all the requests that involved oysters? Tempt me with the jobs until I just had to take one no matter what was going on in my life, no matter how many people might have died? Were you going to get me there and then knock *me* off, too?" Kate remembered suddenly how she had come to take the Spellman job. Beth had said she'd gone to her apartment for her purse and that Faith had called a second time.

It had all been a lie.

Raphael watched the scene through narrowed eyes. He had the sure sense that things were spinning fast out of his control. Somehow, he knew, he was in the process of losing her. Right here. Right now. It made no sense but there it was—and the feeling was strong. And damn it, he had too much else on his plate right now.

He hadn't wanted it to happen like this.

"Kate. Calm down. It wasn't Beth's DNA that matched."

She scarcely heard him. She felt so *stupid!* So used by an employee she'd trusted, and so naive in Raphael's eyes! He'd thought he had to protect her. That she couldn't stand up to the truth.

She *mattered*, he'd said. But he didn't know her at all.

Suddenly, she understood all of it—their conversation this morning, and the way he'd held himself back from touching her all those days before she'd taken matters into her own hands. She thought of Anna again, and knew, somehow, that he would not have shielded that woman. He would never have thought it was necessary. Not Anna, the polished, smart, savvy attorney.

A woman unlike herself, Kate realized with a deep,

sharp pang. *She* was a woman with crazy hair he kind of liked, a woman it was okay to roll around in the sheets with for however long they had to stay together—assuming she insisted on it—but who would never be allowed to share his dangerous, slimeball-filled, killer-riddled life. That was what he'd been trying to tell her this morning. She was a woman he had to keep tucked on the side, a woman he had to coddle and lie to. She was too much of a draining responsibility to be anything more.

Not a partner, not someone he could love, not even a friend. A liability. Kate put a steadying hand on the nearest desk.

Well, she would know all of it now. She wouldn't be coddled anymore, damn it. "Whose DNA matched?"

Fox and Raphael exchanged looks, and both were grim.

"Mandeleone let Allegra go out to get her hair done," Fox said. "When nothing happened for days after the McGaffney hit, when it didn't appear that she was in any real danger and that you were actually the target, Mandeleone relaxed a bit, dropped his guard."

Allegra? Kate felt staggered.

"Mandeleone dropped the ball," Raphael said harshly.

"And she went to the Spellmans' instead of to the hairdresser?" Kate's head spun. "She wasn't in the van waiting to grab me. She was in there looking for the rock salt. But it wasn't there—it was at home—and she woke Belle up and—and she shot her!"

"The gun might have just discharged when she was struggling with the pooch," Fox said comfortingly. He flicked a glance at the other woman. "I've known her a long time. I can't seriously see her shooting to kill an animal. She's not that cold."

Allegra tipped her chin up as though to deny his judgment.

"Let me finish up here," Raphael said. "Then I'll take you home and we can talk."

Home. Kate knew which place he meant. He was talking about her once-upon-a-time haven, her own small apartment. Now, at last, she knew that was for the best.

She found her voice again. "Can't I go now?"

"What?" Raphael scowled.

"I want to go home now." She laughed a little shrilly. "Who's going to kill me at this point? You've got the diamonds and you said everyone knows it."

"Actually, they're in a vault downstairs." What difference did that make? he wondered, something kicking at his chest, something he hadn't seen coming. Now *he* was nitpicking. What the hell had she done to him?

"That's my point. I have nothing anyone wants any longer. I'm not in danger. There's no more need for police protection." It would be easier this way, she realized frantically. One of the cops could give her a lift home. Then she would never even have to say goodbye to him. If that made her a coward, then so be it. She seized on it. "There's nothing for me to do here. You don't need me. Just let someone give me a ride."

Raphael looked at Beth, at Janaya and at Allegra, who continued to glare at him coldly. He felt his adrenaline trying to drain and leave him. So much to do yet, he thought. It would take a few hours just to break Allegra all the way, to get all the details of her complete involvement. Already he knew she wasn't going to go down easily, DNA proof or not.

Hours, he thought. What right did he have to make Kate hang around until dawn? She was right. There was no real need to keep her close anymore.

He didn't want to let her go. And she couldn't wait to get out of here. But then, he'd pretty much known that all along.

Temper replaced his adrenaline—and how the hell could she do *that* to him again and again? This woman could evoke both a headache and heartache with scarcely a glance.

"Martin, give her a lift. You're off shift right about now anyway, aren't you?"

The man who'd been standing next to Janaya nodded. "Yes, sir."

"Okay, then. She's all yours."

His voice was so cold, so practical, so flat. Kate fought against the urge to make a sound. Whatever came out of her throat would be wretched. She followed the officer to the door without looking back.

Then she passed Janaya, and she caught the other woman's frightened eyes. She needed to get away from Raphael, but not so much that she could abandon someone who mattered to her. She turned back one last time. "Janaya had nothing to do with this, you know."

Raphael was already directing Allegra and the other detective into an interrogation room. Fox was taking Beth Olivetti away. Raphael glanced her way impatiently.

All she wanted to do was leave him, to get away from him now that this was over. "Thanks for the input, Sherlock. I'll keep it in mind."

His response fractured something inside her. Kate clamped down on it hard so it wouldn't show. She nodded once, smartly, and left with the police officer.

Chapter 17

It was twenty past four in the morning when Raphael left headquarters. Dew had started to bead on his Explorer. The sky was still black, but dawn tickled its edges. He got behind the wheel and sat for a long moment as the wipers cleared the windshield.

There was always a bone-deep fatigue when he closed a case, when the energy that had carried him through the hunt washed out of him. But this was different. This was a hollow kind of pain.

He wanted to go to Kate. He did not want to go back to his empty town house. *What in the hell had she done to him?*

Suddenly, Raphael was as angry with her as he had ever been. It only spiked his temper more that she wasn't even here so he could let her know about it. The second—the *nanosecond*—the coast had been clear, she'd gone racing off. And in her wake, the life he'd liked perfectly fine just one short week ago seemed suddenly empty.

"So what are you going to do about it?"

"Huh?" Raphael felt his muscles jerk inside his skin. His neck snapped as he turned his head to look at the passenger seat.

It was the dog. *The dog?*

"Well?"

"Well, what?" Raphael answered automatically. Then he realized he was talking to a dog.

He shoved at the driver's side door with all his strength and leaped out of the Explorer. He stood beside it a moment, digging the heels of his hands into his eyes. He was *beyond* exhaustion. He was hallucinating that a dog was talking to him.

He leaned forward an inch, then two, and looked cautiously into the car. Belle was still there.

"Here's what we've got," she said. "We've got a lady who's crazy about you. You're crazy about her. So you're just going to let her go home?"

Raphael stared. Belle had a man's voice. She had a *familiar* man's voice. Belle's voice was coming from behind him.

Raphael jerked out of the vehicle again and turned around. Fox stood behind him.

"What's wrong?" Fox asked. "You look like you've seen a ghost."

"Uh, nothing. Nothing at all."

"So, are you going to go after her?"

Raphael's jaw hardened. "No way. I'll be damned if I'm going to tag after her like some kind of homeless puppy, sniffing and wagging my tail and begging for her attention. Not in this lifetime. Not for any woman, and sure as hell not for one who couldn't wait to be rid of me."

"She didn't want to go."

"Sure, she did."

"Wrong."

"She left!"

"Like she had a choice."

He wasn't going to answer. No way, Raphael decided. He stuck his hands in his jeans pockets and glanced at the stars.

Fox kept coming. "It's all a crock. You know it and I know it. All that slop about Anna. Sure, you've felt guilty about her. Yeah, I'll bite that but you're not half as scared about what could happen to Kate as you are over what could happen to you now that you've met her. Hey, pal, what's worse, worrying about her or living without her the rest of your life? Because if you don't go after her, that's about what's going to happen. She came after you once. I don't see her doing it again. Now it's your turn."

He was dispensing advice now? The man who dated a different woman every night, searching for Ms. Right? Raphael slid behind the wheel again, giving serious thought to running Fox over.

Then he realized that Belle was no longer in the passenger seat.

Nor was Fox standing beside the Explorer any longer.

Gone? Both of them? What the hell?

He twisted around and craned his neck to look into the back seat. Nothing. He got out of the truck again and went around to the back to spring the door and peer into the cargo area.

More nothing.

"Get back here, you nasty little beast!" The dog had been here. Fox had been here. Damn it, he was sure of it.

Fox thought he was afraid of what Kate could do to him? She'd already done it! He was losing his mind without her.

Raphael got into the Explorer and shoved the SUV in gear.

He drove for the bridge. The dog, that cranky—okay, weird—little mongrel would be there where they'd left her. *And what did he think that would prove?*

He was losing his mind.

But Fox's words kept ringing in his head. When he got home and found Kate's van still in his driveway, the sight hit him like a punch. Then he opened the door to his empty town house, and the silence was like a wall.

How could a woman *do* that? It was like they had some kind of innate power that when they left a place, they could just suck all of themselves out of the air, also. There was no scent of her here any longer. The air was still, like all the currents of her being had left it. Raphael swore aloud and went to look for the dog.

He went upstairs to his bedroom. Kate's overnight case was still on the chair in the corner where it had been for the last many days. Every item inside was folded with military precision. He stared at it and waited for the usual annoyance. It didn't come. *Hey, pal, what's worse, worrying about her or living without her the rest of your life?*

"Pooch!" he called out. "All right, listen, you nasty little monster, come out here now. Angel, my foot."

There was only silence.

Raphael made a quick tour of the town house. His head was pounding by the time he finished. He tried to remember if they had taken Belle to headquarters this morning— maybe he just didn't remember. Maybe she really *had* been in his truck—not talking, of course—and she had run off without him noticing.

No, he thought, they definitely hadn't taken the dog with them. She should have been here. Dogs just didn't disappear out of closed and locked town houses into thin air. Then again, they didn't talk, either.

It was all the excuse he needed. Five minutes later,

Raphael found himself driving over the bridge toward Kate's apartment.

Kate couldn't sleep without his snoring. *How could that be?* No one could get so used to something in one short week that she couldn't live without it!

She'd live without him. She'd be fine. He'd just been…a hiccup in her life. And probably, she reasoned, rolling over in bed for the countless time, the stress of the whole week, the danger, the bizarre circumstances had magnified everything she thought she felt for him. She certainly didn't love him. In another week, she'd look back at all this and marvel at how easily she could lose her mind.

Kate pressed her face into the pillow and cried.

She wept until her eyes burned and her throat ached. *He was gone.* Her pulse thumped in misery. Her heart sounded like a drum in her chest. Then she lifted her face from the pillow, craned her neck, and frowned.

It would have been poetic if her heart really had pounded like that while it broke, she thought. But it wasn't her heart. It was someone at the door.

Her gaze flew to the bedside clock. It was not even five-thirty in the morning.

Panic seized her. Maybe she'd cut off the police protection too soon. Maybe someone didn't believe that Raphael really had the diamonds. Or maybe there was more to all this than the gems. She hadn't stayed long enough at headquarters to find that out. Maybe someone felt she really needed to be killed, after all. But would they knock on her door to do it?

Kate pressed a fist to her mouth and put her feet to the floor. She should call Raphael. Yes, that was what she would do. She gave a small cry of panic, then his voice drifted into the apartment.

He was out there in the hallway shouting loudly enough to wake up every neighbor on the floor!

"Kate, if you're in there, open up! Five seconds! Then I'm breaking down the door."

Kate scooted off the bed and ran to the living room before he could make good on his promise. She flung open the door. "Are you out of your mind?"

He looked exhausted, Kate thought, something shimmying in the area of her heart. It was all she could do not to offer him coffee.

She looked like she'd been crying, Raphael thought, and his heart moved in his chest again the way it had been doing from the first moment he'd set eyes on her. It took everything he had not to reach out for her.

Raphael looked over her shoulder into the apartment. There was no sign of the Chihuahua. Had he really expected there to be? Like the little beast was on some kind of sunrise mission, sprinkling golden angel dust and words of wisdom on both of them? He felt like a fool. He stepped inside, past Kate, anyway. "Where's the dog?"

Kate looked at him and scowled. "We left her at your place."

"She's not there."

"She has to be there. Where would she have gone?"

"I'm telling you, she's not." There really had been something weird about that beast, Raphael thought. "You know, we never really talked about this, but do you think…"

"She really is an angel?" Kate came inside and closed the door behind her.

"Well…yeah."

Suddenly, Kate's skin pulled into gooseflesh. She remembered that Belle had done the same thing to Shawna in the end, disappearing into thin air on the streets of New York. In that moment, Kate knew it really was over, only this time there was no happy ending. "I guess…you know…it's possible."

"But a *Chihuahua?*"

They looked at each other, then they shook their heads and spoke at the same time. "Nah. No way."

Kate almost smiled. She pressed a fist to her lips so he wouldn't see her mouth tremble. "You should go."

"Yeah." Raphael hitched his weight but stood where he was. "I got the rest of the story after you left. I was right. McGaffney turned traitor. It was one of his own guys who killed him."

She didn't care, Kate thought. He had to leave. She could not stand being this close to him, knowing how he felt about her. But she found herself nodding woodenly. If there was one thing she knew, it was that he wouldn't leave until he was good and ready. Better, she thought, to let him say what he wanted to say, then goad him toward the door again.

Apparently, she thought, she was better at goading men than she'd ever realized. And all it had brought her was heartache.

"Those diamonds were hot," Raphael said. "They were stolen. They would have been fenced, but McGaffney grabbed them and tucked them away to cool off. He told his associates they'd been stolen right from his safe. Joe figured it for a scam. He was the one who sent Allegra in that night."

Something sad shifted inside Kate. "She killed McGaffney?" Allegra's grief had seemed so genuine. Nothing was ever as it seemed.

"No. Joe did."

Suddenly, she made the connection. "Joe? *Bonnie* Joe? From the restaurant?" Her gaze flew to him. "We were right there in that restaurant with a cold-blooded killer?"

He almost smiled. "We were right there in that restaurant with a whole lot of cold-blooded killers. I'd guess that most of the men in that room had blood on their hands."

And yet he'd taken her there with him anyway, Kate thought. So when, at what point, had he decided that she wasn't up to being a part of his life?

"Allegra's job the night McGaffney was killed was to locate the diamonds," Raphael continued. "Which she did. She wasn't in the bathroom when McGaffney went down. She was in the study, looking for the cache. I honestly don't think she thought Joe was going to kill him. She says not. And by the time we got to all this information, we'd already struck a deal for a lesser sentence if she'd just spit it all out. There was no sense in her lying."

Kate was interested in spite of herself. "So how did the diamonds get in my rock salt?"

"When she came back to the dining room, she had the pouch stuck in the front of her dress. She found Phil dead, and you were there. She was supposed to leave the premises right away and turn the goods over to Bonnie Joe outside. But you were in the way, already calling 911. She didn't dare risk it."

"So she followed me into the kitchen and dumped them into the rock salt while my back was turned, while I was on the phone."

"Yeah. Then you sat on her." This time Raphael did grin at the memory of the first time he had seen her. "Anyway, the next thing she knew, the police were all over the place, and Joe took off."

Kate swallowed carefully. "Then I cleaned up the kitchen and took the diamonds with me."

"You can bet *that* wasn't part of anybody's plan."

"Beth?" she asked. That, she realized, she really *did* want to know. "They put her in place *days* before McGaffney was killed."

"Beth's real name is Lilly McCall."

"But you checked her out!"

"I checked out Beth Olivetti. Who, by the way, really is a mother of two with a flair for baking. But she's too busy with her twin toddlers to take on a part-time job. Lilly helped herself to the woman's name, her Social Security number, everything." Kate stared at him, stricken. He'd known it would bother her. She was that way. "It's not that hard to do if you know how. They just checked the registration list at one of the local colleges, found a culinary student who physically resembled Lilly and adopted her personal info so everything would mesh when I checked her references." He began to pace. "It was all set up from the beginning. Allegra suggested to Phil that he should call Dinner For Two so they could be alone together, but all she really wanted was to pour a lot of your wine down him so she'd have relatively unrestricted access to the house. Lilly was supposed to have been at Mc-Gaffney's that night, too. Her purpose was to keep you out of the way while all this went down. You were necessary to the meal itself, but you were supposed to stay in the kitchen. Lilly was supposed to have been going back and forth to the dining room."

Then McGaffney had let her choose the menu, Kate thought, and she hadn't needed help. "But why not just grab McGaffney off the street and…you know, throw him in the back of a big, black limousine and put a gun to his head and make him tell where the diamonds were?"

This time Raphael couldn't help but laugh. "That might have worked on TV."

Kate sat straighter, snapping her shoulders back indignantly. "Why not for real?"

"He would have told them anything to save his life. He wouldn't have told them where the diamonds really were. It would have been a wild-goose chase."

"Ah." Some of the air went out of her.

"Allegra was under some pressure, too, in the end. There were a few who didn't believe she'd spilled the gems into your rock salt, who thought *she* was trying to make off with them. Luckily for her, she's Joe's current lady. Still, that would only have protected her for so long. She was desperate to get the diamonds back and turn them over to the family before somebody decided to take *her* out."

"She was desperate enough to try to kill Betty Morley," Kate whispered.

"She claims she was just trying to scare her into running from the room. If Betty had done that, Allegra would have grabbed the rock salt and would have been gone."

All the last, little pieces, Kate thought.

Raphael realized there was nothing left to explain.

He needed to go back to the door. He needed to let himself out of here, get back in his Explorer and go home. He needed to sleep for a day, he told himself. He'd stop on the way and buy another six-pack of beer to replace what she'd guzzled when she'd suddenly started changing on him. Maybe he'd get some cereal, something easy to eat that didn't need to be cooked.

The prospect was damned annoying.

"Don't shut me out." Even he wasn't sure if the growl in his voice was from temper or desperation. "Don't shut the door on me now just because this is over. I never wanted that. Damn it, I told you yesterday morning that I didn't want it!"

Kate stared at him. The change in topic had her heart galloping.

"Okay, you want me to spill my guts? Fine. The best thing that ever happened to me was being assigned to you. You came into my house and you—you made it smell good."

Kate choked. "*Smell* good?"

"With all that stuff you were always cooking." *With the scent of you.*

Kate made a small sound of pain. Raphael panicked. Words again. He couldn't find the right ones. He wasn't reaching her. "You made it *feel* good! Damn it, I'm trying to tell you that I want you to come back there!" *I want you to come back and stay.* It rocked him. But in that moment, he knew it was true.

Kate clapped a trembling hand to her mouth. "Go away."

Something wild erupted inside him. "That makes no sense! What kind of sense does it make for me to leave? We're good together. We're *great* together! We balance each other." He thrust a finger at her. "I'm good for you, whether you want to admit it or not. You haven't done that sniffing, *tsking* thing in days now. See? I loosen you up."

She couldn't take anymore. Kate shot to her feet. "I'm not some sex toy!"

Raphael's jaw dropped. "Who said anything about sex? I didn't get to that part yet."

Don't, Kate thought desperately, *please, please don't.*

"But as long as we're on the subject, I dare you to stand there and tell me that part wasn't terrific, too. It was better than terrific. Don't forget I was there in that bed with you, honey, and on the sofa, and on the floor. And I'm here to tell you that you thought it was pretty great then."

She was dying inside. Yes, Kate thought helplessly, she was simply going to die. "I am worth more than that," she said with exquisite care.

And then he understood. It was a woman thing. She was going to go and do female logic on him. "Yeah," he said cautiously. "I didn't say you weren't." He thought about it. "No, I never said you weren't. I said you were a great cook. I said—"

He broke off and ducked when a magazine from the coffee table somehow made it into her hand and came sailing across the room at him. "Now what the hell was that for?"

"Get out!"

"Not until we finish this!"

"We *are* finished!" No, she thought, they weren't. Not until she pulled his limbs off with her bare hands.

Kate threw herself at him. In some distant part of her mind, she knew she was crying again, great gulping sounds of it. But fury rocketed through her at the same time. She pounded her fists against his chest. "I don't want half a loaf! Damn you, I'm not so goofy in love with you that I'm going to settle for crumbs! I'm worth more than that!"

Everything inside him went still. "You're in love with me?"

"I'm not just going to come over once in a while and make dinner for you and—and organize your mess of a life and jump into bed with you while you go out with other women, the kind you don't have to coddle!"

"You're in love with me?" He managed to catch one of her wrists.

She twisted it free and hit him again. "For your information, I think I've done a damned fine job of dodging bullets this past week! I've been *spectacular* at it! I wasn't even scared most of the time!"

"You're swearing again." He wiggled his brows at her. Damn, he felt good.

"I don't know where you ever got the idea that I couldn't take it, all your…your slimeballs and creeps—but if you think that, then you don't know me at all!"

"Let's get back to the part about you loving me."

"I don't want to be someone you keep on the side, all tucked away because I have to be protected from the harsher side of your life! I am *not* a liability!"

He finally caught both her wrists, grinning. "No, but you'd make a great wife."

"I'm—" She broke off, her blood draining, the room tilting. "What did you say?"

"Are you finished coming unglued?"

"I never come unglued."

"Honey, that was unglued." He grinned. "I like it. It does things to my heart."

Kate drew herself back and away from him while she still had some pride left. She blew an errant curl off her forehead and hugged herself. She was not going to read anything into that comment. He was just referring to her...her capabilities again.

Those she was painfully sure of.

"I would make a very good wife." She sniffed. "However, if it's all the same to you, I'll save those talents for..." *She would not cry again.* Damn it, she would *not.*

"Yeah?" he prompted.

"For someone who wants me to share his life." She drew her spine straight. "His *whole* life."

"Is being scared to death for you allowed?" Suddenly, he was sober. His heart burned. "Kate, I meant what I said yesterday. It would kill me if anything happened to you, if anybody went after you."

She was shaking inside. "You didn't say that yesterday."

"Yes, I did."

"No." She shook her head hard. "You said you weren't going to let it happen. That you'd make everybody think I didn't matter so it wouldn't happen. Then you lied to me all day about Beth and Allegra."

Raphael frowned. "I didn't lie to you about Beth and Allegra."

"You definitely lied to me."

"I just didn't have time to discuss it! I had an investigation to wrap up!"

"You were protecting me!"

The heat around his heart roared up to fill his head. "I've been doing that since this mess started! I hid newspapers from you! So get used to it! I figured the truth was going to hurt you, that you were going to try to blame yourself somehow—which you did—and I was going to be able to give you my full attention when it happened!"

Kate opened her mouth and closed it again. Her temper cracked and flew out of her. And down deep, at the core of her, there was, indeed, hope. It trembled.

"That's why you didn't tell me what you were thinking all day?"

His eyes narrowed warily. "Yeah."

"You called for Beth—Lilly, I mean—and Janaya's DNA after we got to headquarters so I wouldn't hear you."

"What of it?"

She nodded shakily. "Uh…nothing. Okay. I can accept that." *He cared.*

"Then you'll marry me?"

The floor dropped out from beneath her feet. "What?" she whispered.

She wasn't going to make this easy, he thought. But then, why should that surprise him?

Then suddenly he realized it was the easiest thing in the world.

"I want you in my home. In my life. All the time. Every day, every morning, every night." She gave a small cry. He didn't know if that was good or bad. He decided to go for the practical approach. It had always reached her before. "You said you loved me."

She nodded, shook her head, then nodded again while his heart stopped. Then she clapped a hand to her mouth and a tear spilled over to trace down her cheek. "I do. Oh, I do."

"That's the natural, accepted progression of these things, Kate. When you love someone, you marry them."

"You love me?" The hope swelled into her chest and hurt.

He threw a hand up. "Well, what do you think this has all been about?"

"You love me." She breathed it. And in that instant, she felt beautiful.

"I love you." He waited. And then she smiled, brighter than the sun. "I'll never stop worrying that someone's going to hurt you. I'll never stop calling you five times a day to make sure you're okay. But I can live with it. If you can."

She would cherish it.

Kate began to say so. Oh, there was so much she needed to say! But suddenly, there was a commotion outside, below her opened window.

She'd know that bark anywhere.

Kate ran to the window. She pushed up the screen and leaned out. Raphael put a hand on her shoulder and leaned out behind her. Belle stood in the alley, at the bottom of the fire escape. When she saw them, she barked again once, sharply. She wagged her tail, then she waddled off— all two or three extra pounds of her.

"Now how in the hell does she do that?" Raphael muttered. "You know, vanish from one place then turn up in another?"

"We don't need her anymore," Kate whispered. And something happened to her blood, a quickening, a tingle. She came inside and closed the screen. "She saved my life."

Raphael pulled back from the window, then he took her into his arms. "No. She saved mine."

* * * * * *

SILHOUETTE SENSATION®

AVAILABLE FROM 18TH MAY 2001

THE ONCE AND FUTURE FATHER Marie Ferrarella

Detective Dylan McMorrow delivered heartbreaking news and a baby to Lucinda Alvarez. Then, with a killer watching her every move, he was honour-bound to protect her, even *before* he learned the truth about her newborn…

WHO DO YOU LOVE? Maggie Shayne & Marilyn Pappano

2-in-1

Two brand-new stories featuring lovers with hidden identities by two favourite best-selling authors.

THE WILDES OF WYOMING—ACE Ruth Langan

Ally Brady relieved a handsome stranger of a thousand dollars, never realising that he was Ace Wilde—her new boss! And Ally's need for money had Ace wondering if she was the saboteur plaguing his family.

THE DETECTIVE'S UNDOING Jill Shalvis

Cade McKnight was a private investigator hired to uncover the truth about Delia Scanlon's heritage, *not* to spend time under the covers with the sexy spitfire, who aroused more than just his protective male instincts!

WHO'S BEEN SLEEPING IN HER BED? Pamela Dalton

Mitch Reeves was handsome, protective, electrifying—a perfect husband. So why couldn't Katerina Reeves remember she'd married him?

THE TEMPTATION OF SEAN MacNEILL Virginia Kantra

There was a naked man in her bed and he nearly made her forget all about her kids in the car, the mountain of luggage to come in and the men who might be pursuing her…

AVAILABLE FROM 18TH MAY 2001

SILHOUETTE®

Intrigue
Danger, deception and suspense

INNOCENT WITNESS Leona Karr
URGENT VOWS Joyce Sullivan
THE STRANGER NEXT DOOR Joanna Wayne
UNDERCOVER PROTECTOR Cassie Miles

Special Edition
*Vivid, satisfying romances
full of family, life and love*

WHOSE BABY IS THIS? Patricia Thayer
TO A MacALLISTER BORN Joan Elliott Pickart
THE SHEIKH'S ARRANGED MARRIAGE Susan Mallery
A MAN APART Ginna Gray
THE PRICE OF HONOUR Janis Reams Hudson
MARRIED TO A STRANGER Allison Leigh

Desire
Intense, sensual love stories

BACHELOR DOCTOR Barbara Boswell
ROCK SOLID Jennifer Greene
WIFE FOR HIRE Amy J Fetzer
THE BABY BONUS Metsy Hingle
A ROYAL MISSION Elizabeth August
IN NAME ONLY Peggy Moreland

0501/18b

Silhouette Special Edition®
and
bestselling author

Susan Mallery

present

Desert Rogues

A sensuous new mini-series set under the hot desert sun

Meet Khalil, Jamal and Malik—strong, sexy,
impossibly stubborn princes who do as they
see fit. But life in the royal palace is about to
change when they each claim a tempestuous
American bride!

THE SHEIKH'S KIDNAPPED BRIDE
(May)

**THE SHEIKH'S ARRANGED
MARRIAGE**
(June)

THE SHEIKH'S SECRET BRIDE
(July)

*Escape to El Bahar—a majestic land
where seduction rules and romantic
fantasies come alive...*

0401/SH/LC13

Silhouette Stars

Born this month.

Bing Crosby, Tammy Wynette, Michael Palin, Glenda
Jackson, Sid Vicious, Salvador Dali, Janet Jackson,
Gabriela Sabatini, Toyah Wilcox, Priscilla Presley.

Star of the Month.

Taurus

The year ahead is full of challenges and although
you normally resist change you should feel
ready to move on. Relationships are strained in
the early part of the year but once you
understand what you need from those close to
you life will become easier, with someone
surprising you with their depth of commitment.

SILH/HR/0501a

Gemini

Relationships are the focus of this month and some of you will be making a stronger bond with that special person. Home matters are also highlighted with a change of scene looking likely.

Cancer

Your energy levels are high and it seems there is little you can't achieve. Success brings its own rewards and you will be in demand both socially and at work.

 Leo

Personal relationships need to be handled carefully to avoid conflict as it may be that you are not communicating your true emotions. Any new activity will reduce the stress and help you find a positive way forward.

Virgo

Romantically an excellent time and you will realise just how important those close to you are. Finances are still improving and you may make plans for a trip away, possibly further afield than normal.

Libra

Energy levels are high and you need to find creative outlets in which to express yourself. Mid-month relationships prove difficult and you may need to step back for a while.

Scorpio

There are many opportunities to further your career and increase your personal finances. There may be some domestic upheaval but the outcome should lead to greater understanding and happiness.

SILH/HR/0501c

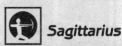 **Sagittarius**

A social month but be careful not to overcommit yourself as you may need some time out to restore energy levels. Romance is well aspected and there may be someone new in your life.

Capricorn

Romance and travel are well aspected so take the time out to indulge yourself and your spirits will be lifted. Finances receive a welcome boost towards the end of the month.

 Aquarius

You may be open to disappointment and expecting too much of yourself so try to be more realistic about what you can expect to achieve. A letter brings the chance to travel late in the month.

Pisces

Socially an excellent month and as finances are looking good you may take the opportunity to entertain in lavish style. Romantically towards the end of the month there could be a chance to improve relationships.

 Aries

Life is about to take on a new and exciting meaning with personal luck putting you on course for success. Romance is just around the corner and may be found in the most unexpected places.

Look out for more
Silhouette Stars next month

FREE!
2 Books
and a surprise gift!

We would like to take this opportunity to thank you for reading this Silhouette® book by offering you the chance to take TWO more specially selected titles from the Sensation™ series absolutely FREE! We're also making this offer to introduce you to the benefits of the Reader Service™—

- ★ FREE home delivery
- ★ FREE gifts and competitions
- ★ FREE monthly Newsletter
- ★ Books available before they're in the shops
- ★ Exclusive Reader Service discounts

Accepting these FREE books and gift places you under no obligation to buy; you may cancel at any time, even after receiving your free shipment. Simply complete your details below and return the entire page to the address below. *You don't even need a stamp!*

YES! Please send me 2 free Sensation books and a surprise gift. I understand that unless you hear from me, I will receive 4 superb new titles every month for just £2.80 each, postage and packing free. I am under no obligation to purchase any books and may cancel my subscription at any time. The free books and gift will be mine to keep in any case.

SIZEB

Ms/Mrs/Miss/Mr ....Initials ....
BLOCK CAPITALS PLEASE

Surname ....

Address ....

....

....Postcode ....

Send this whole page to:
UK: The Reader Service, FREEPOST CN81, Croydon, CR9 3WZ
EIRE: The Reader Service, PO Box 4546, Kilcock, County Kildare (stamp required)